1941

Oliver Stanley

Book Guild Publishing
Sussex, England

First published in Great Britain in 2008 by
The Book Guild Ltd
Pavilion View
19 New Road
Brighton BN1 1UF

Typesetting in Garamond by
Keyboard Services, Luton, Bedfordshire

Printed in Great Britain by
Athenaeum Press Ltd, Gateshead

A catalogue record for this book is available from
The British Library

ISBN 978 1 84624 303 5

Oliver Stanley was educated at Oxford and Harvard universities. His first visit to France was as a soldier during the Second World War serving, like the hero of *1941*, in the Allied armies of Liberation. In what remained of his misspent youth, he joined the Inland Revenue, then changed sides in the tax wars and became a banker. He has written books and articles about taxation and finance, and has been a chairman and director of many companies. *1941* is a prequel to his first novel *Hôtel Victoire*, published by Book Guild in 2007, which also reflects his passion for France and the French.

By the same author:

Hôtel Victoire, The Book Guild, 2007

Prologue: 10 May 1941

At 2300 hours, on 10 May 1941, a Messerschmidt Me 110 was sighted on radar screens over the Firth of Clyde, south of Glasgow, Scotland, and the air raid sirens sounded their familiar warning, driving the people of Glasgow out of their beds and into their shelters. During the previous week, there had been heavy raids on Liverpool for seven successive nights. In London, 3,000 people had been killed; 2,000 buildings, including the House of Commons, had been destroyed and the whole country was terrified.

Because that night there was a heavy mist, no attempt was made to intercept. There were no British fighters airborne and no anti-aircraft batteries in action, but, inexplicably, the Messerschmidt was seen to crash in flames at 23.09, shortly after having being identified.

David Maclean, a ploughman at Floors Farm, near Eaglesham, out late to shoot rabbits, first spotted some movement on the ground close to his cottage. He aimed his shot-gun, shouting, 'Run, yer little rabbit, run!'

Then, seeing it wasn't a rabbit, he shouted, 'Hands up, yer rotten, trespassing Sassenach bastard!'

David found he'd captured a German pilot, who'd broken his ankle in landing by parachute. But he was delighted to be taken prisoner.

In David's cottage, offered a cup of strong tea, he said, 'Thank you, but I do not drink tea at night. My name is Hauptmann Alfred Horn and here are some photographs of my wife and family.'

'Och laddie! I don't understand your filthy language.'

'Is not my wife beautiful? You see that fat little boy? He is

1

my eldest son. His name is Wolf-Rudiger and he is aged three years. Handsome, is he not?'

'He looks a bit like Alice's little boy, doesn't he, David?'

'No he doesn't, mother. That little bugger's a German little bugger.'

They argued as to what should be done. Meanwhile Corporal Jock Mackenzie, Signal Corps, who had been tracking the plane, sent a Home Guard platoon to Floors Farm where they took the prisoner to Greenock police station. When they got there, he addressed the desk sergeant in English.

"I wish to speak to the Duke of Hamilton. I have an important message for him.'

The sergeant was cross at being woken up in the middle of the night. Ultimately, the Night Duty Officer at the local barracks in Paisley, a Major Donald of the Argyll and Sutherland Highlanders, was sent for.

At the police station he questioned Horn, who repeated, 'I am the authorised representative of the *Reichsführer* and the government of the Third Reich, and I carry an important and confidential message for the Duke. It is about the future relationship of our two countries.'

'And I'm Charley's Aunt,' replied Donald.

But he decided it wasn't any business of his, and wanted to get back to bed. Next morning, he took Hess to a local hospital to have his ankle set.

The duty doctor, who was delighted to ventilate his knowledge of the language, said in German, 'Please state your name, number and rank.'

'I am Rudolf Hess, Deputy Führer of the German Reich and I wish to see the Duke of Hamilton as soon as possible...'

'Och yes, laddie! And there's a fellow in B Ward, who thinks he's Jesus Christ, and he's going to give me the keys of heaven!'

'...Please arrange for me to be taken to him. You will be rewarded – perhaps even honoured by the Führer.'

'Just straighten your leg, would you?'

2

'You are an idiot. Look at this document! You will see it is addressed to the Duke.'

He produced from a concealed pocket a thick sealed envelope addressed: 'The Duke of Hamilton, Scotland, Personal and Private', which he refused to hand over.

'It's to be given him personally.'

Donald observed, 'He looks like Hess, with those thick eyebrows.'

'Well, I'll set his ankle. Lie down, please. After that you can take him to the Duke of Plaza Toro for all I care.'

'Hamilton's a pacifist. I remember now he wrote to *The Times*, just after the war broke out saying Hitler was an honourable chap, and we should negotiate with him.'

The doctor was too busy to take any notice.

'I will see your arrival is notified to the Duke,' Donald said.

He put through a call to his Headquarters, saying he believed Hitler's Deputy had landed in Scotland with a secret message. Every successive retailer of this signal was greeted with laughter and scorn, but ultimately, someone got through to Squadron Leader the Duke of Hamilton, at Tactical Wing HQ, where his squadron of Hurricanes was based. The Duke was alarmed: a ghost from his past had come to haunt him. Before the war, he'd been strongly pro-German, because he'd liked Wagner's *Ring* cycle, and had visited Hitler in Berchtesgarten, where he'd been graciously received. Anyway, the Hitler régime had represented a bulwark against the Marxists and the Labour Party, who wanted to destroy the existing social order everywhere in the world but particularly in Ayrshire, where he owned his splendid estate. Since inheriting it from his forbears, he'd been determined to preserve it intact against the forces of revolution and darkness. Now it was likely that the message contained evidence which would cast doubt on his loyalty. Would he ever escape from the stigma of being a member of the Anglo-German Fellowship Association? Were the Intelligence Services now having him investigated? What was going on?

Despite his reluctance to become involved, the Duke knew his duty. He went first to inspect the crashed Messerschmidt and then to meet Rudolf Hess at Maryhill Barracks, Glasgow. In an empty barrack room, they saluted one another. The Duke spoke in German.

'Good morning, Herr Hess.'

'Good morning, Your Grace. How are you nowadays? How very nice it is to meet you again.'

'Let me try to remember. We met in Berchtesgarten, wasn't it?'

'Yes, with the Führer at my side.'

'It was the Anglo-German Fellowship Society, wasn't it?'

'Yes. It was in the autumn of 1936. At the Olympics. Those were golden days. To ensure they will return, please open this envelope and read its important contents.'

'Is this a document which rakes up the events of the past? You understand that I don't want to be put into an embarrassing position.'

'I can assure you there is no problem.'

The Duke could not read all the elaborate German text. Dazed and confused, he telephoned the Foreign Office, then, in response to instructions, flew to London to report to the Prime Minister, Winston Churchill.

The Prime Minister's secretary, Sir John Colville, met Hamilton at Northolt aerodrome, and conducted him directly to the Prime Minister at his country house, Chequers. There the Duke had to wait for a couple of hours in the hall until dinner was over; lack of food and sleep, worry and fatigue made him restless and bad-tempered By the time he was shown into the dining room, he'd made up his mind to treat Churchill like the jumped up *nouveau* that he was.

The Prime Minister was smoking a cigar and drinking brandy with his guests, who included Spears and Sir Archibald Sinclair. He had been expecting the arrival of a messenger and was not surprised to hear about Hess. But he was determined that the whole matter should be treated with derision. He presented a genial exterior as he greeted Hamilton.

4

'Hello, Your Grace! You're late for dinner, you know. Pity you couldn't get here earlier. What's this extraordinary tale you've come to tell me? I like a good after dinner story.'

'It's this, Sir: the Deputy German Führer, Rudolf Hess has flown to Scotland, and given me this message to convey to you. It's from Hitler.'

The company roared with laughter, as if this was a great witticism.

'Is this some kind of foolish joke?'

'No, sir, it's true. I have the message. It's from Hitler himself.'

'Rubbish man, you've been overdoing it, I expect. Sit down and have a glass of brandy.'

'Prime Minister, why don't you read this document?'

He pushed it into Churchill's hand.

'I can't. It's in German.'

'I think what it says is...'

'I don't care what it says. It's a trick of some kind.'

'Sir, it's certainly Hess.'

'What makes you so sure?'

'I've met him before – in Germany.'

'Have you indeed? Well, well!'

'It was years ago,' the Duke said defensively. 'It was all different then.'

'That may or may not be so. But, Your Grace, we must have this fantastic story of yours fully investigated.'

After Hamilton, feeling foolish and dejected had been ushered out, Churchill sat back in his chair and roared with laughter.

'There you are, Edward, it worked,' he said to Spears.

'Brilliant, Prime Minister! An absolutely brilliant concept of yours. This may have changed the whole course of the war.'

'Let's drink a toast to that!'

'What do we do now, Prime Minister?'

Churchill thought for a few seconds.

'What we shall have to do is demonstrate to the country our profound scepticism about the whole affair. We must make out we believe this fellow to be a fraud. We must tell the Press and the Americans we think he's a lunatic or an imposter, or both.'

'That shouldn't present any problems. We can get Beaverbrook on side. And what should be done with him?'

'Lock the bugger up safely somewhere. Where he can't make trouble! In a psychiatric hospital would be best, where no one can get to him, and he can't get to anyone.'

'And Hamilton?'

'We must take steps to ensure that whatever he says about this affair is not credible. It will be necessary to ensure he is discredited ... completely.'

'And then?'

'We must carefully plan how best to send the signed and sealed document back to Herr Hitler – perhaps through conventional channels. No, perhaps not. Perhaps some special courier has to be found. And that will be an important task.'

Churchill ordered Hess to be treated as a lunatic or a war criminal and isolated in a convenient house not far from London. He was sent to Mytchett Place near Aldershot, which was converted into a fort with barbed wire fences and slit trenches, Not so much to prevent Hess's escape, as to deter visitors, particularly journalists, 'whilst his mental health was being studied'.

Life became difficult for the Duke of Hamilton. He was attacked by the Communist Party as a friend of the enemy; he tried to sue for libel. The popular press was unsympathetic. It was also alleged that before the war he'd had a homosexual relationship with a high ranking Nazi and that Hess had told him he was being blackmailed. All these slurs remained unproved.

Churchill issued a statement to the Press:

'The Prime Minister remains doubtful as to the real reasons for the visit of Herr Hess, if indeed it be Herr Hess, and as to the prisoner's state of mind ... on which medical reports are being sought.'

This was after the Intelligence Agencies, however, had privately authenticated Hess and reported that there was some reason to suggest his visit had been carefully planned, but this fact was never revealed. At first, Hess's flight to Scotland was made the headlines:

HESS QUITS HITLER, FLIES TO SCOTLAND
No 3 NAZI LANDS BY CHUTE

However, Churchill's friend, Beaverbrook arranged for speculation in the London papers to be muzzled. The radio comedian, Arthur Askey, had entertained the whole country with his satiric song, 'Thanks for Dropping In, Mr Hess!' but Churchill ordered this to be withdrawn. False stories were given to the Press about a split in the highest ranks of the Nazi Party. The story ceased to be news much sooner than might have been expected...

Within a week a detailed report on Hess's arrival was put before the XX Committee to decide what further action to take. The function of this Committee was to advise the Prime Minister on how to win the war through duplicity and cheating. It met regularly in the War Rooms in St James's, a cavern littered with different coloured telephones, teleprinters, decoding machines – and paper: piles of it covered every working surface and flowed onto the floor.

The Hess situation, not yet code-named, was the last item on the Agenda. Churchill was wearing his battledress and smoking one of his longest corona coronas. Crowded round the table, elbow to elbow, were Spears, his ADC, and heads of various intelligence-gathering agencies – MI6, MI5 and Military Intelligence, each with an aide. Freshly clipped moustaches and highly polished Sam Browne's testified to the importance of the occasion. Departmental heads tended to regard defeat of the Axis powers as rather less important than defeat of rival agencies. Soon it would be peacetime again, and one had to give attention to the course of one's future career. But in the presence of the Prime Minister debate was modulated and uncontroversial.

After minutes of the previous meeting had been agreed and

all preliminary items dealt with, Churchill said, 'Now as regards the Hess incident. Let us begin at the beginning. You have all seen the file. It is the object of his coming which is the first issue to be considered. As you all know from the reports, he has been carefully questioned, but no substantial or credible explanation has emerged. What possible reason might there be for the unexpected visit of our guest, Herr Rudolf Hess?'

Some members of the Committee were well prepared for this question and began speaking together,

'Chairman, there are the psychological aspects...'

'Chairman, we need to consider...'

'One at a time, gentlemen please!'

'Chairman, we have received detailed reports from our agencies of announcements made on German radio programmes, and in the Berlin Press. Hitler has issued a statement to the effect that Rudolf Hess had been pronounced medically insane. Two of his adjutants, Leitgen and Pintsch have been arrested and handed over to the Gestapo, but it is not clear what charges are to be brought against them. The Berlin Press has suggested that Hess believed he was in the grip of supernatural forces... Though, of course, we have no way of confirming the truth of all this.'

'Those facts are noted.'

'Sir, there are technical aspects to be considered: our experts have expressed themselves doubtful as to whether Hess could have been acting alone. We know he took off from Augsburg, and he would, they believe, have needed to land somewhere to refuel. The plane he used has been examined and it appears to have been a new aircraft. The guns had never been fired. Also, they believe he could not have navigated so accurately in the dark without help. He might have used radio navigation, perhaps the Kleve beam, to bring him so close to where we think he wanted to be – the airfield at RAF Acklington. All these factors together suggest that this must have been a concerted plan and that Hess had official Luftwaffe sanction.'

'Most interesting! Noted!'

'Chairman, we can but speculate about the psychological motive. Might it be possible, for example, that Hess had quarrelled with Hitler violently on some major policy issue, so that he came to believe, rightly or wrongly, that his life or freedom was being threatened? Under this extreme pressure, his best course of action might have seemed to be to escape from the clutches of his former friends: to fly here as the only viable alternative to death or imprisonment?'

'Mmm ... one distinct possibility.'

'Or, Chairman, here is an alternative hypothesis: it may be he decided he no longer believed in the possibility of Germany winning the war, and wanted to avoid the stigma and penalties of defeat by joining the victorious side.'

'Mmm ... yes indeed.'

'What reasons have been adduced for his having come to such a conclusion?'

'None, in particular!'

'Chairman, the reports prepared by our doctors cast doubt on his medical condition. They suggest a state of mind bordering upon insanity. His flight may simply have been an act of wild, hopeless desperation generated by an unsound mind.'

'Hmm ... yes. What else, gentlemen?'

Silence.

Then a junior major piped up.

'Sir, might he have been carrying a message of some kind?'

'What kind of message?'

'Sir, I don't know. I was merely speculating that some private message, perhaps from Hitler himself, might have been the reason for his visit...'

At this Churchill intervened.

'But he has been repeatedly questioned, and has produced nothing of substance.'

Silence.

'Are there any other possible constructions to be put on this situation?'

Another silence.

'Very well, gentlemen. It may be that the flight to our country of Herr Rudolf Hess, Deputy Führer simply demonstrates to us the presence of a worm in the German apple. That would be a piece of encouraging news. If any new facts emerge, I wish to be kept fully informed.'

'Indeed, Prime Minister.'

'Now, I think the only possible course of action is simply to lock the fellow up in solitary confinement, and wait to see if isolation encourages him to tell us what he's really come for.'

'Indeed, Prime Minister.'

'And put out a statement to that effect.'

There were general nods of approval.

'How will this extraordinary matter be designated?'

'As Operation Determinate.'

'Very well.'

The meeting broke up. It was time for a pink gin at the club.

When the others had left, Churchill sat at the conference table, hugging himself with delight. He'd succeeded. The Double Cross Committee had been absolutely and comprehensively double-crossed!

He said to Spears: 'A courier has to be found. He will be given an important task.'

PART 1

24 July 1940

There used to be a popular song in England called 'When They Sound the Last All-Clear!' It promised that after the war ended there would be no more air-raids, the world would be at peace, we'd meet our lovely wives and girlfriends again, live with them for ever and all be happy. Now the last all-clear has sounded and that's how it is for me! Looking back over the desperate events of the last five years I believe I've been very lucky! How incredible they've been! Since 1940, I've lived in a world that sometimes seemed all danger and death.

When the war began, Paris – City of Light – was my home, and I loved it. It had been my birthplace, and the centre of my universe. I walked the boulevards, met my friends in cafés, and assumed I'd live there for ever. Ann-Marie was my loving, beautiful wife; she became the mother of my son, Ethienne. We'd been married a year, then separated by the war, but always content to be together. Now we're far apart. After I suddenly deserted her, later – much later – I learned she became a *collaboratrice*, sleeping with the enemy: German officers, who'd captured and were occupying my city. All that was my fault, and I sometimes feel enormous shame and guilt. In retrospect, I know I shouldn't have left her alone, but in the spring of 1940 it seemed the only thing to do. I felt the call – as people say – to go and continue to fight for my country, and that – my God! – I've certainly succeeded in doing.

Then, when I was sent back to Paris, I tried to help her, but couldn't. We were too far apart even to communicate with one another. We'd gone different ways and our love and friendship had died – casualties of the war! Now I don't know what has happened to her. I've been told she's with an odd type called Henri Rouget. I don't know whether she's made a new life for herself, but I sincerely hope so. And then there's my son. I wonder what's become of him . . .

Is it true? Have I really abandoned everything important: home, wife, friends, loyalties, language? Sometimes, I convince myself my present world's not real but all fantasy! On reflection, that can't be so, because during those years an irreversible transformation occurred: I grew up. When my life dissolved into nightmare at the beginning of the war, I was an innocent boy soldier, worrying about the creases in my trousers and whether I'd get a medal. I obeyed orders without question, trusted people to do what they said they'd do, believed what I was told, and was so weak that when caught doing something wrong, I ran away. But I've painfully learned that's not the way to live happily, or even to live at all. 'Experience', it's called!

I also ask myself just what triggered this dramatic upheaval in my life: was it the war, the defeat of France, and my flight to England? Perhaps . . . to some extent! Or was it just my growing up, rather belatedly? Was that the cause? Or the result? In 1940 I certainly wasn't a child, I was an engineer and a commissioned officer in the French Army, I'd fought the enemy in the field, I was happily married and I'd fathered a child – perhaps two.

Now I'm faced with the decision whether to stay here in London, or go back. I can't imagine what will be there for me in my beloved Paris. My former life has been destroyed. Do I make this weird country, England, my home for ever? I never imagined that question would ever arise. All I can remember of the moment when I set foot on English shore . . . is a sensation of triumph!

It was 24 July 1940. My sight of England represented for me sanctuary, but also – *mon Dieu!* – emphasised how far I was from my home in France, my family and friends. I might have been lonely, terrified or suicidal but didn't have time! The fisherman in the boat just dumped me on a beach – not at Dover, but somewhere isolated – with a curt nod. I didn't know where to go or what to do. I had no money, couldn't speak the ridiculous English language, and knew no-one in England, except the General himself. I'd met him once in action.

He'd been a colonel in charge of a brigade when I was a junior reserve officer. We'd stood side by side facing the enemy, and he'd congratulated me on my success in battle. He must have been confusing me with some one else. That meeting had been my inspiration to escape to England, find him, and join the Free French. I had a profound belief in him as the true leader of our people in the fight for freedom and democracy. What a bloody stupid innocent I was in those days!

England was an unknown land where I soon discovered that comic people spoke a barbaric tongue. Like the fishermen who'd said to me: 'plice!' … 'plice!'. I didn't know whether this meant *'s'il vous plaît'*, or whether I should look for police, or keep away from police. I walked into the summer dawn, got tired, lay down, fell asleep, woke up desperate for something to eat and drink, with a blistered foot, and half crazy from hunger and fear.

Then I got to a town. There was no one about, except some British Tommies who marched past singing 'Roll out the barrel…' What was a barrel? A gun? I wondered. I wandered through silent streets of little red houses. Some were boarded up. Others had bottles of fresh milk on the doorstep. What could it be for? I drank some and felt better. An old lady saw me and shouted angrily. I tried to speak to her, but she went into her house and slammed the door.

The sky was not so peaceful. A fleet of bombers, Heinkels and Dorniers passed over the town. I know now they were headed for London, being intercepted by Hurricanes and Spitfires. When I looked up, I could see dogfights overhead. I was back in the front line. The sound of gunfire reminded me of the battle for France, where I'd been fighting two months earlier. I'd been at

Weygand's army HQ. He'd had forty-five divisions to hold the line from the Somme to the Aisne, but in only a few days, we'd been broken and all started running west. Yes, running. At the recollection of it, I started running through those quiet streets to escape the Boches, just as I'd run in my own country. Soon, I thought, England would collapse and I might just as well have stayed in Paris and avoided that terrible crossing, sea-sick all the way...

But that first day in England was a day in which everything changed, and the Goddess of Good Luck suddenly appeared by my side giving me all her support. The police might have arrested me, and with no English and no papers I'd probably have been shot as a spy. Instead England offered me a first taste of its generous hospitality – a taste I've never forgotten.

I spent the whole morning wandering through the fields and villages of Sussex, pre-occupied with finding something to eat. Visions of crusty baguettes and ripe camembert filled my mind. Back in our apartment on Boulevard Raspail, my wife Ann-Marie and my mother would be having lunch: coq au vin, perhaps, and a carafe of *ordinaire*. For dessert, they'd have *crème caramel* or *fraises de bois*. Missing all that made me cry for home.

A little earlier, I'd have met my friend Daniel at the Café de Sports for our early morning aperitif: a *cinzano*, which Gaston, the old waiter would have served correctly on a saucer, with a single twist of lemon peel and a cube of ice. We would have clinked glasses, muttered '*à la tienne!*' lit our Gauloises and told stories of our sexual adventures during the previous night. Daniel was a good listener, and he liked to hear about my matrimonial life with Ann-Marie, despite the fact he'd fancied her himself at one time. Or perhaps because of that. We'd argue about intellectual theories, exchange news and gossip and watch girls passing by, speculating on their potential as lovers. The recollection of those familiar events made me think again what a terrible mistake I'd made in leaving Paris. The landscape around me had become unreal. I was no longer a soldier, just a lost child.

14

But now I'd got to a town, so I automatically looked for a restaurant. My plan was to have a decent lunch on the terrace, *coq au vin*, preferably, so as to make me feel at home. With no money to pay, the police would be called. Then I could go to prison on a full stomach. I walked more quickly, and the green fields of England were replaced by streets of little red houses, with dirty shops on the corners. But not a single restaurant. Unbelievable! Not even a *terrasse* café in the square of what looked like the city hall. It was baffling. Surely, somewhere, the barbaric English must eat. I put my nose in the air and followed a strong odour of cooking food. Through deserted streets I trailed until I found the source: a busy shop on a street corner. I watched, trying to understand what was happening. Apparently, they had this bizarre practice: you bought your food ready cooked in the shop and took it away. How obscene! A board outside told me that something was priced at '5d' and something else at '2d'. Extraordinary!

The shop was called EDNA'S. I stood watching the women busy serving. There were two of them: one fat and ugly, with a cloth tied round her head and swollen hands; the other a tall, thin blonde, very English looking. I might have taken her for an aristocratic lady had she not been wearing a dirty blue apron. They both had cigarettes in their mouths and talked to their customers without taking them out.

After a while they saw me, winked through the shop and giggled. When the shop emptied, they beckoned me in.

The fat one called Edna said, 'Where have you come from, handsome?'

And the other said, 'You're a cheeky bugger, whoever you are!'

I could hardly understand them, but I replied, '*Bonjour Mesmoiselles*! It's a nice morning, is it not?'

I could speak only a few words of English, but in my urge to communicate to anyone I made an eloquent speech in French.

'My beautiful little darlings! I beg you to attend to me, a French visitor to your country. Believe me, when I say I adore you both. You represent my heart's desire, all I've ever wanted from a woman. Please accept that my hunger for both of you is enormous and so, incidentally, is my sexual organ. Never before have I seen a restaurant like yours and food as you serve it. It is astonishing that two such gorgeous creatures should be performing so humble a task. However, it is not for me to criticise. Other nations, other customs...'

The two girls stared at me without understanding a single word. I went on.

'If you will accord me a little of your food to satisfy my tremendous appetite, I will accord you in return an important length of my prick to satisfy yours. For me it will be a first taste of England. For you, a first taste of *la vraie* France: penetration by a genuine French penis, an experience you will cherish in your memories for a long time...'

They began to understand the exchange I was offering them.

'He's a froggy,' said Edna.

'Come over from Dunkirk, have you?'

'He's just said he's starving, poor lamb.'

'And he wants to give us a bit of you-know-what.'

'I bet he would, the dirty young devil.'

'Given half a chance!'

'Wouldn't mind a bit of that myself.'

'You and me both, dearie.'

I thought it interesting that women always immediately understand offers like that. And English women were apparently no different from French ones.

Edna and Freda laughed until they cried. They gave me some fish and chips in a newspaper called *The Daily Male* (no it was *The Daily Mail*), and I ate them all. The taste of the rancid fat was disgusting, but it was the best meal I've ever eaten. I felt so much better that I leaned over the counter, took the cigarettes out of their mouths, and gave them each a kiss full of enthusiasm and forecasting more to come. They seemed to like my kisses because they gave me some more chips.

Edna said, 'You can see he was hungry for it, poor little sod.'

'And that's not all he's hungry for.'

'Well, he's not the only one.'

'Wonder if he's got a friend.'

I pointed to myself and told them my name was Albert. They repeated it: 'Alberre!', and said it was a lovely name.

'We're going to have a party,' they said, 'and you're invited to it.'

When the shop closed at two o'clock, they led me upstairs, put on the gramophone and we waltzed to the tune of 'I'll be with you in Apple Blossom time'. I danced with each of them in turn, and when I took a rest they danced with each other.

'What do you want to drink?' they asked, pointing to a glass.

'*Un verre de rouge, s'il vous plaît.*'

But that was an order which they couldn't fulfill. Instead we drank a curious cocktail called 'gin-and-orange', clinking glasses and shouting each other's names. After two or three drinks, the girls sang the song I'd heard the marching soldiers sing – 'Roll Out the Barrel!' – and I did my imitation of Charles Trenet singing about the happy times of his lost youth. 'Que reste-t-il de mes beaux jours?' It's a song about secret meetings and stolen kisses and Freda and Edna seemed to enjoy it very much.

All the time, they smoked Woodbine cigarettes and drank gin. I lost count of time and space. England was better – much better – than I'd imagined!

'*Vive l'Angleterre!*' I shouted. '*Vivent les belles anglaises!*'

Outside we could hear the air-raid sirens and the anti-aircraft guns. We looked out of the window and saw vapour trails in the sky. Spitfires chased Heinkels. Once there was a great crash – a bomb had landed close to the town, but we didn't care. We all threw ourselves in a heap on the floor and the girls laughed so much they couldn't get up.

I explained to them carefully how seductive they were, and how their two different physical shapes complemented each other, but they didn't understand.

Edna said:, 'He is a one, isn't he?'

'He's a card!'

'He's got a dirty mind.'

'Yes, isn't it lovely?'

I told them I wanted to make passionate love to them both and illustrated this by moving my hips in and out. They perfectly understood and made similar gestures. Edna and Freda were happy to share everything because, I thought, in England, men were rationed. My worst problem was that they giggled hysterically most of the time, making it difficult for me to concentrate on what they were saying. Sometimes they called out their husbands' names: 'Ooh Bob!' or 'Again, Jim!' Much later, I learned that Bob and Jim were in the Royal Navy and had been at sea since the first day of the war – September 3rd 1939. Left alone since then, the poor creatures were desperate for all I could provide.

I'd had a strenuous night and morning and began to wonder if I'd last the course.

Then a terrible thing happened. I suddenly got very tired and fell asleep. When I woke up I found that the girls had tucked me up in a big bed and climbed in as well. I woke up, confused but happy. I was grateful for a sleep and some more Woodbines. The girls had been hoping for a more positive performance and were disappointed when I indicated they'd have to wait for another day. They gave me a cup of a revolting brown liquid, which I drank. Then they argued as to what should be done with me. It sounded as though Edna wanted to keep me as a pet, but Freda said this wasn't practical. So they got the local school teacher, Miss Everson, to come and speak to me in French. Progress was slow.

She asked me, '*Pourquoi êtes vous venus ici?*'

'I have come to join the Free French army of General de Gaulle.'

'Oh, oui!'

'In London.'

'Oui.'

'I must go there.'

'Oui.'

'I must go there now.'

'Oui.'

Gradually, they understood and Miss Everson telephoned the Free French HQ at St Stephen's House. They wrote down the address and gave it to me to show to a taxi driver. They gave me one of Bob's clean shirts and one of Jim's jackets, which was too big. They gave me two packets of Woodbines and some English money: big coins called 'half-crowns' and little ones called 'bobs' and 'tanners'. Miss Everson explained the values, leaving me hopelessly confused. At the railway station, Edna and Freda bought me a single ticket, though they would have liked to get a day return. When the train arrived, we all parted tenderly and I nearly succeeded in embracing Miss Everson as well as the two girls. It was an emotional moment, because they'd been so good to me. I'll never forget them, I thought.

For a long time afterwards I wanted to go back to the shop and make love to them again – even to eat their fish and chips. I knew I owed them a big debt of gratitude and was ready to pay it off. I did succeed in returning once to Hastings a long time later, but that was a terribly sad occasion.

On the lonely train journey to London I began to think about my own lovely young wife Ann-Marie. She was only seventeen and I'd loved her passionately. I felt guilty about having been so unfaithful to her, but this sensation soon passed. She would have forgiven me, I decided. After all, I was a soldier, we had been parted by the war, and I wasn't responsible for that.

When I'd told her about my plan to escape to England and renew the battle, she'd said, 'Albert, I love you, but, darling, you're a bloody fool. How can you be so crazy? You've been home what? A week? You've told me how lucky you were to get away without a scratch and now you want to put your life in hazard all over again. For what exactly? Tell me that.'

'In order to redeem my failure at the battle of Montcornet.'

'Montcornet! Nonsense! And what about me and our child? You're rushing off to war all over again, with your *tricolor* waving, leaving us behind.'

'You must understand, Ann-Marie, I'm continuing the fight for France.'

In the end, she accepted that, but, my God, she needed persuading. We'd just finished dinner: *blanquette de veau*, and burgundy 1938; then *haricots verts*. One always remembers the details. Rationing and shortages hadn't yet begun in Paris. The boches were there but mostly kept to the Grands Boulevards and the Champs Elysees. And the brothels in Clichy, of course. There'd been no fighting in the city and life seemed relatively normal. The trees in the Luxembourg gardens near our home were in full flower.

We'd been sitting opposite one another at the big kitchen table in my parents' home on Boulevard Raspail. It was cozy and familiar: I'd lived there since childhood. Ann-Marie seemed more beautiful than ever, and I wanted to make love to her all the time. It would be terrible to leave her, but she couldn't come with me. Not with her baby due in a month. I knew she'd have a boy. He'd become an engineer like his father. I explained to her what I felt. Well, more or less what I felt.

'The war's not over yet. The English will go on fighting. Churchill says they'll never surrender. De Gaulle is in England training a new army.'

'You're crazy, Albert. De Gaulle will do nothing. And the British will betray us again.'

It was useless arguing with her. But there was nothing for me to do in Paris. I couldn't get a job because I had no civilian papers, so I had no money. And my mother wouldn't give us any. She didn't have much. I'd looked in the box she kept under the bed. So I couldn't go down to the café and have a drink with my friends.

I wanted to come home next time with honour and glory not shamed by defeat.

But there was another important reason for wanting to get away. There was this girl called Cecile, who, by an unfortunate coincidence, was in the same situation as Ann-Marie. And she was threatening to claim her rights and make a terrible fuss. I was afraid she'd hear I was back from the front and turn up at the apartment. If I got away, someone else could take the blame. Everyone knew she'd slept with scores of men, but she was a really nice girl.

Ann-Marie gave me a tearful goodbye. At night in bed, she cried on my shoulder, which I found very touching. I told her to be brave and share my love for *la belle France*. Then, at dawn, I'd walked out of the apartment, while she slept, and taken a train to Calais. I'd had a story all ready to explain where I was going but no-one challenged me. There I'd got a ride in a boat with some fishermen who, surprisingly, turned out to be English. They were doing a deal in cigarettes and making a packet out of the war.

I went back over these events during my train journey to London. At the railway station I'd seen the name of the town for the first time. It was 'HASTINGS'. That was where my ancestor William had landed in 1066. I wondered if he'd had the luck to meet two such lovely girls. Probably not! But he'd been able to conquer his new domain, which was what I had to do. The train finally stopped and I got out. The sign on the station platform didn't say 'London' which was what I'd expected, but VICTORIA: *Victoire!* That, I thought, was a good omen.

June 1940

'CHANTONS QUAND-MEME!'

That was what the posters shouted. They'd been stuck up all over Paris and expressed the confused mood of the people. The silly bastards who ran the country were telling us to sing. What a joke! Despite the golden sunshine which bathed the elegant boulevards, I felt more like crying than singing. My husband, Albert, had been at the front since the panzers attacked on 10 May and I hadn't heard a word from him. Had he been killed, I wondered? You'd have thought he'd have written a line to ask about our baby. Well, *our* baby, so far as I know! So far as *he* knew...!

The geraniums in the Jardins de Luxembourg were in full bloom. 'Bright emblems of a carefree world' was how the newspaper described them. What they didn't say was that it was a fast vanishing world. The German armies were approaching Paris, and I didn't find it easy to close ears and mind to the rumble of artillery. Apart from all that political shit, I'd had really bad luck. I'd been careless. Only on one night – but I'd got pregnant; due in a month. It had all been a colossal mistake ... Albert away at the front. Sometimes I felt happy because I knew it was going to be boy. But mostly I hated the little bugger, my bloated stomach, and sickness every morning. And I hated Mama – Albert's, not mine – who was so bloody pleased about it. She fussed around me like an old hen cackling. But it was too late to do anything now.

Albert's clandestine return from the front gave me quite a fright. He appeared one day at dawn, looking dirty and desperate. His uniform was covered in oil. We sat together on the bed, all day, hands clasped, saying little. I couldn't get him to talk to me. Nor to make love. Whether that was because of my pregnancy I couldn't tell.

When I asked what had happened to him, he just stared into the distance and said, 'Nothing.'

'What is it, Albert, that has upset you?'

'Nothing.'

'Were you wounded?'

'No.'

'Were you in the fighting?'

'Yes.'

'Was it terrible things you've seen?'

'Yes.'

'Tell me what they were.'

He just looked away.

'Tell me, Albert. Say something.'

Then he had a spasm of shaking, so I seized his hand and put my arm round him. He'd become a total stranger, unrecognisable as the elegant young officer who'd gone off laughing, saluting and kissing me goodbye. War changes people, I discovered.

After a few days I began to get pissed off with him. I stopped asking him questions and talked about our baby.

'It's going to be a boy, Albert, I know it is. Isn't that marvellous? I expect he'll grow up like you, always smiling. We'll have to learn how to look after him.'

But he didn't seem to be listening, and I couldn't get through to him.

On Sunday, I went to Mass at *Basilisque Nôtre Dame des Victoires*, my favourite church. It was crowded with people, sobbing and praying for the return of their loved ones. I got very upset. I prayed to the Holy Virgin for guidance: what to do about Albert; and for my baby and myself. Somehow, I wasn't confident my prayers were going to be answered.

After three or four days, Albert seemed to become more normal. He began to talk to me, to ask me how I was, and when our child was expected. I stopped worrying for a day or so, but it was a short respite. I'd sat for months, like all the other girls in Paris, thinking '*J'attendrai toujours...*'

My waiting had been rewarded and he'd come. Now, suddenly, he told me he was going off again! That left me stunned and hysterical at the same time.

23

I asked him over and over again: 'Why must you go now? Why so soon? Wait a few months and see what happens.'

But the stupid bastard wouldn't listen. Instead, he started telling me about his cowardice and terror during the battle of the Meuse. It was when they'd turned back from Lislet. He'd not been able to withstand the continued effects of the diving *stukas*. They'd come down perpendicularly, he told me, on individual tanks in his squadron, sirens screaming, bombs whistling, like birds of prey. Then there would be an explosion. Another of his friends had been blown to pieces. One by one, they'd been picked off. He and Captain Idée had been the only two of nine to get back to base. Idée told him he attributed his survival to the medallion of St Thérèse which he wore on his wrist and repeatedly kissed. Albert had no such support. Soaked in sweat and vomit, he'd collapsed on the base of the turret. All communication systems had failed and it had been his driver Francois who'd navigated across open country with no map. Guided by instinct he got them back to base camp on the River Serre. There they were shelled from the opposite bank. Within a few minutes, Francois had been killed by stray shrapnel – before Albert had had time to shake his hand and tell him he'd recommend him for a medal. It was then he started shaking and running and he hadn't stopped until he'd reached Boulevard Raspail. I told him he'd done nothing to be ashamed of, but he just wouldn't listen.

The government bunked off to the Loire, shouting over their shoulders that Paris was an 'Open City'. Then Reynaud decided that the wine and restaurants were better in Bordeaux, so he moved his government there, where they could stay in five star hotels. Pétain broadcast to us: '. . . it is with a broken heart, I tell you it is necessary to stop fighting.'

Politics is a lot of shit, if you ask me.

On the 18th we heard on the wireless that the Germans had entered Caen, Cherbourg, Rênnes and Le Mans. They told us to stay home, and leave roads free because the flood of refugees was 'compromising' military operations. Albert wanted to listen

24

to de Gaulle speaking from London. No-one had heard of him before, but now his name was on everyone's lips. What he said was very cunning: 'France has lost a battle, but not the war. The government giving way to panic has surrendered the nation into slavery. I, General de Gaulle, am inviting French officers and soldiers, wherever they may be, to join me.'

Albert was ripe for all that, and he fell for it like a ton of bricks. The next day, I couldn't stop him listening again. Now de Gaulle claimed he was speaking in the name of France, and we all had a duty to continue the war. To lay down arms and surrender any piece of the French land to the enemy would be a crime against the nation. As I told Albert, it was easy for him to say that, sitting there in England, drinking tea with Churchill. But Albert thought he was a hero.

Next morning, whilst I was asleep, he buggered off without as much as an '*Au revoir!*' For a while, I thought he'd reappear. Everyone said the police were turning back anyone trying to leave Paris. The big exodus had stopped and people began coming back. I felt I'd been a fool to let him go like that, but what could I have done? It was the Holy Virgin punishing me for my sins. I prayed to her to forgive me, but I'd committed one sin she just wouldn't tolerate.

After Albert had gone, I stayed indoors all day, thinking my baby was about to be born. Night after night I listened for his footsteps on the stairs, but he didn't come back. After a bit, I thought I might get him back when the Germans invaded England and put Winston Churchill in the tower of London as they'd promised. Soon the whole war would be over, and things would get back to normal. Then it all changed again. By July, people began to say the British weren't going to give in. Churchill spoke on the wireless in his terrible French telling us they'd never surrender: easy for him with the Channel in between!

Of course, Albert had gone off once before, but this was different. He'd wanted to go. Was that because he felt so guilty about running away home? I think men love going off to war, flags waving, trumpets blowing. First they want to be heroes, like that crazy de Gaulle now. Then they run away like Pétain. It's all a big adventure for them. But what about me? And my baby, Ethienne?

One morning, I took Ethienne to the Jardin de Luxembourg, and sat with him in the sunshine. Both of us cried for a while: he was just exercising his lungs, but I was suffering from post-natal depression, and a sense of grievance against the world. Men stopped and asked if there was anything they could do, but none of them invited me out to lunch. A baby in a pram was a big turn-off. The I saw my friend Génevieve, looking very pleased with herself, and I waved to her.

She said, 'Bonjour, chérie, do you like my new frock?'

'No, not much!'

She never listened to a word.

'It's a gift from my new lover, Jean-Michel, who is very rich. He's making lots of money selling things to the Germans.'

'What things?'

'You know, everything: wine, cognac, jewellery, girls – everything. He sells at ridiculous prices and gets paid in marks. So he buys me anything I want. You know … silk stockings.'

'Silk stockings!'

Talking to her didn't help much.

When I told her about Albert buggering off, she said, 'He's gone to have a good time with the English girls. They're all sluts, you know.'

'You don't know what you're talking about.'

'Good riddance is what I say. Plenty more fish in the sea!'

'Shut up, you silly cow!'

'Think about yourself, not him.'

She was a stupid cow but she had a point there. Everything had been getting worse since Pétain signed the Armistice on 22 June; and after the Germans hung a red banner over the Chamber of Deputies: 'Deutschland siegt an allen fronten!'

Germany victorious on all fronts!

26

I'd known I was having a boy. He'd arrived on time and looked just like Albert. That was what I said to my mother-in-law, who couldn't see any likeness. I didn't really know who he looked like. It could have been any of the men I was friendly with in the autumn of '39. I'd been generous then, with boys going off to the front, but I'd learned better. I decided to call my son Ethienne Alphonse Lucien, so that later he could choose what name and what father he wanted.

I didn't enjoy having a baby. He kept waking and wanting to be fed. He hadn't done my figure much good either. But the big question was: what were we going to do for money? Albert hadn't brought any back, and his bloody Mama had spent all the savings she'd kept under the bed. That's what she told me, and it was true because I looked. Not that there was much to buy. You needed tickets for bread. Meat wasn't sold on Mondays, Wednesdays or Fridays. The *pâtisseries* were open only two days a week.

When I went to church I explained to the Holy Virgin that Ethienne was getting on my nerves. Of course I loved him, but the bastard just yelled when he wanted his feed. I asked Her for help and guidance, but she didn't seem to have much to offer.

One Saturday evening, I came to a decision. I wouldn't be betraying Albert because he'd betrayed me first. So I dressed smartly and went over to Opéra. I had one dress that fitted, my figure was coming back and I was wearing my last pair of silk stockings. At apéritif time, I sat on the terrasse at the Café de Paris with a *sirop*. There were Germans everywhere on the *Grands Boulevards*, saluting each other like crazy. Everyone said they were very friendly. They smiled at girls, helped old ladies across roads and gave sweets to children. There were posters on the walls telling the 'abandoned people' to put their trust in a German soldier. What a joke!

Theatres, cinemas and cabarets were reopening for them. The shops had customers with money to spend. Paris was coming back to life. As they passed, they said: *'Guten Abend, Fraulein!'*

and others things which one didn't need to know German to understand. They were all thinking how I'd be in bed, and what it would cost. Unlike coffee, girls were not in short supply.

My object was to land an officer a *Hauptmann* or higher. Everyone said they were given thousands of francs and could buy all the coffee, food, wine and cigarettes they wanted. I began to study German badges of rank to make sure I sold out to the highest bidder.

Two young corporals came to sit on the next table, grinned at me and asked: 'Why are you all alone, *Fraulein*?' 'Aren't you perhaps looking for a little friendship this evening?' 'May I offer you a cigarette?'

They went on to tell me that now Germany had won the war we could all be good friends. Soon, they'd be going back to their home towns, but meanwhile they'd like me to show them everything Paris offered. Everything! They were polite, not bad looking, but they weren't what I wanted. I didn't answer them, and after a few minutes got up and walked off. Behind me, I heard them say: 'Stuck up little French bitch!' 'Wouldn't touch her with yours!'

What I wanted wasn't to be found on the Boulevards. The high ranking officers were either being invited into politicians' homes for parties in Neuilly, or were screwing in expensive brothels in rue de Provence. So I borrowed Mama's old fur cape and a cigarette holder, which made me look very sophisticated. I was lucky.

In a café near Gare St Lazare, I started talking to a woman about twice my age, who said, 'This isn't your *quartier*. What d'you think you're doing around here?'

'That's my business. No law against coming here for a drink, is there?'

'You want to be careful. The locals won't like you muscling in on their territory.'

'I don't understand.'

'I think you do. There are those who think they've got all the fishing rights in this pond. Outsiders aren't welcome. Sometimes they get a razor slash to warn them off.'

28

'I'm not fishing.'

'You look like you are. You'd do better to go through the usual channels.'

'What are they? And, by the way, would you like a drink?'

'Thought you'd never ask! I'll have a *vin blanc sec.*'

'What channels are usual?'

'I can introduce you to a very fine place. Top of the league! Everything well arranged. There's never any trouble. But it costs a percentage.

'How is it organised?'

'It's a hotel where the Boches officers are billeted. Most nights they have parties. The *patron* gets them girls.'

'What does he get?'

'A cut!'

'What's it called?'

'Are you crazy? I get my cut, too, you know.'

'I've got no money.'

'I'll trust you if you say you're on.'

'I'm on.'

'I knew you would be.'

Adeline, as she was called, took me to the Hôtel Victoire – only one star, no restaurant, but elegantly furnished with pretensions to style. Double doors led to a marble pillared hall, behind which stood the patron. He was correctly dressed in striped pants, dark jacket and silver tie. Everything about him demonstrated he was a professional hôtelier, calm, trustworthy, and with formal manners.

'Monsieur Henri,' Adeline said formally, 'may I present my long-standing friend, Mademoiselle Ann-Marie?'

'Delighted to make your acquaintance, mademoiselle, and may I welcome you to the Hôtel Victoire?'

'Which victory, monsieur, does the name of your hotel celebrate?'

'That is an intelligent question, mademoiselle, and you will be relieved to hear that the answer is the victory of the battle of Austerlitz – a victory over the English.'

Then he asked me with equal gravity, 'Shall we have the pleasure of your company one evening?'

'I hope so.'

He told me I was invited for Saturday evening. I should wear one of my smartest dresses and behave correctly, no matter what happened.

'You will like it here in the Victoire: you will be treated as an honoured guest.'

I laughed at what seemed to be a joke, but afterwards I realised he'd been quite serious.

Next time I met my friend Géneviève, I told her about Monsieur Henri.

'I sat watching him for a while, trying to understand what he's really like. He had some clever books on his desk.'

'You shouldn't go to such places, Ann-Marie. You'll get into terrible trouble.'

Silly cow!

On the next Saturday evening, dressed in my best, I pushed open the double doors of the Victoire and sauntered in. Monsieur Henri ushered me into the lounge, which was crowded with German officers, drinking, smoking cigars and laughing loud and long at their own wit. I smiled carefully at them all, thinking, 'Well, fuck them! I'll take them for everything I can, before they get a sniff of it.'

General von Studnitz, the Commander-in-Chief arrived with a flourish, monocle in place, his chest aglow with medals. You could see he was an arrogant bastard because he put up his highly polished boots on a sofa. Monsieur Henri told me his headquarters was at the Crillon in Place de la Concorde, but he regularly visited his officers' billets to 'maintain morale'. His aides crowded round him determined to be seen laughing at his jokes. He spoke excellent French,

'Monsieur Henri, my comrades in arms are thirsty. Be so good as to bring some more champagne, and some lovely girls to go with it!'

'Immediately, Herr General!'

'To me, he said, 'We are delighted to meet you. It is good of you to favour us with your charming company this evening.'

I gave him a radiant smile.

'It is good of you to invite me.'

'It is our pleasure.' As if addressing a troop parade, he went on, 'You will be aware that Paris is a city famous for supplying two excellent commodities – wine and women – to the victorious armies of past centuries. Here, at the Victoire we celebrate victories over the English. We are the victors now. And to the victors, the spoils of war!'

As if this were a signal, they all began singing 'Lili Marlene':

'Vor der Kaserne, vor dem grossen Tor,
Stand eine Laterne und steht sie noch davor...'

I sat watching and listening, calculating how to achieve a successful career in this unfamiliar society. The officers danced around Adeline and other girls, smiling and talking, but Robert, the hotel page, was also attracting a lot of attention. He was a nice looking, blonde boy, with a cheeky smile, wearing a brass-buttoned short tunic and tight trousers which outlined his bottom.

Much later, when I knew him better, I asked Monsieur Henri why the Germans had been so interested in Robert.

'Homosexuality, the physical attraction of man for man is not to be condemned,' he replied. 'It is only one element in the diverse compound of human nature.'

At first I didn't understand him.

'You must recognize there is no fundamental distinction between desire for the same sex and desire for the opposite sex,' he continued. 'Both are capable of being satisfied by a relatively simple physical act producing a sense of pleasure, apotheosis and release. Love, on the other hand, is a different phenomenon. Love makes one miserable for, by definition, it is a sense of longing.'

'For what?'

'Mostly for the unattainable.'

'I have never been in love. There were times when I thought I was in love with Albert, but I wasn't really.'

'Who is Albert?'

'He is my husband. But he has left me.'

'Why?'

'He said he wanted to join de Gaulle in England, to go on fighting for France.'

Monsieur Henri looked at the Germans sitting around in his hotel and quickly changed the subject.

'Like you, I have never been in love. Nor is it one of my aspirations to be so.'

'What are your aspirations, Monsieur Henri?'

'I believe in learning and service to the community. My principal aim is to equip myself with the capacity to heal the sick. That would be a more worthy profession than that of hôtelier.'

'Is that what you're studying all the time. Medicine?'

'Yes.'

'You're going to become a doctor.'

'A healer.'

Monsieur Henri seemed amazingly cultivated and wise, and I was flattered and delighted when he suggested a drink in his private room. I expected he would try and seduce me. Instead, he spent an hour telling me about his medical research. I didn't know whether I was relieved or disappointed.

July 1940

My first day in London was at first disappointing, then dramatic. I spent the night on a bench in Victoria station, and next morning found a taxi to take me to St Stephen's House. The city looked miserable; there were sandbags everywhere, but it hadn't been bombed yet. That came later. All the traffic went on the wrong side of the road. Extraordinary! When I got to our HQ, it was like coming home. Everyone was speaking French. A corporal told me to wait because Colonel Palewski never came in before noon. So I waited...

The only furniture in the room was a trestle table, two hard chairs and, in the corner, what looked like a barrel of Bordeaux. I felt tired and dirty. When I can't present an elegant face to the world I lose confidence. I needed to shave and hadn't had anything to eat or drink since Hastings, so I stuck my head under the tap and turned it on: delicious! *Chambertin* probably, but I couldn't place the year. Some of it ran down my shirt. My head began to spin so I had another drink and lay down on the floor. Through the partition I heard an angry conversation.

'Each day they order me to return to France. Yesterday they informed me I was 'compulsorily retired'. I have also been commanded to 'place myself under arrest'.

'That would be difficult to accomplish.'

'Now they have announced that the Supreme Court has convicted me for desertion under fire and sentenced me to four years in prison.'

'One might have expected worse, General: deprivation of citizenship or death by hanging.'

'Thank you, Colonel, for that frivolous and insulting comment.'

'I apologise, General, but it wasn't meant as a joke.'

As they came in, I scrambled to my feet, and slipped, which made a poor impression. The general's beaky nose and disappointing chin were unmistakeable. He seemed enormously tall and had an unbalanced walk. His nose was powerful, almost Bourbon, his ears stuck out, and he wore a new two star general's uniform and old-fashioned leggings. He looked at me: stiff, immobile and remote. Following him was a squat, middle-aged Jew with Colonel's badges and a scarred face. He grinned at me, but the General didn't. He looked at me like I was a lump of shit and said, 'Have you been drinking?'

'No, General. Lack of food and sleep during my escape from Paris, closely pursued by enemy forces...'

'What is your name and rank?'

'Albert Leconte. Lieutenant.' I'd rehearsed my speech to him. 'You won't remember me, General, but I served under you at the HQ of 4th Armoured. I stood with you on the ramparts of Laon by the church. I was holding the map when you formulated your brilliant plan to strike at the road junction at Montcornet and...'

'I don't remember you. Active or Reserve?'

'Active, sir.'

'Passed Staff College?'

'No, sir.'

'Where were you?'

'School of Engineering, sir.'

'Where were you during the campaign?'

'I was transferred from your HQ to Captain Idée's Company – to command a B tank. We cleaned up at Chivres and then at Bucy...'

He stared at me.

'... but were halted at Lislet. They were piercing our armour and ... there were Stukas.'

'So you turned and ran for it.'

I struggled to look him in the eye. Not easy because his was about twelve centimetres higher than mine.

'No, General. Your command was to retire in good order, lacking infantry support. The intercom systems failed, but I navigated over open country back to base camp on the river –

the Serre. We beat off enemy air attacks, and downed four Junkers 87s. Sir, we didn't lack the fighting spirit. I listened to your appeal of 18th June. You said France was undefeated and the Empire was behind you. That is why I escaped to join you here. To continue the battle.'

I stood to attention, making this speech. He managed a nod, and a twitch of a smile. What a cold fish!

After he'd gone back to his office, the old Colonel asked, 'How did you get here, exactly?'

I gave him an edited account, to which he seemed not to listen. Later I learned he was a man who didn't miss much.

He said, 'You will pledge your allegiance to our cause with a glass of wine...'

'Willingly, Colonel!'

'...later. Now sit down and pay attention. The General is glad to see you.'

I must have raised my eyebrows, which he noticed.

'You have much to learn. I am the General's *chef de cabinet*. You will report everything to me. There is a lot of work to be done. I've just come from Tunis. Admiral Emile Muselier has arrived from Gibraltar. He is senior to de Gaulle, so we have a problem. He is a rogue and we must watch him carefully. The British have recognised de Gaulle as chief of the free French force, and will guarantee us pay and rations. That is important. We have to work on a constitutional document.'

Palewski grinned like a maniac.

'The key figure in all this is called "Spears". He is head of the British Mission, a major general and a cavalry officer. He is astute and devious. He is arranging dinner parties for us to promote our cause – and his own – in influential British circles. Not all of them are supportive. Amongst the military class, we have enemies. Do you understand me?'

'Not entirely, Colonel.'

'It is a complex political situation. Some of the British want to make peace with Vichy. You will attend meetings with them

regularly and be appointed Meeting Secretary. Do you understand English? Have you met many English people?'

I thought of Edna and Freda.

'Only a little, Colonel. I've met some hospitable English, who gave me a warm welcome to their country.'

'That is good. Were they aristocrats?'

'Not really.'

'It is essential we establish credibility with the ruling class – to influence them in our favour. Without their support, we have no power.'

'How is this credibility to be established?'

'I will put you in the picture, as the English say. By meeting them at dinner parties, picnics and balls; in Whitehall; at The Connaught; The Travellers' and their homes in Belgravia. By explaining the great capacities of our General, who is a leader of courage and patriotism. By impressing them, charming them, flattering them, and, when necessary, making passionate love to their wives. In England, wives dominate husbands and tell them what to do. You will recount amusing stories, read them poetry and offer them the culture and wit of France.'

'In your view, Colonel, I'm equipped to do all that?'

'With a little training, yes!'

'How do you know?'

'You are young, handsome, and, hopefully, virile. It will be your duty as an officer in the French army to flatter and fuck for France. Does that dismay you?'

'Certainly not.'

'You're not a homosexualist?'

'No, sir.'

'You will understand, Leconte, that many of our English colleagues have that perversion – a practice they learn at schools. Or maybe it's the terrible food in England.'

'Yes, sir.'

'You must understand also that I cannot satisfy all the ladies of London myself. And there is no one else in these HQ upon whom I can rely. I need a reserve striking force. It's not a tough job, Leconte, for a young man like you. Why do you look so worried?'

'Not worried, Colonel, but perhaps surprised that duty and pleasure will be so agreeably combined.'

'You will meet the *Amis de Voluntaires Francais Libres*, a committee of high ranking ladies – not beautiful but with spouses influential in government circles. If they adore you, they'll mend your socks.'

I thought that there had been nothing exceptional about this briefing so far. In my experience, generals and colonels are always arrogant and full of themselves. They regularly tell you not only how to fight their battles but also who to fuck, what to eat and how to lead your life generally. Then the Colonel began to introduce me to our colleagues, including Vice Admiral Muselier, a jokey little *Marseillais*, with a reputation for being dangerous. He'd once punched a general in the face at a High Command Committee. Whilst I was saluting him, the adjoining office broke into a tumult of confused shouting. News had come through that the British had arrested the crews of our battleships in harbour at Portsmouth and Plymouth and marched them into prison camps.

Muselier went purple with rage, waved his arms in the air and shouted, 'It's all the General's fault. I've told that stupid prick a thousand times that he must assert himself. Does he ever listen? No!'

Crisis followed crisis. Next morning, they told me Muselier had got a signal that the British had opened fire on our ships at *Kiers el Kebir* and in nine minutes the whole fleet had been destroyed. Unbelievable! Vichy had broken off diplomatic relations with London.

Palewski read the cable aloud, then said, 'All this demonstrates how little the English understand the political situation. When they have a problem, they produce an absurd solution. This gives Pétain another lever against us. It makes us accomplices in the murder of French sailors. That is the downside, but there is an upside.'

'What's that, sir?'

'The British cannot now make peace with Vichy. So they must turn more to us. You will accompany me, Leconte, to the General's office.'

On hearing the news de Gaulle gave a strangled cry of pain and rage.

Palewski added, 'When Churchill announced the action in the House of Commons, they gave him a standing ovation. So it must be good news.'

'To joke on an issue like this amounts to insubordination. Why am I surrounded by such fools? I shall resign. I shall give up my mission. I shall retire to Canada and spend my days contemplating the injustices and stupidities of the world. You are dismissed, both of you. Get out!'

Palewski was unperturbed. He saluted in his vague and friendly way and we retreated.

'Don't worry, we'll get Spears to placate him. But since the British call him the Constable of France, we've now got to arrange for him to broadcast to the French people.'

Constable, I thought! The accent was on the '*Con*'.

'Telling them what, sir?'

'You ask too many questions, Leconte. As a punishment you will produce a first draft of the General's speech.'

I'd never written a speech in my life but succeeded in producing a version which everyone agreed could have been written by no one other than the General.

'. . . there is not one Frenchman, who has not heard with pain and anger of this hateful tragedy. . .'

Only Palewski gave me credit, and we began to work together. I'd made the General into a Man of Destiny, to be promoted by the British like – Palewski said – a bar of soap. It didn't do him much good in France. Vichy condemned him to deprivation of citizenship, forfeiture of assets, and death by firing squad. Still

– as Palewski said – it might have been the guillotine.

A week later, we had a Bastille Day parade in front of the statue of poor, old Marshal Foch. The General took the salute, looking uncomfortable, because, Palewski said, he needed go to the lavatory. Not at all. It was the sight of his FF infantry marching to the sound of the Marseillaise played unrecognisably by the band of the Irish Guards. They all needed a shave, and their uniforms and weapons were dirty. I'd been given a battledress which didn't fit. When presented to Spears, he stared through me, giving a curt nod. He was on the saluting platform with the General, and I heard him say to his ADC, 'What a ghastly band of ruffians!'

At that time in England we all sang sentimental songs about meeting on some future sunny day the girl we'd left behind. Life would be beautiful then and, in the meantime, you were supposed to keep smiling. Every night, instead of smiling, I thought about Ann-Marie, and whether I'd ever make love to her again.

But after three weeks in London I became so immersed in my new world I had no time to meditate on the past. I grew a moustache, drank tea with milk, smoked woodbines, and transformed myself into a pragmatic Englishman. I learned English, including useful swear words, like 'fuck!' and 'bugger!' which I used regularly. Palewski, who treated me like his son, was well established in London society, and he took me to grand homes in Belgravia for dinner, saying, as we arrived: 'You will make polite conversation with the men. And behave yourself with the women.'

'Yes, Colonel.'

'No "farting" to use an English idiom.'

He didn't always practise what he preached.

'How do you d … o … o … o … o?' they shouted, as we arrived, sounding like cocks crowing.

'S … o … o … o … o pleased to meet you!'

I hoped to be given gin and orange to remind me of my first hostesses. But no! There was champagne, which wasn't bad,

39

considering the British had just been driven out at Dunkirk, and seemed to be losing the war. We gulped it quickly and soon stiffness and formality were replaced by giggling, because Palewski was telling one of his favourite stories, usually surrounded by girls, on whose bottoms he casually rested a hand. The one not holding a glass.

Of course, the houses enormously impressed me, because they were like museums, with oil paintings and tapestries on the walls, oriental carpets and glittering silver. I was less impressed by their inhabitants, who chattered like birds, laughing at jokes I didn't understand. No-one shook hands or told anyone their names. When I introduced myself as 'Leconte', they looked at me oddly.

Palewski introduced me to Nancy Rodd, his current mistress, supposed to be clever and amusing. Her husband was in the army so she was distributing favours elsewhere. She called him 'Colonel' all the time and was absolutely besotted by him. What I couldn't understand was that her mother, Lady Redesdale, the hostess, seemed pro-German.

She told me, 'It won't be long before you can go home.'

'Do you think so, Madame?'

'Yes, Hitler will soon win the war, everything will be wonderful and they'll get rid of all the Jews.'

Palewski pretended not to hear. It seemed Nancy's sister called 'Bobo' had been a girlfriend of Hitler's! When Britain declared war, she'd tried to shoot herself, managed to get a bullet into her brain – supposing she had one – but failed to finish herself off. Another crazy sister was married to a fascist called Moseley and had been put in prison with him. The whole evening was spent laughing and shouting at nothing at all. All the girls had high-pitched neighing voices, and big teeth like horses. What a family! Unbelievable!

Palewski, a terrible snob, admired them all. He spoke excellent English because he'd been at Oxford before the war, and managed to sound exactly like an Englishman. I heard Nancy say to him: 'Oh I do love you so, Colonel, darling!'

40

To which he replied: 'Oh I say, that's most awfully kind of you.'

But you couldn't help liking him. The following week he took me to dinner for a special briefing. Before he could begin, I told him how amusing I thought his English mistress was and how much I admired her.

'I tell you, Leconte,' he replied, 'you need to find an English *petite amie*. She will be your best language teacher, and you'll learn other interesting things as well.

'Thank you, Colonel. I will do as you command.'

I was learning how to behave in England, a country where manners were very different from those at home.

During dinner Palewski expounded to me Operation Menace, the brain child of de Gaulle, for which I was nominated to be Intelligence Officer. We were to send an expeditionary force to land at Dakar, in French West Africa, where the locals would flock to join us. What a crazy idea! Disaster could confidently be predicted from the outset. My main task was to liaise with Spears, a model English cavalry officer, complete with bristling moustache, stinking pipe, clipped intonation, and elaborate manners. We never let our reciprocal hatred show.

Next morning, Palewski, Christian Fouchet, a lieutenant, René Cassin, a lawyer, Maurice Schumann, a journalist and I gathered for a briefing.

'Mon cher Colonel, you must concede it is impossible for your scheme to be taken seriously...'

'What is important to recognise is that this map is ten years out of date...'

'The British will never accord us supplies to make such a crossing...'

'At least the General has confidence in my evaluation of the supply situation, which you have not...'

It was all to be treated as Highly Confidential. None of them had ever seen action and I became terribly depressed about the whole project.

A week before sailing, the General summoned me, saying: 'You will accompany me and act as my interpreter.'

Our mission was to Simpson's to order the General's tropical kit. The tailor, disconcerted by the General's height, explained it would take three weeks.

I responded, 'This order, my good man, needs to be ready in seven days for our departure to West Africa.'

We sailed from Liverpool in a Dutch liner, the *Westerland*. Just before departure, Palewski sent me with papers to be delivered to the joint British commanders on HMS *Barham*. I stood on the deck outside Vice-Admiral Cunningham's cabin listening to their conversation:

'I'm afraid that French chap, de Gaulle, is going to be the real menace on this show.'

'Not sound, eh?'

'Quite!'

'The problem we've got on this show…'

'Yes?'

'Don't know how to express it, really.'

'You can be frank with me, old chap.'

'Well, my reading of the SitRep is that this whole sideshow has been forced on us by the PM to prove to that pompous French chap we're backing him.'

'No-one believes in it, I agree.'

'Quite useless.'

'Won't accomplish anything!'

'Quite.'

'Important we don't consume resources unnecessarily.'

'Quite.'

I knocked, went in, saluted, handed over the papers. They nodded to me without speaking, so I did a smart about face and went out, feeling thoroughly depressed.

At his briefing conference next morning the General announced that we were going to liberate part of the territory of France; that the honour of France was at stake, etc. It lasted nearly an hour. Afterwards, as I paced the deck wondering if a torpedo would soon strike, Palewski fell into step.

'Well, my young friend, what is your current assessment of our mission?'

'I am not hopeful, Colonel, of a brilliant military success.'

'Aha! You are making progress. And what is your assessment of our leader?'

'I have to confess, Colonel, I perceive some small weaknesses.'

'Aha! You are gifted with great insight.'

In the Atlantic, the weather turned foul – and so did all the relationships on board. We received a coded signal saying the enemy was forewarned, our expedition accordingly cancelled and we were to return to base. At first the General screamed that we'd wrongly decoded the message. Then he sent back a signal protesting, rejecting the decision and saying he'd take full responsibility. So we sailed on...

When we got to the African coast, we landed one single troop on the beach at Dakar, which turned out to be heavily fortified and defended. Our small force was repulsed with heavy casualties.

I heard Cunningham say to his colleague, 'Rather as predicted, I'm afraid.'

'Not a good show, what?'

'Mistaken strategy, old boy.'

'Quite.'

It took us three weeks to sail back to Liverpool, shadowed all the way by U boats. Night and day I lay in my bunk, waiting for the explosion which would signal a torpedo hitting the boiler room. It never happened. The only thing that hit me was a stream of vomit from the sea-sick occupant of the bunk above me.

17 May 1941

Slowly the old Avro Anson taxied along the Hendon runway, and, staggering slightly, gained altitude. It had been painted black which matched my mood. Sitting in its bomb-bay, I shivered in my thin civilian suit, made in Savile Row, but tailored in French style, and bearing a label *'Fabriqué en France'*. I looked down on London, wondering if this was the last time I'd ever see it. Somewhere there, Palewski, who'd nominated me for this crazy mission – another one – was safe in bed with his repellent Nancy, saying: 'Oh I do so love you, you delightful girl!'

Well, fuck him, as the English say. My compensation was I'd soon be back in *la belle France*. If the outcome of my mission was fatal I wouldn't die exiled in England. And I'd get a decent glass of wine again and a cup of coffee. If the Boches had left any in Paris! But from my new perspective, London life now seemed calm and sweet, although at the time it had seemed comic, disagreeable and absurd. All my colleagues were too busy quarrelling to organise anything. Muselier had been arrested by the British. I'd escorted the General to the Foreign Office, where their Foreign Minister, Anthony Eden, sat at a desk in an elegant room, looking debonair and smoothing his moustache.

'My dear General,' he began, 'something lamentable has occurred. We have received proof that your colleague Admiral Muselier is in touch with the Vichy authorities; that he attempted to transmit the plan of our Dakar expedition to Darlan, and he is planning to hand over a battleship. The PM has ordered he be confined to Pentonville prison, together with two other French officers and three ladies all found in bed with him when he was arrested. We have thought it right to appraise you of this unfortunate affair.'

He produced some papers, supposed to be evidence, which de Gaulle grabbed. I thought that, in his fury, he was about to tear them up. Then he said, 'Some enormous error has occurred. We hold your government responsible. Your insulting allegations are false. We reserve our position.'

We proved that the alleged proofs were forged and the British backed down. Soon after, Muselier was arrested again, this time for pursuing girls into the Ladies' Lavatory in King's Cross station. When released, he blamed de Gaulle for victimising him and told Eden that de Gaulle suffered from acute megalomania!

Quelle pagaille! As for de Gaulle, he saw himself as the saviour of our country and regularly proclaimed: 'I am Jeanne d'Arc' – without a flicker of a smile.

When the British heard him, they sniggered. His only relaxation was in hating people, both the British and his colleagues, including me.

Now all that had become remote.

Whilst we'd been walking across St James's Park, Palewski had said, 'Leconte, you seem restless in London. Did you not enjoy Lady Peel's reception? London salons do not please you?'

'London has its charms, Colonel, but I'm beginning to feel guilty.'

'About what?'

'That I should have left my home and family for this relaxed style of life. My efforts to persuade Spears to modernise the equipment of the Fifth Battalion have proved fruitless. They have decided that Lee-Enfield rifles manufactured in 1911 are the only available weapons. Ammunition is limited, so no firing-range practice...'

'What you describe are important functions...'

'And dancing quicksteps with your friends, the Mitfords, seems a discipline unlikely to liberate Paris from the German jackboot.'

'You are spending too much time in the ballroom and not enough in the bedroom.'

'There is a wartime shortage of beautiful girls.'

'You are too discriminating, Leconte. The English have a useful maxim. One does not examine the mantelpiece whilst poking the fire. Anyway I can tell you that you will soon put all this behind you.'

Next day, I was summoned with Palewski to the Cabinet Office, for a 'Special Briefing'. Spears was there, with other British officers and a civilian in a dark suit. They nodded to me but no one was introduced. Palewski began.

'Leconte, the Commander-in-Chief has authorised me to ask you whether you will volunteer for a special mission of utmost importance and great risk.'

'Of course, Colonel!'

They all stared at me, as if expecting an eloquent speech.

'I am not unfamiliar, Colonel, with the risks of battle.'

'Very good, Leconte. Can you confirm as a matter of life or death that you will respect the confidence to be imparted to you?'

'Of course, Colonel.'

They continued in this pompous manner for a while, until finally Spears picked up a red telephone and whispered into it. A door at the end of the room opened and in walked Winston Churchill, wearing his khaki battledress and smoking his big cigar. He sat down and twinkled at me, looking rather like a friendly bulldog, but slyer and more devious. Without any introductions, he plunged in.

'You must recognise, er ... Leconte, that we urgently need your French empire to come to our support. At present its leaders are poised between Vichy and ourselves. They can be tipped either way. You have resources which we need – a fleet of warships anchored in the Caribbean.'

So intense was his glare and so commanding his presence, he made the coveted resources appear to be personal property unreasonably withheld by me.

'It has been reported that you participated in that expedition to Dakar, which was...' (he coughed), '...not entirely successful. But you will have appreciated the objectives. Now we must act more positively to influence your French colleagues in Africa and elsewhere to abandon Vichy and put their resources at our disposal.'

He paused and I held breath as if hypnotised by a snake-

46

charmer. Churchill looked at Spears, who took up the story.

'Information has reached us which leads us to believe that Vichy might not oppose the remaining French territories declaring themselves for the Free French cause, following the lead of *les trois glorieuses*: Chad, Congo, and Cameroons. At the outset we were doubtful whether this could be true. Now it has been confirmed. But Vichy needs to be offered an inducement, tendered in a convincing manner. Your role would be that of a delegation, carrying documents, offering that inducement.'

Then the civilian took up the story and told me about communications between ambassadors in Lisbon and what a diplomatic triumph it had been. I looked from one to the other of them, wondering whose turn it was next.

'So we need a courageous officer to go secretly to Vichy carrying this contractual document setting out the terms of the arrangement. You, Leconte, have been nominated for the critically important mission. You will remain in Paris until London has carried out its side of the bargain. Then you will be released and returned to London via Lisbon. You will be guaranteed personal immunity as an emissary carrying a flag of truce. However, the risks are obvious. You will remember Vichy has passed a death sentence on all Free French...'

Briefly I had a surge of enthusiasm. Selection for an important mission was good for the ego. And I'd get home again. I could hear the sounds of Paris, smell the fresh baguettes in the *boulangeries* and the Gauloises in the metro. I'd see the geraniums in the Jardins de Luxembourg and the chestnut trees along the Seine. I felt a longing to be there. When would I go? Tomorrow? To get back to my real world, I'd take any risk.

And yet... Doubts began to form. Somehow, Churchill's rhetoric seemed to lack the ring of truth. My impression was that he'd been reciting lines in a drama at the *Comédie Française*, and the others were his chorus. Something was missing. But they were waiting for my reply:

'May I ask, Sir, what the inducement is to be?'

Palewski replied first.

'You understand, Leconte, it is better you have limited information. What you do not know you will never be able to tell.'

Churchill broke in.

'He must be put in the picture. Leconte, your loyalty to General de Gaulle has been noted. It does you great credit. It has also been reported you are a perceptive, alert young officer. One who recognises facts, however unpleasant. You will have recognised, alas, the General is not, and can never be, an effective Commander-in-Chief. Reply frankly. Is that not so?'

I nodded. It was no use pretending otherwise. I knew Churchill and de Gaulle had quarrelled bitterly. There had been an occasion when de Gaulle had given an interview to the American Daily News asserting that Churchill was afraid of the French fleet. Churchill had ordered all relations with de Gaulle to be cut off. Then de Gaulle had denied the interview had ever taken place, which had increased Churchill's rage. Eden and Palewski had acted as peacemakers, claiming de Gaulle had gone off his head. Churchill went on.

'Alas! General Charles de Gaulle, Constable of France, will never secure the total loyalty of the forces under his nominal command.'

'Constable,' I thought again. With the emphasis on the 'Con'.

'They are too diverse and miscellaneous. He is a man of great qualities, but with an unpredictable temperament. He is not at ease with the great task which has been thrust upon him. Therefore, it would be a sympathetic act to relieve him of it.'

He paused allowing me to reflect that that was a particularly duplicitous remark.

'The General has many times offered … no, promised … no, threatened to relinquish his command and retire to Canada. We are proposing to tell the Vichy government that that is his wish. The Free French force in London will be disbanded. The General and his family will leave for Canada forthwith. Vichy will withdraw the sentence of death which their Courts have pronounced on you and your comrades *in absentia.* Your new headquarters will be established on the island of Miquelon. You may be aware that that island and the isle of St Pierre lie some twenty miles off the coast of Newfoundland. Your French warships will sail there under their own steam and pass under Free French control.'

Churchill drained his glass, got up quickly and ended with a rhetorical flourish.

'Captain Leconte, you are being entrusted with a dangerous mission. You will need all your courage and endurance. Much depends on your success. For the future of your country and ours. Good luck and God speed!'

He grasped my hand warmly, walked to the door, where he turned, beamed at us all and held up two fingers of his hand in the V for Victory sign he had invented. What a showman! Then he disappeared like a stage magician through a secret exit. We all stood up. The meeting had ended, leaving me with a thousand unspoken questions and struggling to absorb what I'd been told.

Over the next few days I tried to get Palewski to talk about my mission but he avoided me. Instead of practising the *palais* glide, I was given two sessions of parachute training, which consisted of jumping off a six foot wall into a field. The instructor repeatedly counselled me: 'Bend your knees, Sir, and roll over as you hit the ground.'

By the time I'd learned the technique I had acquired several bad bruises and jolted my spine. Then I had one practice jump. From take-off I was gripped with fear. But my nightmare was short, because almost without warning the despatcher opened a hole in the floor and pushed me through. After the first terrifying moment it was exhilarating. I could see rural England stretched out. Then I pulled the shrouds, and landed neatly. Back in the officers' Mess with a gin in my hand, I felt enormously elated. I'd become one of the Gods, who look down on earth-bound mortals below and decide to join them for a short vacation.

Then I got my orders. I was to carry in a briefcase a sealed dossier to be handed to General Weygand. To protect me from the Vichy death sentence I would resign my captaincy and become a civilian. No back pay! I was given a document to sign, making me liable to the Official Secrets Act and a lot more theatrical nonsense which the British so enjoy.

What I found impossible to believe was that de Gaulle would quietly retire. His outbursts had been threats not promises. As I was to be held hostage until he did, my prospects didn't seem good. I might remain a prisoner until the end of the war. Or be shot as a traitor. I'd looked at the map and found the islands of Miquelon and St Pierre, the only remaining outposts of a great French Empire in the North American continent. To base the Free French HQ there seemed absurd. Although I'd been 'invited' to volunteer, the truth was I hadn't been given much choice. Looking back on the encounter with Churchill, I couldn't quite hear myself saying: '*Mille regrets, mais merci, non!*'

And it was too late to say that now.

The Anson buzzed through the night. We'd crossed the Channel and were losing height. I tried to see the ground below and caught a glimpse of a river. There was no moonlight and the timing of my jump was to be determined by map-reading. The dispatcher spent most of the flight anxiously checking map and watch. Suddenly, he opened the flap in the floor and pointed into the night. I took a deep breath and dropped into the fierce slip-stream, the brief-case strapped tightly to my wrist. My parachute opened with a crack. In no time, trees, walls, hedges were looming up and I narrowly missed them; then a stream and a field. I remembered to bend my knees, rolled over clumsily and banged my bottom.

1941

Sitting at my desk between the white marble pillars in the hall of my hotel, I reflected yet again on my lamentable profession and dreamed of escaping back to the *Ecole de Médecine*, a world which seemed far away. There, ten years ago, I'd been happily pursuing medical studies when my father had died. That event, at the end of my first year, had disjointed my life, switching me onto a new track. On the same day I lost father, career and motivation. His death had been tragic: he had fallen not down but up the cellar steps, clutching a bottle in each hand, and had toppled amongst the empties. Both bottles – *St Emilion* 1927 – had broken, so he'd expired in a lake of claret. What a death! Not inappropriate for an hôtelier. No guests were present. '*On mourra seul,*' as Pascal says.

Although I'd argued, I hadn't been able to resist Mama's insistence that I assume Papa's role as patron of the Victoire. It was my filial duty, she claimed. She is very strong-willed. What does Horace say? 'Delicta maiorum immeritus lues': For the sins of one's ancestor one must suffer, though guiltless.

But I haven't absolutely given up my calling, and have been studying homeopathy, the science of treating like with like. I believe in bringing to illness a substance, which, in a healthy person would produce symptoms similar to those displayed by the person who is ill. The effect is to stimulate symptoms, not suppress them, so the body learns to reject the disease. But healing patients is my vocation only when I'm not attending to the needs of my clients. There's always an ample supply of patients. Sometimes it seems the whole of mankind is a diseased race. Womankind too. More interesting in some ways!

I enjoy watching both species at play. And in my hotel I have a changing caste of players to keep my attention engaged. I observe with scientific detachment both their exhilaration at success and dismay at failure. Currently appearing in a dramatic star part is a new, young and pretty female lead called Ann-Marie, whose triumph in attracting the attention of Major Max Braunich has made her continuously breathless with excitement. Frankly, I was surprised at her success, not because she's unattractive – far from it, blonde, with come-and-get-me looks. Its Braunich I'm surprised at, because I didn't think he'd want a girl like that. One of the junior officers on Von Studnitz' staff, I'd categorised him as well-bred, cultured, ambitious, not one to waste time and money on tarts. After I'd introduced them he stood talking to her for an hour about his interest in music and how he loved to play the cello. He spoke excellent French, using the subjunctive perfectly. Now he seems devoted to her. During the first week of their affair they lay in bed every afternoon, with the casement windows open. As their room was next to mine, I could overhear their intimate conversations.

'What would your wife say if she could see what we're doing, Max?'

'I've told you a thousand times I don't have a wife!'

'Push harder, Max! And I've told you a thousand times I find that hard to believe.'

'How you French girls love being provocative!'

'How do you know? Have you fucked many French girls?'

'Thousands, but only one that counts!'

Their room looked on to the central courtyard. Through the open window, I could see the *femme de chambre* struggling with the laundry and an old man digging at a patch of earth. Was he trying to grow vegetables? Their bed stopped creaking and all went quiet. I could imagine Ann-Marie snuggling down, relishing the warmth of Max sleeping by her side. She was a lovely girl.

On the table, I could see Max's belt, holster, gold watch and a pile of 100 franc notes. On the wardrobe door hung his uniform; his black glossy boots stood inside the door having just been carefully polished by Robert. She'd only to ring the bell and Robert would bring up champagne and two glasses on a tray. That would be 12,000 francs.

After a few minutes, one of them stirred in bed.

'Will you play the cello for me some time?' she asked.

'Of course, my darling, I'll play for you a Beethoven sonata – beautiful, relaxing music which makes one forget the world and the war.'

'I thought all you Germans were so pleased with the world and the war that you wouldn't want to forget them.'

I didn't think that was a clever remark to make.

'I am not pleased with the war. None of us wanted it. It was forced upon us.'

She quickly changed the subject.

'We can go to music concerts here in Paris, you know, Max.'

'I know. At the *Salle Pleyel*.'

'I've never been.'

'Really! I shall arrange for tickets. We will go, just the two of us, and we'll hold hands, whilst the music swir-l-s-s around us.'

'Like children!'

'Like innocent young lovers!'

They laughed together and he kissed her.

'*Je t'aime*,' he said spontaneously.

'Say it in German for me.'

'*Ich liebe dich*.'

'What other languages can you speak?'

'I can speak a few words of English.'

'That will be useful when you conquer that country.'

'Perhaps.'

'Perhaps "useful" or perhaps "conquer"?'

'Perhaps both. The English are an odd race: very different from us. Not part of Europe at all.'

'How do you know?'

'I lived there. In London: I was at college there.'

'When was that?'

'Ten years ago. I was eighteen.'

'You've had such an interesting life, Max. Did you enjoy England?'

'Very much. The people were good to me.'

53

'The French are good to you too.'

'Germany is also a good country. The best of all. We will become the true leaders of Europe, after the decadent Anglo-Saxons have been defeated.'

'I'd like to see Germany, and where you live in Berlin.'

'So you shall, my darling. I will try to arrange for you to come to my home and hear me play my cello.'

'You don't have it with you here?'

'My darling, you can't take a cello to war. It's not like a flute.'

'Then perhaps we could buy one here in Paris.'

'That is a good idea. Could we go to a music instrument shop?'

'Why not?'

'Let's go tomorrow.'

When, later, she consulted me at my desk, I feigned surprise at the enquiry.

'A cello! It is possible I can put you in touch with a knowledgeable gentleman. He is an expert at what is now called "System D".'

'What does that mean, Monsieur Henri?'

'For *débrouiller*, you know – managing somehow to get things done. It is becoming a fine art.'

Much later, she told me what had happened. Buying a cello proved to require a series of complex transactions, involving the exchange of francs for butter and sugar, and the use of those goods as currency. It became an exciting treasure hunt, which helped to bring them together. They went hand in hand from one dusty back room to another, throughout Paris, searching for a perfect specimen. The instrument they finally bought looked and sounded beautiful.

She showed it to me proudly, saying, 'It will be the first piece of furnishing in our conjugal home.'

That was never to be, but at least, buying a cello was a helpful introduction to System D which became for us all a way of life for the next five years.

During this period, I was studying the works of Charles Fourier

(1772–1837), a Utopian philosopher, and was much influenced by him. He believed that Paris is a city of love, lust and passion located in a culture which prides itself on its capacity for logic and reasoning power. He also believed that the planets regularly copulated amongst themselves, so spawning civilisation as we know it. He set himself the task of classifying passion and came up with thirteen different varieties: the five senses; honour; friendship; love and parenthood; concordance; intrigue; variety; and finally unityism, a sort of egotism turned inside out. I believe, as he did, that in a perfect future all these passions would be duly satisfied. And that it is my task in life as a healer – to secure they are satisfied in the lives of my patients; in the life of Ann-Marie, for instance, whose problems, frankly, obsess me.

To secure this satisfaction, according to Fourier, no woman should have less than four husbands or lovers concurrently, or, failing that, in rapid succession. He called this the butterfly passion for variety, creating sexual and moral harmony. In an extraordinary exemplification of this theory, Ann-Marie did have four lovers concurrently, and, later in our relationship, she recited to me in detail the histories of them. The results were dramatic but not as successful as Fourier would have predicted. The first was Major Max Braunich. In the privacy of my consulting room, she told me how that ended and the second relationship began.

'My affair with Max went well for several weeks. I was radiantly happy and my looks improved. On my nineteenth birthday, Max gave a party for me at the Victoire. He and his colleagues raised their glasses and voted me 'La plus belle fille de Paris'. General von Studnitz kissed my hand. In the afternoons I waited for him to come home, and put out baguette crumbs for the sparrows. Mostly they'd disappeared: flown off to England – some said – to continue the war. Like Albert. Sometimes, when I was lonely, I wondered what had happened to the silly idiot.

Then, one evening, Max arrived back looking very pleased with himself. He was unexpectedly early, and I was still in bed, smoking and reading. During the day I led a lazy life, for without

55

Max and his bundles of 100 franc notes I couldn't go to the shops.

He said, 'Prepare yourself, my darling. I am the bearer of extraordinary news. It is both good and bad. I am both delighted and desolated by what has happened today.'

'What?'

First, I will tell you the good news: I have been promoted. Six months early. You see before you Colonel Max Braunich. It is in recognition of my work in Paris; particularly my regulations to secure that the Jews must register themselves and their businesses. That has been considered exceptionally successful.'

'Max! That's wonderful! We'll have champagne.'

'You will have guessed already what is to be the bad news: I am to be transferred to the East – to command a regiment in the field. Staff work is all very fine for a time, but not for ever. So, in a sense, that is good news too, but I am desolated at leaving Paris.'

Nothing had ever been said about our settled way of life coming to an end, and somehow I'd come to believe it never would. Not while the Occupation continued – and after that my plan was to go back with him to Berlin for ever. We would get married, which would be legal because I'd claim to be a war widow. Max was handsome, cultivated, generous and from a good German family. He had taken me to concerts, theatres, shown me the tourist sights of Paris and taught me to listen to Bach and Beethoven. So I was terribly upset at the thought of losing him. I burst into tears.

'No, no, no, that's terrible! What will become of me? How will I survive without you?'

'Now, my darling, it's not as terrible as all that. War is full of lovers' partings. I know it seems cruel now, but soon you'll come to accept it.' He added as an afterthought, 'We'll both come to accept it.'

'How? When will we be able to meet again?'

'Who knows? That is war.'

'Can't I come with you? We planned that once. You promised that I should come to Germany so that we could stay together. You can't just go off, when we've had such good times together. And been so close! Where will I live?'

'Don't imagine I haven't thought of all that, my darling, and made plans so that you will remain here, snug and secure, with no worries.'

'How? What plans?'

I wasn't pretending to cry; I didn't need to pretend.

'It has not been difficult. You know my colleague Hans-Otto has always liked and admired you. He thinks, as I do, that you are very beautiful. He is kind and clever. We have worked together for a long time and I'm confident you will come to love him as you have loved me.'

Hans-Otto, Max's assistant, was a sycophantic bastard, who laughed at Max's jokes, but was otherwise totally without a sense of humour. He was always trying to look up my skirt; anyway he was only a Hauptman, and I didn't want to sink that low. So I went on crying inconsolably.

'So you think you can pass me on to him just like that?'

'He has promised to take over the expenses of this suite.'

'So you think you've sold me to him!'

'Nonsense, my darling. What I mean is he has said many times that when I'm posted...'

'He wants to take me over. Is that what you're going to say?'

'No, no, no! He has many times confided that if we were not already lovers he would have made a pass at you. He admires you very much.'

'What about me? You think I can just drop one lover on Tuesday and start with another on Wednesday?'

'Look, Ann-Marie, I know you're upset, but let's not talk about it now. Let's go out and have dinner, just the two of us. We've still got another whole week together.'

I hesitated. Pride and anger almost made me refuse to go. He was treating me like a possession, showing neither love nor respect.

But I caught myself in time. Where would I go without this suite? Back to Albert's Mama? That would be hell now. What alternatives had I got? If I had a row with Max and turned down Hans-Otto, I'd have to start again from scratch with whatever German bastard I could find. Better the devil you know…

What really made me angry was that Max was so ready to pass me on like a pet he couldn't play with any longer. Maybe soon he'd be pining for me. No, he wouldn't! He'd be back with his wife and he'd have forgotten all about me. What a typical German shit he turned out to be! And how naive I was thinking he was going to take me back to Germany with him. Next time I'd know better. Never trust men. All they wanted was to get between your legs, and then, when they'd had a good go at that, they pissed off… First Albert. Now Max. And Hans-Otto? How long would he last?

Throughout the next week with Max I never let anger and resentment show through. On our final night, Max played the Beethoven cello sonata movement that I particularly liked, reducing me to tears. That pleased him enormously. Then he went off at dawn, leaving his cello, because it couldn't travel with him. When I recovered, I kicked it to pieces. Afterwards I felt even worse. My bad temper had cost me a hundred thousand francs.

Hans-Otto was gracious enough to allow a few days to elapse before calling on me at the same time as Max used to call. He'd now succeeded to Max's job and behaved as if it were absolutely natural he should succeed to his mistress. He was a fat ugly little bastard with a scar on his cheek. It wasn't a duelling scar: someone hit him with a bottle, he later told me. Quite a reasonable thing to do, in my opinion. He walked with a swagger, and you'd have known he was a Boche if you saw him across the street.

'*Bonsoir, Ann-Marie, ma petite.* How nice to see you and how beautiful you're looking this evening! What a pretty dress! Shall we go out to dinner? Are you nearly ready?'

'Nearly.'

'I'm taking you to the most fashionable restaurant in Paris.'

58

'Marvellous!'

'And the most expensive. Where we'll be seen by everyone.'

'Marvellous!'

He meant Maxims in rue Royale. At Maxims, there was no rationing or shortages. It was said that when Louis Vaudable, the patron, opened the refrigerator, it always contained a bucket of fresh cream. Maxims had become almost a private club for high ranking German officers, and black-marketeers. The menus were of pre-war standard and the wine list ran to twenty seven-pages. Hans-Otto pointed out impressive celebrities at nearby tables: Sacha Guitry, Maurice Chevalier, Otto Abetz, the German ambassador. The waiters greeted Hans-Otto as a regular customer and gave us impeccable service.

We had a dozen oysters each, then partridge, with a particularly good burgundy which Hans-Otto selected, and tarte tatin for dessert. He came regularly with colleagues, he said, but it was more pleasurable having me by his side, looking so beautiful. He really set himself to soften me up.

'I've thought about you a lot, Ann-Marie. I know I can't speak French as well as Max, and I'm not cultivated like him, but I'm sure I can make you happy.'

I didn't say anything, so he went on.

'And we'll have some good times together, won't we?'

'Of course.'

'Whatever you want, you have only to ask me.'

'Thank you.'

'I've brought you a small present as a token of my admiration.'

It was a diamond necklace. I couldn't get a close look at it to see if it was valuable. He put it on me, pawing my neck and shoulders in a revolting way. He'd been eating and drinking greedily and his polite manners began to dissolve in the champagne. Leaning forward so that I could get the full blast of his terrible breath, he said, 'You have beautiful breasts. I'm really looking forward to handling them.'

'That's not a very cultivated thing to say.'

'I've told you I'm not cultivated like that snob, Braunich, and I don't claim to be. I don't know anything about music and all that stuff. And I don't want to. But I can fuck like a rattlesnake.'

I pretended not to hear.

'I've got a really big prick, you know. A metre long! You'll appreciate it. I like girls to sit astride me. That's what I'm going to get you to do, when we get back. You'll enjoy it.'

Again I kept quiet. I hadn't expected such calculated brutality, and wasn't sufficiently sure of myself to scold him. Nor could I get up and walk out. He was sober enough to perceive my discomfort and went on needling me.

'Gone quiet on me, have you, you gorgeous little bitch? Braunich gave you quite a testimonial. Said he could handle your bottom for hours. Gave him a magnificent hard! And that you were a really great fuck. Not that he knows much about it. But I'm looking forward to getting my prick into your arse. Anticipation is part of the pleasure, you know. That's why I like talking about it.'

All I could do was drink, so I drained my glass and demanded a refill. When we got back to the suite I had no problems in letting him make love to me, which he did with animal power. He hadn't the style or consideration of Max, and I couldn't lose myself in the act of love, which I usually did. I decided I hated Hans-Otto and hoped he got killed soon. After I'd fallen asleep he woke me up and forced me to open my mouth to accommodate him. But I refused to bend over for him because I wasn't a bitch or a mare. Fortunately, Hans-Otto had had enough for one night.

As he fell asleep, he whispered, 'I find your body very beautiful. Max was right. You're really a sweet little fucker. I could screw you all night long.' I was supposed to feel pleased. 'You're worth every penny of the room rent.'

Max would never have said anything vulgar like that. At first I couldn't help making repeated comparisons between the two of them. But after a while they began to blend into one indistinguishable German, who appeared at predictable times, possessed a limitless supply of money, and gave me a home, food and drink, in return for exclusive services rendered.'

At the time Ann-Marie narrated these events, I found her story depressing. But worse was to come. An affair with a third lover began in my presence. I had taken Jean-Pierre for a glass of wine at the Café Victoire next door. Jean-Pierre is the son of my *veilleur de nuit*, and I'd known him since he was a child. At that time, he was seventeen, but very tall, handsome and already growing a beard, which made him look older. His father wanted him to be a doctor and was working night and day to finance his education. I thought the boy was insufficiently appreciative of his father's efforts. He was grumbling to me about life at his *lycée* when Ann-Marie came into the café and I waved to her to join us – a colossal error on my part!

She told me later, that after I'd gone back to the Victoire, he said, 'What are you doing this afternoon?'

'Nothing, of course!'

'Let's go for a walk in the Tuileries.'

'Don't you have to go back to the *Lycée*?'

He lied. 'It's a half-day.'

She didn't believe him, but her afternoons were always lonely. They walked past the Madeleine, where the pornographic post-card salesmen were doing magnificent business with the forces of the occupying power, and sat in the gardens, autumnal and deserted.

He wasted no time, but took her hand and said, 'Ann-Marie, I'm madly in love with you! It's *la vraie passion*. I can't think of anything else. I can't do my work at school. You're the most beautiful girl I've ever seen. When you look at me I go to pieces. I dream about you at night. You come naked into my bedroom and we make love together. I know you're two years older than me, but, please, please tell me you care for me, just a little.'

'You ... you mustn't talk like that.'

'Why not?'

'Because I'm in love with someone else.'

'One of those fucking Boches! I don't believe you really care for him.'

'He's a fine German officer.'

'What about me?'

'We're just good friends.' Because he looked so miserable, she added, 'But I do like you very much.'

Taking this as the encouragement he needed, he grabbed her, pushed his tongue into her mouth, and his hand up her skirt.

'Stop it! You're crazy.'

But soon they were back in her bedroom, where he pulled her into the unmade bed. He got into the habit of going there after lunch and regularly missed afternoon school. I showed my disapproval – but they didn't care. They got more and more careless, until one afternoon the key turned, the door opened and Hans-Otto marched in. He saw them, but gave no sign, just nodding and saying imperturbably, 'I am so sorry to intrude. I will return later.'

When he reappeared, Ann-Marie was dressed in her best and sobbing uncontrollably. She'd succeeded in convincing herself that Jean-Pierre had ruthlessly raped her. What remained was to present this version of events to Han-Otto. But he didn't give her a chance to rehearse her lines.

'You have been a very stupid girl. But even you will recognize this brings our relationship to a close. Sharing isn't in the bargain. This suite confers exclusive rights. Your tenancy is cancelled and you will move out tomorrow. This has been an unhappy day for me, but we Germans are civilized people and I bear you no grudges for deceiving me in a manner typical of your race and sex. We have been repeatedly warned that the French are not to be trusted. Particularly their women. I now understand that.'

'Oh no, you don't understand, my darling.'

'Oh yes, I understand very well.'

He nodded solemnly, walked up to her and slapped her hard twice across the face. Then he grabbed her and threw her over his knee like a child. With one hand, he tore down her knickers, and with the other beat her violently with his gloved hand. She struggled to get away and tried to kick him, but he was too strong for her. Finally, he pushed her, sobbing with pain and rage, onto the floor. Then he stepped back.

'You know, Ann-Marie, I really enjoyed that. It was good fun. I feel much better now. I should have beaten you regularly. Your bottom is very attractive when it is pink. I am quite tempted by it.'

He surveyed the damage carefully, grinned at her and walked out.

May 1941

At eleven in the morning on the day after Albert flew to France, the XX Committee met in the basement war room to review operations. Spears represented the Prime Minister, Palewski the Free French, together with other officers on behalf of various secret agencies. The Chair was taken by Head of Military Intelligence, a donnish old fellow, with the rank of brigadier and a row of 1914–18 medal ribbons. It was his practice to open with a review of objectives, ticking them off on a blackboard.

'They are firstly to monitor the progress of those '*ruses de guerre*' already in train; second to devise and structure new stratagems; thirdly to detect comparable deceits which the enemy may try to practise on us. Any questions?'

He turned to the 'Minutes of the Previous Meeting: No 73: to activate Operation Determinate'. This recited that the volunteer carrier had been successfully briefed. The PM's presence was not recorded.

'As regards those who were present, does this appear a true and correct record?'

No-one disputed the minute, so he passed to 'Matters Arising Therefrom'.

'The Committee might like to note that the operation had been set in train yesterday.'

The representative of Naval Intelligence, who hadn't been present at the earlier meeting and felt left out, said, 'There is one aspect. Have the dangers of the mission becoming public knowledge been fully considered?'

'What do you have in mind?'

'Suppose the mission is a success. Knowledge of it, leaking out, may redound to our discredit in, say, the United States.'

'It will not leak out.'

'Would you care to enlarge on that?'

'No-one will be in a position to leak it.'

'What about the junior officer delegated to carry the document?'

'That contingency has been provided for.'

'I see.'

Everyone listened to this discussion attentively, turning their heads from one contestant to the other as if at the Wimbledon Finals. Then the Chairman turned to the next item on the Agenda, which was a delightful and audacious ruse involving a Major Martin, a dead body at sea, forged and misleading papers and concealed identity. It was at an early stage of development and much work remained to be done. The meeting divided into two camps with heated debate. On a narrow vote, it was agreed to go forward.

At the end, the Chairman said, 'This has been a very useful discussion. As you know, the PM regards the work of this Committee as highly important.'

There was nodding around the table. It was encouraging to hear that. Promotions and decorations might be distributed in due course. They got out diaries and fixed the date of the next meeting.

As they were leaving, Palewski button-holed Spears.

'You know, Edward, my dear old fellow, I didn't quite understand what was said about our young friend Leconte.'

Spears went on lighting his pipe.

'What exactly was the implication of "that contingency has been provided for".'

'That everything is under control, I expect.'

'Then you don't know any particular implication?'

'Not my business any more. Nor yours.'

Spears nodded and strode out in a cloud of tobacco smoke leaving Palewski angry and worried, alone at the conference table.

May 1941

As soon as I succeeded in releasing my 'chute, I headed for a clump of trees, rubbing my bruises and clutching my precious brief-case. I'd landed back home in the *Hexagone*. It smelled different. The air was warm and hospitable. I should have been elated, but I wasn't. I was worried and afraid. My heart was thumping like a steam hammer. Had my drop been sufficiently near the stipulated landing point? Would I make the rendezvous? That river I'd seen: it looked like the Loire, one of my favourites when a schoolboy on holiday. But it couldn't have been. Would that I were still on holiday instead of on this absurd mission. Reluctantly, I pushed away the past and struggled back into the urgent present.

The Anson hadn't the range to fly to the Free Zone, so I'd been landed in Occupied France near Nantes. The village I had to find was called Ancenis; my rendezvous was south of the church at a crossroads. I orientated myself on the map and set off through the silent night. After an hour, I realised I'd gone wrong and reversed direction. The code words for my rendezvous were obscure: '*Le temps a laissé son manteau*' and the response would be: '*de vent, de froidure et de pluie.*' Who could have dreamed up such childish stuff? My rendezvous was to be with two diplomats, Colonel DeMoulin and his aide, who'd escort me by car to Vichy. I would personally hand the document to General Maxime Weygand, said to be the most pro-British of Pétain's team, because he'd been given an honorary knighthood in 1918. I would witness his signature, would then be driven to Cerbère, through Spain to Lisbon, and thence flown back to London. At briefing time, it had seemed plausible. Now I was less confident. Spears had once commented that the French were a nation of sceptics. I'd responded: 'To doubt is to be strong.' And Spears had been impressed.

Now I was full of doubt, but not at all strong.

When I finally got there, the escort party wasn't at the church. I sat in the porch. What was I supposed to do? Wait all night?

Suppose by dawn I was still sitting there, shivering and feeling foolish.

It was quiet in the Breton countryside, so I heard a vehicle approaching from far away. It could be a German patrol. The car stopped close to the church and two officers got out. A strong torch flashing around prevented me from seeing their faces, but their uniforms were German. One of them had a pistol in his hand. I crouched deeper into the porch and they brushed past me into the church, the wooden door slamming behind them. Acting on impulse, I ran to the road, and slid behind the wheel of their Mercedes, pulled the starter and drove down the dark road struggling to turn the lights on. After a few minutes I stopped and tried to think. Had I been stupid? Were they the messengers I'd been sent to meet? But they were Germans. Should I go back or go on? I'd lost all power of decision.

I drove on rapidly and turned left at a junction. What a stupid error! Ahead of me was a road block and a sentry. There was a shout of 'Halt!', so I put my foot down and hit the wire at speed. A lurch, a crash and two rifle shots. Wire was apparently caught in a mudguard and the Mercedes wasn't so smooth now. A tyre had been punctured, I decided, so I drove into a clump of trees, switched off the engine and sat shaking.

On the back seat I found a bottle of Martell cognac, helped myself to that and felt better. What now? Sleep was what I badly needed so, warmed by some more cognac, I nodded off on the back seat, hiding my briefcase containing the protocol underneath it.

When I woke it was dawn. Stiff and cold, I tramped back to the road, and set off heading east. It was a fine morning; the dawn chorus had begun and life seemed worth living. I would get to Vichy, rescue my country from the German oppressors, and become a hero. The exercise and the warm sun made me cheerful. This was going to be a repeat of my adventure in England. Soon, I'd find a restaurant and be offered the equivalent of fish and chips – grilled perch from the river – and two lovely girls.

67

Before I'd gone a few hundred metres a German army truck came up behind me, slowed and stopped. The young blonde, grinning driver leaned out and offered me a lift. It would have been suspicious to refuse, so I got in, thanked him, and he drove off. Then – it hit me like a bullet – I realised I'd left the brief case under the back seat of the car. Unbelievable! What a colossal, fucking idiot I was! I had to go back, so I tugged my new friend's arm and shouted. *'Arrêtez s'il vous plaît, Monsieur!'* He nodded and smiled, but clearly didn't understand. In wild panic and desperation I picked up a spanner lying in front of me on the dashboard and cracked him on the head with it. He looked at me in reproachful astonishment for a fraction of a second and then slumped forward onto the wheel. The truck veered on to the right verge, there was a lurch and a crash, and we ended with two wheels in the ditch. I'd succeeded in killing a kindly driver and wrecking another vehicle.

As I walked back to the Mercedes, I repeatedly cursed myself. Shame overwhelmed me. No more dreams of heroic deeds, medals, and strategic success in the face of overwhelming odds. This was what war was really like: crazy missions, in which everything inevitably went wrong; and stupid individuals like me, who, for no reason, panicked, killed and destroyed. However just the cause, the results could never be equally just.

The sun came up and I got hot and thirsty. When, after a two hour walk, I found the car I'd stolen, the two German officers were standing by it, one holding the precious brief-case. I froze, giving them time to draw their Lugers. The taller one jammed his pistol in my guts. He was obviously in a foul temper and would enjoy shooting me.

I put my hands up and said hopefully, *'Le temps a laissé son manteau...'*

His response was in French.

'Please come quietly with us. You've caused enough trouble for one night.'

I said fatuously, 'What about the pass-word?'

'Fuck the pass-word. Get in the car.'

'You are Colonel DeMoulin?'

'Certainly not! Just get in the car.'

'How long will it take us to reach Vichy?'

'We're not going to Vichy.'

'Where are we going?'

'Paris.'

'You are the representative of General Weygand?'

'No.'

'Who do you represent?'

'When we get there, it will be communicated to you.'

'Where in Paris are we going?'

'Abwehr headquarters.'

Now, I thought, I'm in deep *merde*. Presumably, Vichy had betrayed the plot to the Germans. Perhaps, on arrival, I'd be interrogated, tortured and shot. I cursed de Gaulle for nominating me for this mission, and Churchill for seducing me with warmth and flattery. Instead of playing a war hero, I should have told him his proposals were all bullshit. Then I could have gone back to my office in Carleton House Gardens and filled in another set of indent forms. It might have seemed boring then. Now it appeared a secure and fruitful occupation. Reflecting on it, I fell asleep, and was woken by the German shaking me.

'Get out. You can sleep in your room now.'

We were parked in Place de la Concorde, directly outside Hôtel Crillon. German sentries stood by the door with sub-machine guns. I felt a momentary flicker of pleasure at being in Paris, but it didn't last. My captor, who wore the uniform of a Major in the SS, waved a pass, picked up a key from reception and led me into an amazingly luxurious bedroom: double bed, velvet curtains, etc.

'My instructions to you, Leconte, are that you must not try to leave the hotel. But you can ring for food and drink. You will shortly be summoned to a meeting.'

He disappeared before I could reply, taking my briefcase with him. I lay on the bed, too stunned to think. Was I to be tortured to death in a five star hotel with gold-plated fittings? Reality was disappearing under all the plush canopies. I slept again and was woken by a waiter with coffee. It tasted delicious. When I got back from the bathroom the SS Major was sitting on my bed, now grinning at me.

'Wake up again, Leconte. You have a big meeting to attend.'

'With whom?'

'You'll see.'

He pushed me ahead of him down corridors and we walked together into an impressive conference room where several gold-braided officers were sitting round a table. I was relieved to see Weygand, my former Commander in Chief, next to a German general in the centre. It was von Studnitz, but I didn't recognise him at the time. At a side table sat other German officers, some wearing the uniform of the Gestapo. I stood to attention, conscious of crumpled clothes, unshaven chin and being an object of all eyes. How should I respond to interrogation? I seemed drained of all confidence. Weygand, who looked old and tired, addressed me with stiff formality.

'You are Captain Albert Leconte?'

Pretence seemed futile.

'Yes, General.'

'You are the authorised emissary of Winston Churchill, Prime Minister of Great Britain?'

'Yes, General.'

'And do you confirm that the document you brought with you is the Protocol to implement Operation Determinate?'

'I don't know what it is called, General.'

'Do you know its substance?'

'Not precisely.'

'What have been your orders?'

It was too late to dissimulate. Or I was too scared.

'That I would be met and taken to Vichy, not Paris. That you, General, would execute the document on behalf of your

70

government, I would witness it, and return with it to London as soon as practicable.'

They all looked at one another. Then they looked at me with contempt.

'Well, Leconte, you will be interested to hear that is all nonsense or lies. And that you will not be going back to London quite yet...'

Von Studnitz interjected, 'If ever.'

'... but there is every reason to believe that your mission will succeed, and that the current conflict will soon be brought to an end.'

'May I ask how long I will have to wait here?'

'That is not known.'

'May I leave the hotel to visit my wife in Paris?'

'Of course not! You are confined to barracks. And you are now dismissed.'

I was led dejected back to my room.

'I will secure some dinner for both of us,' my escort said. 'May I introduce myself? I am SS Oberführer Erich Reindorf. You are to hold yourself subject to my orders. We shall, I fear, be spending some time together.'

'Captain Albert Leconte, Free French Forces.'

'Yes, I know.'

We shook hands. I began to warm to him.

'Do you play chess?' he asked.

'A little.'

'Good. It may help pass time, which would otherwise be frustrating for us both.'

'It is frustrating for me to be back in my home city and unable to see any of it.'

'You can view the elegant Place de la Concorde from your window.'

'But my wife is not in the Place.'

'What is her name?'

'Ann-Marie.'

71

'Believe me, Leconte, I understand your problem. Many of us have been separated from our wives and families for months.'

He wasn't, I'd realised, a totally unsympathetic character. After roast pork, *haricots verts*, and a choice of *fromages*, all of which were delicious, I fell asleep again, and dreamed of Ann-Marie running towards me, arms outstretched. As she reached me I woke up and couldn't remember where I was. I began grappling with what little I'd been told. At least I wasn't going to be shot. But what I'd been told at Churchill's briefing about de Gaulle's functions as leader being terminated and his leaving London didn't seem to fit in with Weygand's comments or attitude. That must have been a colossal error or, more likely, I suddenly realised, a cover story. It must have been an elaborately staged, deliberate false briefing. So what was the vital document I'd brought? I should have opened it and read it.

In my gold and pink room at the Crillon, the days passed slowly. Rindorf and I played chess. Whilst waiting for me to make my moves, he wrote long entries in a big leather-bound diary.

'Are you recording all the moves in this game?'

'No, in the larger game, played with fewer rules.'

I ceased worrying about the true nature of my mission and settled into a quiet routine, telling myself I must be patient. Soon, I'd get to see my wife and son. I had not been thinking about Ann-Marie, but my new proximity to her made me reflect on our marriage, and my shameful behaviour. My lost confidence began to return. At least I was in Paris, although all I'd seen of it was Place de la Concorde, around which German military traffic revolved. Each morning, to pass the time, I diligently read *Le Figaro*, now reporting a war totally different from the one I'd been experiencing. German paratroops had successfully landed in Crete. The forces of that traitor, de Gaulle, and the British had occupied Syria. Parisian beauties, denied silk stockings, were dyeing their legs with iodine! Hitler and Laval had met and lunched together in Bertesgarten.

Then, on 23rd June, the paper carried a startling black headline:

GRAND OFFENSIVE IN THE EAST

Decisive campaign of the Great Conflict! It would be the most glorious and supreme victory of a nation in arms that the world had ever known. The German forces were advancing into the Russian heartland, virtually unopposed. The Luftwaffe was destroying lines of communication and enemy troop concentrations. It would all be over in six weeks and the barbaric Bolshevist leaders would bow down before a superior civilised power.

When Reindorf, whom I had somehow ceased to think of as an enemy, next appeared he said, 'Congratulations on the success of your mission!'

'What success? What mission? I've told you thousands of times I don't understand what my mission was.'

Reindorf laughed.

'So you say, my friend, so you say.'

All my further attempts to elicit what he'd meant were greeted with laughter and cynicism. He told me not to worry about the world beyond our chess-board. Everything was going to plan. My orders would come in good time. We would drink wine together to celebrate my success. He would secure an assortment of girls for us. Now I went back to speculating again about what could have been the nature of my mission, which somehow seemed to be connected with the Russian offensive. I'd long since discarded the version given me by Churchill. Anyway, it didn't seem to matter now. Things were looking good: the crisp croissants that morning were delicious.

But it was a false dawn. Next morning whilst enjoying *petit déjeuner*, Reindorf appeared looking grim.

'Leconte, you have a big problem,' he snapped. 'You are to attend a meeting immediately. Follow me.'

I put on my jacket and marched to the conference room where von Studnitz and some Gestapo officers were sitting at the conference table. They looked at me with hostility and suspicion.

'Leconte, you brought and delivered to the Reichsführer a document from Churchill and the British government, giving clear and specific undertakings.'

'Yes, I think so.'

'Nonsense! Don't play the fool this morning. We are not in a mood to be amused by your humour. I tell you that you did.'

'Very well!'

'Those clear and specific undertakings have not yet been acted upon and we are becoming impatient. What explanation can you give us?'

'I can't give you any explanation. I don't know anything about the undertakings or the actions of the British government. I was just a message bearer.'

'And what was the message you were bearing? Tell us precisely and in detail the nature of your briefing by the British.'

I was too intimidated to pretend, so I babbled out all I could remember about Churchill's attitude towards de Gaulle and his plan to relieve him of his command, etc. They listened impatiently, and when I'd finished, they conferred.

'Leconte, you are either an accomplished liar or a bloody fool,' said von Studnitz. 'Personally, I am tempted to think the latter. But getting my colleagues in the Gestapo to believe you will be another matter. Your story is a fantasy. Either it is your fantasy or, if you are telling the truth, it is Churchill's fantasy. What do you think, Reindorf?'

'It is possible he is telling the truth. He has seemed to be honest but childishly naive.'

They muttered amongst themselves again.

Then von Studnitz said, 'You are given twenty four hours. If you have no more to tell us, you will be interrogated again with much less civility. I hope you recognise what is at stake. Now get out.'

When we got back to my room, Reindorf said, 'Whatever the truth of your story, Leconte, you're a bloody fool.'

'I realise that now, but what I told them was true.'

'I think I believe you but getting the Gestapo to believe you is another matter. They will pull out your finger nails to get what they want. One by one! Do you understand?'

'Yes.'

'Listen to me, Leconte,' he said slowly and carefully, looking me straight in the eye. 'I can arrange for you to be locked in your room with a sentry outside your door. Or you can give me your word as an officer you will not try to leave the building, or do anything indiscreet. I require your positive affirmation in good faith.'

'Of course.'

'It is your solemn parole.'

'Of course!'

At the time, I didn't understand why he wasn't locking me in my room as he'd done before. Later – much later – I realised that he was a humane man who was deliberately giving me a chance to escape. Perhaps it was to assuage his conscience, but whatever the reason I took it. Later, with fingernails throbbing at the thought they might be torn out, I strolled casually into the kitchen basement, empty in the afternoon, and found the staff exit. There was a *guichet* where they checked in and out, so I crawled on the floor below window level, then walked free into the streets of my beloved city, crossing Pont de la Concorde with the Chamber of Deputies directly ahead. It was a fifteen minute saunter to my own apartment and I forced myself not to run. I began to think about holding Ann-Marie in my arms and making love to her in bed. She was, I recalled, a passionate, enthusiastic and imaginative lover.

Sentries were posted outside Palais Bourbon; the Germans seemed everywhere. Officers passed me saluting each other, and my arm twitched in response. I set myself to avoid meeting eyes. If I were stopped without identity papers I was bound to be arrested. I looked steadily into the distance. All street notices were now in German which seemed bizarre. There were few

75

French vehicles in the streets, only German lorries and motor cyclists. The War Ministry building in Boulevard St Germain was sandbagged and heavily guarded. It seemed crazy that my short walk should take me past so many key Occupation points. At Métro Bac, I turned into Boulevard Raspail and rang the bell outside my own apartment.

By now I'd decided I would beg forgiveness from Ann-Marie for deserting her, and just go back to our old life in Paris together. Everything would be as it was, except that we'd have a child. Then I remembered that the Gestapo would be pursuing me, and my home would be the first place they'd search. Where would I go? Then my mother opened the door.

'Mama! Is Ann-Marie here?'

'Albert! You're home at last!'

'Mama!'

She looked thinner and worried. We embraced and I repeated, 'Where's Ann-Marie?'

'She's gone.'

'What do you mean: "She's gone." Gone where? When?'

'She went months ago. You are well rid of her, Albert. At least, you are safe and so is Ethienne. Where have you been all this time? We've been so worried about you. Why didn't you write? Don't you care about Ethienne?'

We embraced again. My mother was clearly torn between welcoming me home and giving me a good telling-off.

'Look at him! Isn't he handsome? He looks like you. Now I see you together, it's obvious.'

It wasn't obvious to me. Ethienne, as he was called, had a big nose and a silly name. He looked like someone I knew. Yes! Like my best friend, Daniel. But at the time that didn't mean much. When at last I got into the apartment, it seemed exactly as I'd left it a year ago. The same smell of cooking. But Ethienne hadn't been there then. I'd acquired a son, cheerful, with dark curly hair, who grinned at me as if we'd known one another a long time.

'Where's Ann-Marie, Mama?'

'All right, if you must know. I didn't want to upset you. She's keeping company with the Germans. German officers. Sleeping with them! She's a whore, Albert, and you are well rid of her.'

At first, I didn't believe her.

'Mama! How do you know all that?'

'She's been seen. By everyone! In the *neuvième* district. She's in an apartment there, I think.'

'Where?'

'Don't worry about her, Albert. Let her be...'

'Where is she living?'

'In rue Taitbout, I think. It's become a bad quarter. Near rue de Provence. All the whores work there. It's well known.'

'What number?'

'I don't know.'

'Just tell me where she is,' I shouted.

'I don't know the number. She hangs about in a hotel in that quarter, one that's been taken over. German officers are billeted there and that's where she picks them up.'

'Is all this true?'

'Of course it's true. Forget about her. She's gone from the family now. Tell me where you've come from. Those clothes don't fit you properly. You don't seem to know what it's like in Paris. The girls are going with Germans to get cigarettes and coffee. Some people will do anything...'

Until this moment, I hadn't believed that I'd become a father. While I'd been in England, Ann-Marie's pregnancy had become a vague recollection. Nothing had prepared me for the phenomenon of a son: this living, breathing creature. I stared at him, searching for my own likeness. All I could see was a cheerful baby, who stared back.

'How have you managed?' I asked my mother lamely. 'What has been happening to you?'

Mama collapsed into hysterical sobs and I clumsily tried to comfort her.

77

'Now Mama! Ethienne is watching and he is wondering what's going on.'

She recovered quickly.

'Have you come from England? I've been so worried about you.'

'Yes. Listen. I've got to go.'

'Go! Go where? You're crazy, Albert. You've only just arrived. Don't you want some food? Where are you going? When will you come back?'

'I've got to find Ann-Marie.'

'Don't go, Albert. Ethienne needs you. So do I!'

'I must, Mama. I'll come back, soon, I promise.'

'Go then! Wait! Aren't you going to kiss your little son? Hold him for a moment.'

Gingerly I picked up Ethienne, who clung to me and then said, 'Mama, mama.'

'I can't believe he's real.'

'He's real enough. And he's crawling now. You should see him eat – when there's anything for him.'

'I'll bring something next time I come.'

'When will you come back?'

'I don't know. Soon!'

When I tried to hand Ethienne to his grandmother, he gave a yell, clung to my neck, then struggled to get down. Then he clung to my knee.

'If you see Ann-Marie...' I hesitated. 'Tell her that I'm looking for her.'

'I won't see her, and if I did I wouldn't speak to her. Haven't you understood? She's living like a whore with the Boches.'

'I'll try and come back tomorrow.'

I kissed my mother, hugged Ethienne and closed the door on their cries of protest. As I ran down the stairs I could hear my son shouting: 'Mama, mama!' Would I ever hear him shouting 'Papa?'

Struggling to come to terms with what I'd been told, I set off for the *neuvième* across the Seine. Passing Café des Sports on the other side of the boulevard, I couldn't help glancing at the familiar terrace table, still sunny in the later afternoon. There I used to sit with my friends, arguing, gossiping and watching life go by. It was there I'd first met Ann-Marie, who had seemed the most seductive girl in the group, and when I'd secured her, my friends envied me. Daniel, my closest friend, confided he would have liked to contest this prize and I wondered if they hadn't spent rather too much time together after I'd been called up.

I could see Gaston, the waiter, wearing his white coat, still standing in the doorway to welcome customers. As I watched, an extraordinary thing happened. Daniel sauntered around the corner, sat down and pulled a book from his pocket. Gaston hastened over and took his order. I hesitated but I didn't dare wait any longer in case our eyes met, so I walked off rapidly towards the river. I realized I'd been right. Ethienne looked like Daniel. I'd seen father and son in one afternoon. Ann-Marie had slept with him before we were married. Or after? I tried to work out dates. Anyway, my mother was right. She was a terrible slut and all my love and anxiety for her began to evaporate.

Walking north past Concorde again, I gazed at an unfamiliar world. On Avenue de l'Opéra few shops were open. Notices on windows asked 'Etes vous en ordre?'

Without any identity papers, I was conscious my answer would be 'Non!' Was the Gestapo already hunting for me? If they caught me they would inevitably assume my guilt, although I didn't know of what exactly I was supposed to be guilty.

Other notices on windows announced that Jewish businesses had been closed by order of the authorities. Long queues were forming outside the *boulangeries*. Where could I hide? I asked in a café where the military were billeted and was directed to the nearby Hôtel Victoire, a small, unprepossessing place. I pushed open the double glazed door and entered a shabby hall with marble pillars. An elegant fellow in a formal suit was sitting at the reception desk.

79

June 1941

After the defeat of France last year, the name of my hotel has begun to seem ironic. Perhaps I should change it to 'Hôtel Vaincu'. Nowadays, in France, all nomenclature is changing. We have had to learn the German word *ersatz*, meaning low quality imitation. But now *nationale* is used as a euphemism for *ersatz*. As well as *revolution nationale*, we have *café nationale*, *sucre nationale*, *tabac nationale*. Our great leader, Marshal Pétain, victor of Verdun no longer claims to offer us *Liberté, Egalité, Fraternité*, but only *Travail, Famille, Patrie!*

My life and work has become more demanding and more disagreeable. Every room, even the honeymoon suite, is now rented long-term to an officer of the occupying forces on the HQ staff of General von Studnitz. They are all having a splendid vacation here and regularly tell me they adore my city. Hitler would flatten London without a second thought, but not Paris.

They are demanding guests, calling for hot water, cold champagne, fresh towels and clean girls at all hours of the day and night. I am neglecting my medical studies and my patients. But Marshal Pétain has instructed us to *collaborate* with the German authorities – another new word coming into general use. And it's quite a profitable activity being an hôtelier at this time. But my mother practices the habits of a squirrel and never allows me to handle the takings. She keeps all the cash locked away, and wears the keys on a chain around her waist. My father was the target of her continual reproaches which is why, I believe, he tripped and fell. Since his death I've become her target, and I've come to hate her.

In the mornings I sit at my desk greeting my German guests and reading *Le Figaro*. Its current joke is that the French national slogan should be: *Trahison, Famine, Prison*. When this morning, Ann-Marie appeared, I saw her face was discoloured and swollen.

'Monsieur Henri,' she asked, 'can I talk to you?'

'Of course. Please sit down. Have you had an accident?'

'I've got a little problem, Monsieur Henri. You see, Hans-Otto doesn't love me any more. We have had a quarrel. He has been horrible to me. You know what Germans are like.'

'I'm very sorry.'

'So I've decided to leave him.'

'I'm sorry to hear that.'

'I wondered if I could take my own room here. I've got a few francs saved up, which will last a while if the rate isn't too high.'

I thought about the implication of her words and her body posture. She was certainly an attractive girl, with generous curves in exactly the right places. I would have found her irresistible, except that her charm was weakened by what might tactfully be called 'negative exclusivity'.

'It would be a pleasure to invite you here but, unfortunately, the whole hotel has been commandeered by the military.'

I preferred to avoid the word 'Germans'.

'Isn't there a small corner I could use for the time being?'

'I will try to think about some arrangement which might suit you.'

'I have to move out today.'

'I see.'

She came round my desk, put her head on my chest, and sobbed dramatically.

'Oh, Monsieur Henri, I know you'll help me because I'm desperate.'

I was stimulated by her proximity, but disengaged her gently.

'You can rely on me, Mademoiselle Ann-Marie. We will find you somewhere. Now let me think. There is a small store-room in the basement, where the laundry is kept. Maybe you could camp there for a few days, until you have been able to make a different arrangement.'

'Oh, Monsieur Henri, that would be marvellous! You have always been so kind to me.'

'I am sorry we cannot offer you anything more comfortable.'

81

'It's just what I need until I have a new friend.'

I felt I'd better give her a warning.

'You know, Madamoiselle, I regard young Jean-Pierre as if he were my own son. His father has worked hard in my hotel to maintain him as a student. He is in attendance here every night, seven days a week. We hope soon Jean-Pierre will go to medical school, which I myself would liked to have done, but could not. That is why I have allowed myself to have high ambitions for him.'

She must have realized this was a discreet warning, and she got the message. She'd have to give him up. That was the price of the room, and she'd have to pay it. I wondered if she'd ask 'Why are you telling me all this?', but she didn't dare. Instead, she said, 'He is a very charming boy.'

'Quite.'

'And I'm very fond of him.'

'We all are.'

There was a silence.

'Would you like to see the storeroom? It's very small, and uncomfortable. You may prefer other alternatives.'

'I have no choice.'

'I see.'

In the afternoon she moved in – a big step down from her luxurious suite. No window, no view, and nowhere to put her cases of beautiful clothes. In the evening she appeared smartly dressed to join the officers who gathered every night in my salon for champagne apéritifs. On her way, she glanced into the office and saw my mother, who was opening the safe. Her polite '*Bonsoir, Madame Rouget!*' went unanswered. Mama never condescended to notice Ann-Marie's existence; she simply ignored her.

Fortunately, Hans-Otto wasn't in the salon that night. But a large circle of his colleagues stood around, with glasses in hand but in sober mood. I couldn't understand exactly what they were talking about, but it sounded as if some dramatic offensive was about to be launched. On England?

'It was late last year the Führer made the critical decision to attack,' said one senior officer.

'Really?'

'Directive twenty-one has just been declassified. It reads: "The bulk of the Russian army stationed in Poland and Western Russia will be destroyed by deeply penetrating armoured spearheads. Russian forces still capable of giving battle will be prevented from withdrawal. The final objective is to erect a barrier against Asiatic Russia on the general line Volga-Archangel." That was issued by the Führer in December last.'

'He has taken personal command.'

'For better or worse!'

'The General Staff had difficulty in persuading him to delay until now.'

'No, it has been a wet spring in Poland. We've been waiting for the ground to dry.'

'Late June is the best date. The days are longest.'

'Napoleon chose twenty-fifth June for his invasion of Russia.'

'He didn't exactly make a success of it.'

'The Führer wanted to settle with Churchill first!'

'There'll be no deals with the Russians. The Führer has said they are to be treated as *untermensch* – subhuman. It's to be a war of total extermination.'

'What's puzzling about the decision is that we may be fighting on two fronts.'

'The Führer has said we are simply anticipating their planned assault on Germany.'

'It is claimed that the Red Army is weak and inadequately equipped. So it will be another glorious joy-ride for our troops – a lightning victory!'

'We'll have the Panzer VI in full production with the 58mm. They'll have no answer to that.'

'More importantly the morale of our troops is at peak.'

'Of course.'

'In twenty-one days, we'll be in Moscow.'

One or two of the Germans looked doubtful but concealed their reservations. Ann-Marie stood by herself for half an hour, being ignored. Then she went off to bed, and I heard her crying until she fell asleep. I was tempted to go and comfort her.

The following morning, *Paris Matin* reported that operation BARBAROSSA had begun at dawn the previous day. Waves of Heinkels and Dorniers had destroyed the Russian air-force on the ground. The largest invasion force in the world – one hundred and sixty divisions – was advancing in three separate thrusts. Three million German soldiers would become conquerors by Xmas.

The language in *Figaro* was similar. The sub-human Bolshevist threat to Franco-German civilization would soon be lifted. The government was forming a Legion of French Volunteers to fight side by side with their German allies. It was hoped 100,000 young Frenchmen would come forward. After all, half of Napoleon's 1812 army had been Germans. The logic of this escaped me.

When I showed Ann-Marie my copy, she boasted, 'My friend, Colonel Max Braunich, was transferred to the east. He will be there.'

'Without doubt.'

Later, much later, I learned from one of his colleagues that the Colonel was that day lying on his back, silent, staring at the sky. It seemed that at dawn, a stray German shell had scored a direct hit on his headquarters, killing him, his driver and his wireless operator. But, of course, at the time, I knew nothing of all that.

'Doubtless he will be having his morning coffee.'

'With some other girl, you mean, Monsieur Henri?'

'He won't have time for all that in the middle of the battlefield!'

'The Germans always seem to have time for it.'

'You may be right, Madamoiselle Ann-Marie.'

'What about you, Monsieur Henri. Do you always have time for it?'

'Not in the morning. Love-making for me is a nocturnal activity.'

'I will remember that,'

22 June 1941

The Doublecross Committee was convened in the War Room at short notice at eleven hundred hours on 22 June 1941. There was full attendance, and extra chairs had to be sent for. The Chairman opened with his usual statement of aims and objectives but he was so impatient that he rattled through them, his excitement making him stutter. Operation Determinate was briefly mentioned in the course of: 'Matters Arising From The Minutes of the Previous meeting'.

The Chairman said: '. . . we have learned the Vichy government wholly welcomed the initiative and expressed themselves ready to sign, and do all possible to influence the Germans. We know that Weygand took the Protocol to Berlin for Hitler to consider. But now, gentlemen, we must get to the main business for today. Reports have come through reliable neutral sources that at three hundred hours this morning Luftwaffe bomber squadrons began to attack Soviet forward air bases. Many Soviet aircraft have been destroyed on the ground. At the same time, German panzer columns have invaded Russian occupied Poland in great strength and crossed the frontier into the Soviet Union. These formations are advancing against relatively weak opposition. There are no reports of a formal declaration of war or any similar announcement.'

His normally impassive audience was moved to cheer. In the excitement Determinate was forgotten. Instead, the Committee began to speculate on future events.

'Does the Committee suppose that the Soviets will now seek to conclude an alliance with Britain?'

'That must be the obvious step.'

'Then what will be this Committee's advice to the War Cabinet?'

'That will require careful consideration, perhaps by a sub-Committee.'

Everyone was far too euphoric to raise disagreeable questions about Operation Determinate – as to whether to abandon de

Gaulle and the Free French. Palewski began to think that the sooner all that was forgotten the better. He slipped out of the War-room as soon as he could, for his afternoon *rendez-vous* with his darling Nancy. She got impatient when he was late, and he failed to hear the Chairman reminding the meeting of the need for confidentiality.

Next morning, he gave de Gaulle an edited version of the meeting. De Gaulle, as always, was furious and set himself to use the material to embarrass Churchill.

A month later, on 27 August, the *Chicago Daily News* carried an attention-grabbing headline:

ENGLAND AFRAID OF FRENCH FLEET!

There followed an exclusive story by George Weller, Foreign Correspondent, to whom General de Gaulle, commander of the Free French Forces, had given an exclusive interview. He was report as having said: 'What England has been carrying on is a deal with Hitler in which Vichy serves as a go-between. What happened, in effect, is an exchange of advantages between hostile powers, which keeps the Vichy government alive, so long as both Britain and Germany are agreed it should exist.'

On the following day, this colossal and unsustainable falsehood was brought to Churchill's attention by his Press secretary. Furious, the PM shouted to his cabinet colleagues, 'Is he daring to suggest that I, Winston Churchill, have done some kind of deal with the evil Nazi, Adolf Hitler?'

'That appears to be the implication, Prime Minister.'

'Then he has clearly gone off his head.'

'So it would seem, Prime Minister.'

'We must act robustly and at once.'

'Indubitably, Prime Minister.'

The Press Secretary, summoned, proposed that a denial release should carry the clear implication that de Gaulle had been 'overworking' and had become mentally disturbed.

'This is only the beginning,' Churchill bellowed. 'We must force from him a full retraction and apology.'

'Very good, Prime Minister.'

'All support for the Free French is to cease. Resources, intelligence material, broadcasting facilities are to be suspended. The whole relationship is to be treated as at an end.'

The tactic was completely successful. All de Gaulle had to rely on was Palewski's oral report, and even he realized his position was hopeless. Then Churchill summoned him to a meeting in the Cabinet Room – Churchill in his shabby battledress to demonstrate he was a man of the people, and de Gaulle in elegant blue uniform and polished boots. They glared at one another with mutual hatred. As a mark of his contempt, Churchill refused to speak his terrible French and Sir John Colville his private secretary was called in to translate.

'*Mon générale, je vous ai invité...*' he began, when Churchill interrupted him:

'I didn't call him '*Mon*' general, and I didn't say I'd '*invited*' him. I summoned him.'

Colville walked out and another interpreter had to be found to translate the exchange of insults. Churchill told de Gaulle he'd committed 'an unacceptable deliberate public provocation.' De Gaulle backed down and replied that the interview was fictitious, had never occurred, that he was making representations to the newspaper. Finally, he offered his profound apologies.

Before he left, Churchill gave him a cigar, in the hope it would make him sick. He told Colville: 'That fellow makes me hate all French. He is now lying comprehensively. It is by no means surprising his enemies have cashiered him, denationalized him and sentenced him to death. I understand exactly their attitude.'

And Churchill secured his revenge. Getting into the bath in his rented house in Kent, De Gaulle clumsily broke it and hot water flowed through the ceiling. He ran downstairs naked, frightening the housemaid. Afterwards he conducted a long feud with his landlord for compensation. Neither Spears nor Palewski were available to help: both had been transferred abroad. De Gaulle wrote to Colville asking him 'to use his influence'. Colville found an opportunity to mention this to Churchill. Together they tore up the letter and used the strips to light cigars.

After the Committee meeting, Churchill instructed Spears that the Determinate file be closed. Amongst all the comings and goings of junior officers at Carleton Gardens, Albert's absence went unnoticed. His personal file was marked: *Decommissioned and discharged from duties. Pay and rations to cease with effect from 30 May 1941. No forwarding address. Next-of kin: not known.*

His mission had slipped into history.

July 1941

I was sitting at my desk reading a classical work on homeopathy by Christian Hahnemann when Albert Leconte came into my hotel. At that time I didn't, of course, know who he was.

'Bonjour, Monsieur. Can I help you?'

'Madame Ann-Marie Leconte? Is she here?'

I put down my book.

'Who shall I say is asking for her?' I said formally.

He hesitated.

'An old friend.'

'I will make enquiries, if you will kindly wait a moment.'

I went down to the basement, knocked on the storeroom door and said, 'Mademoiselle Ann-Marie, there's a young man asking for you.'

'Who is it?'

'He says he's an old friend.'

'What does he look like?'

'He is dark, clean shaven, perhaps shorter than average, worried about something.'

She followed me into the lobby yawning. She and Albert stared at each other for some seconds, both stunned into silence, neither knowing how the other would react and waiting for a cue. I realized then who he must be.

'Do you wish to sit in the hotel lounge?' I enquired to break the tension. 'It is not in use at present.'

For a moment, she seemed on the point of throwing herself into his arms, when he said abruptly, 'So it's true then. It's all true.'

'What's true?'

'That you've left home and are sleeping with the Boches.'

There was another awkward silence. I thought she was coming close to admitting guilt and begging forgiveness. Instead, she raised her voice.

'It was you who left home, you bastard. A year ago. It was

you who deserted me, leaving me with nothing! Only a baby to feed. Now you reappear from nowhere and start throwing accusations at me!'

I pretended not to hear and went back to my book.

'You don't deny it. You're sleeping with the Boches.'

'Where've you been this last year, I'd like to know? Just come back from England, have you? And how's your precious friend, de Gaulle, getting on? You've made a mess of things, Albert. It's you who've fucked everything up...'

Leconte smacked her across the cheek – not hard, but it was the one still bruised from whatever had happened a few days ago, and she screamed with pain and anger.

'Fuck off! I hate you, you bastard! You've ruined my life!'

Woken from her post-prandial doze by the scream, Mama appeared from behind her plush curtain, her flow of malice against the world generously released.

'What's going on? Get that disgusting creature out of here, Henri. I've told you once. I shan't tell you again.'

'Yes, Mama.'

I turned helplessly to Ann-Marie, now sobbing, and said as gently as I could, 'It would be best if you left now, Mademoiselle, and I'll speak to you later.'

'Get her out, I say!'

Ann-Marie screamed again, turned and ran out through the door, leaving Albert and me looking silently at each other, somehow drawn together in a curious complicity. He took a slow breath.

'I'm sorry, I behaved badly,' he said. 'But you'll perhaps understand why I'm so upset.'

'It wasn't your fault. The Germans are consuming everything now: food, wine, even our women. But you should follow and look after her. She is very vulnerable.'

'Has she been staying here long?'

'Not long.'

'She's very young.'

'I know.'

He looked down the road, but there was no sign of her, then at his watch.

'I will try to come back.'

'She won't be here,' Mama shouted. 'Whores aren't welcome here!'

'Don't worry, Monsieur, I'll look after her and see she comes to no harm.'

Somehow, Mama's bullying had drawn us together.

'Au revoir, Monsieur, and thank you.'

'Wait! Where are you going?'

Although we'd exchanged only a few words, we trusted one another.

He hesitated before saying, 'Back to London. I'm on the run from the Gestapo.'

'Have you got friends, money, papers?'

'No, nothing.'

I was driven to help him. He was young and vulnerable, just like his wife.

'Wait a moment!' I fumbled in my locked drawer. 'Take these!'

I gave him my reserve of nearly 5,000 francs and I got out the Swiss passport left by a tourist in 1938. After he'd gone, we found it under his bed, and kept it. The photo didn't look much like Leconte, but it was faded and he had a moustache.

'And take this...'

'Thank you: you've been a real...'

At that moment a grey Mercedes stopped outside, and two of my Wehrmacht staff officer clients came into my hall. I bowed, smiled, and handed them their keys. Although Leconte didn't get a second glance, I could see he felt threatened.

'The Gare St Lazare is only a few minutes' walk from here,' I said. 'You turn left out of the door, then right and then straight on!'

'Merci, Monsieur. Au revoir.'

He shook me warmly by the hand.

'Adieu and bonne chance!'

I went into the nearby Café Victoire and found her there, looking sorry for herself.

'How are you, Mademoiselle? What can I offer you to drink?'

'A sirop, please.'

'Now tell me about Albert. How long since you've seen him?'

'I don't know. We quarreled.'

'I'm sorry.'

She took a deep breath and tried to recover herself.

'You're a good friend, Monsieur Henri. Now let's forget Albert and talk about something else. How goes life at your elegant hotel?'

'Busy with the military as you know. Every room is taken.'

'So you're working very hard.'

'Certainly.'

'But you relax sometimes?'

I nodded. Since my youth, I'd found relaxation at No. 122 rue de Provence. Now that establishment had put up a sign: MAISON RESERVEE AUX MILITAIRES ALLEMANDS.

So I'd been obliged to give my custom to the more expensive: 'Chabanais' whose sign read:

MAISON OUVERTE AUX MESSIEURS LES FRANÇAIS

It was, however, an agreeable place, with some rooms decorated by Toulouse-Lautrec.

Our conversation seemed to have reached a dead end, when I realized she'd put her hand on my leg and slid it up so it was resting on my fly. I looked at her directly.

'Unfortunately, I have to return to my reception desk.'

'Perhaps I could call on you later in the afternoon, when things are quiet at your hotel.' I looked doubtful, so she added, 'We could continue our conversation.'

'Between five and seven. Those are the best times.'

'Until five, then.'

'Au revoir, Mademoiselle!'

'What is your room number?'

'Number one.'

'Of course.'

During the afternoon I was too busy to think about her or her husband. She arrived punctually at five wearing a dress, black stockings and high-heeled shoes. When she came in I was writing at my desk and treated her as if she'd come for a medical examination.

'Please go behind that screen and take off all your clothes except your shoes and stockings,' I said.

She obeyed and emerged a few minute later looking very desirable. I was tempted to tell her she was beautiful but, instead, led her by her hand to the bed and gestured that she should kneel and bend forward – a posture that seemed appropriate for our relationship. He bottom was beautifully shaped and I caressed it. Then I stroked her neck and pendant breasts. He legs moved further apart, and she began to breathe more deeply. As soon as I penetrated her, she seemed to enjoy my slow rhythmic thrusts and responded. So we achieved satisfaction together. Afterwards she lay down on the bed, and I went back to my desk to write the details of my experience whilst fresh in mind. For many years I have kept a record of Physical Engagements, which I hope ultimately to write up as a case-book. But I read my record principally for my own pleasure.

After a while she turned and said, 'Tell me a little about yourself.'

'My life hasn't been very interesting. I was born here in the hotel, delivered, my mother claimed, by the hall-porter wearing his white gloves.'

'Did you go to school in the quartier?'

'Yes, but my schooling was short. As soon as I was tall enough, I started work in the hotel. I recollect my childhood in pill box hat and brass buttoned tunic, delivering messages about secret assignations amongst my clients.'

We laughed together for the first time, and I began to find it easier to talk to her.

'I hadn't wanted to be an hôtelier. My ambition was to become a doctor. But the early death of my father forced me to abandon all hopes of that, and I had to help my mother who dominated my youth. She has always managed the financial side, negotiated with the authorities, etc.'

'Really?'

'She loved my father and wears black always in his memory.'

'So I have observed.'

'And since his death, hates everyone in the world: you, me and all clients.'

I found myself talking to her very frankly.

'Before the war, business was often poor, and the hotel half-empty. Now I wish it had a restaurant permit, and more stars. Then I could sell it for a fortune and return to my medical studies.'

'What about your mother?'

'You are right. All that is just a dream.'

'You have never married?'

'Never.'

Neither of us spoke for a few minutes. Then she tried again. 'Monsieur Henri?'

'Yes.'

'I need somewhere to live – nothing pretentious, just a little room, where we could meet each other regularly.'

'It makes me sad to say you can't stay permanently in the Victoire.'

'I know, but can't you find me an apartment nearby? You could come and see me regularly. You'd like that, wouldn't you? I would be very kind to you and there is so much we could do together.'

'That would be difficult.'

'Why?'

'It's my mother, you see. The fact is... she doesn't give me any money.'

'None at all!'

'Only a few francs a week.' Then I had an idea. 'But there is a place I visit on Saturday nights: the Chabanais. It is like a gentleman's club. Some eminent people go there. Do you know what I mean?'

'I think so.'

'Well, maybe I could arrange for you to have a room there. They know me well because I'm a regular visitor.'

'Do Germans go there?'

'Certainly not!'

'Would I have a job there?'

'Well, if you wanted to assist, that would be welcome and the work is well paid.'

'And you would come and see me there? Please, Monsieur Henri!'

'Every Saturday night, I promise you.'

It was already after six o'clock. Shall we stroll round and I'll make some enquiries on your behalf?'

She went behind the screen and dressed hastily. Just before we left my room, I realised she had a special quality about her and I kissed her gently.

She clung to me and I said, 'I am glad you came. Your visit has been an important one.'

July 1941

Walking blindly towards Gare St Lazare, I was nearly run down by a German truck, and heard the driver curse me as a stupid French pig. He was right. And Ann-Marie was right. I had no cause to be angry with her. I'd screwed up my life and hers. I should never have left her and gone off to that absurd country – England! If I'd stayed with her, she'd be happy, and I wouldn't be on the run, terrified of every German who walked past me in the street. It had all seemed simple then: I was going to join my heroic leader – De Gaulle, fight for my beloved country, redeem past failures, cover myself in glory. (Oh, yes! And get away from Cecile.) I knew where I was going, where my loyalties lay, who was my enemy. Now I knew nothing. I'd become a pawn in some international game, but nobody had told me the rules. I had been given the task of carrying an important message, but what was it? To whom did I now owe allegiance? That idiot, de Gaulle? That liar, Churchill? Weygand? Everyone had been moving me around their private chess boards. And all this time my married life had been in total collapse, and my lovely wife had become a whore.

My last reflection, before reaching Gare St Lazare was that the only individual to whom I owed any debt was Reindorf: he had allowed me to escape, and I'd walked out without a word of thanks.

In the railway station there were Germans everywhere: sentries with bayonets, officers in restaurants, others with enormous suitcases getting porters to carry their booty.

When I got to the ticket office, I said, 'Calais, single, second class.'

'Identity card, *laissez passé* and certificate of demobilization please.'

'I gave him my Swiss passport, but he didn't look at it.'

'Foreigners aren't permitted to travel to the coastal Zone Rouge. Surely you know that?'

'No, sorry!'

I stood thinking what to do. The Germans probably knew my home address. They'd go and question my mother. I'd left a clear trail behind me. By now they would already be at the Victoire. I walked quickly into the Metro and bought a ticket. Everywhere posters asked: '*Etes vous en règle?*' I was conscious of being out of order in several respects. On examining the passport given me by the friendly hôtelier I realized I'd become Michael Hinziger of 13 rue du Cendrier, in the Canton of Geneva, Suisse, aged 32; height: 1m 80; colouring: dark; eyes: hazel. In the photograph, he looked older, a worried little man, which was what I'd now become. I decided to head for Ashtray St, Geneva, and buttoned the passport carefully into my pocket, thinking my life could depend on it.

When I showed my passport at the ticket office in Gare de Lyon, the clerk just laughed. But he was quite friendly.

'If you want to go home, you must first apply to the Swiss Embassy for their authorization in duplicate, which you will take both to the *gendarmerie* and the *kommandatur* for a stamped travel permit.'

'How long will that take?'

'About six weeks, probably.'

Whilst standing by the newspaper shop, struggling to think where to go next, I noticed a German military policeman looking at me curiously. He came towards me, said something in German and put out his hand. I didn't understand, but I got out the passport and gave it to him. He looked at the photograph and then at me and then at the photo again. Fear gripped me like a vice. My mouth moved but I couldn't speak. Grudgingly, he gave me the passport back, nodded, saluted and went off.

An old man standing by said, 'He's looking for deserters from their army. Some of the Boches don't want to go and fight the Russians. They want to stay in Paris for ever. Wouldn't you?'

'Certainly.'

What I meant was 'Certainly not!' I took the Metro to the end of the line, Place d'Italie, and stood in the road amongst other shadowy figures trying to thumb a lift. A lorry full of bricks and rubbish stopped and the driver gestured me into the back. I buried myself in the stinking rubble, which was fortunate because we were soon stopped at a checkpoint. I heard a sentry asking for 'Papers!' and then we sped away. I risked looking out. Paris had ended abruptly and rural France surrounded the road. There were lines of poplars, and cows in green fields. I began to relax, fell asleep, and when I woke it was just dawn.

'Auxerre, on the River Yonne. Do you want to stop?' the driver shouted.

'Thank you, yes.'

I got down, and shook his hand but he didn't want to speak to or look at me. Perhaps he knew he'd risked his life giving me a lift.

The town was barely awake. Opposite the railway station – my target – was the Hôtel de la Gare. There were no Germans about and I was the only customer. The patron, fat and talkative, served me coffee and a slice of bread.

'Here you are, my friend.'

I hadn't eaten for twenty-four hours so it tasted delicious: hot and strong.

'Just a little bird of passage, are you?'

'Yes, I'm heading south.'

'You didn't come by train then.'

'No, I got a lift.'

He looked at me carefully. I began to worry. Why so many questions?

'I wouldn't stay here too long, if I were you.'

'Why not?'

'There's a Boche patrol comes through every morning to check passengers at the station. They stop here for coffee.'

'My papers are in order. But thanks, anyway.'

'It's nothing. Are you going to take the train?'

'If there is one. I'm travelling to Geneva.'

'Is that so? Well, fancy that!'

'Is there a train?'

'It's eight-twenty towards Dijon. But they're always later nowadays. Listen! Arrive at the last minute, when it's in the station. Buy your ticket and jump on as it's leaving.'

'Thanks. Where's the nearest church in your town?'

'Church?' He looked startled, then nodded. 'In the main square. But unless you want to say a few masses to the Virgin, you could stay in my kitchen. Wash a few dishes, maybe.'

'That would be ideal. Thanks very much!'

'It's nothing. My sister married a Jew. He's a tailor. Has a nice little shop in rue du Pont – just across the river.'

Clearly, he was used to refugees passing through, and had immediately identified me as one, albeit of a wrong category. No point in denying my origins.

'They've just told my brother-in-law he's got to sell his business to a non-Jew and deposit the money in a blocked account. Anyway, no one will buy it, so he'll just have to close it down.'

'I suppose there's a lot like that.'

He looked at me carefully.

'He thought he was safe, because he'd been in the army in the last war. He was a sergeant, decorated for bravery and all that shit.'

'Really?'

'But now he's been told that won't help him. It's a crazy world we're living in, not like it was when I was young. If you'd told me a few years ago there'd be no coffee, I'd have thought you were mad.'

'Yes.'

I began to get anxious that the German patrol he'd mentioned would arrive at any moment and find me still listening to his talk. But I couldn't bring myself to cut short his friendly chatter.

'My sister is going crazy with fear. She thinks they're going to come and take her away to prison. And their children: two boys – nine and six. They can't do that, can they?'

'Of course not!'

'What are your people doing about it? Anyway, here he is. Bonjour, jeune homme!'

They shook hands. The man who'd come in was burly, with a moustache rather like Hitler's. He had dark shadows under his eyes. The patron went back to the bar, served him a coffee and whispered in his ear for several minutes. Then the brother-in-law came over to my table, sat down and stared at me.

'You're not Jewish.'

'No.'

'Why did you tell him you were?'

'I didn't.'

'But you're on the run?'

'Yes.'

'For you, it's all right, maybe, to run. Me, I've got a family. How can I go off and leave them?'

His brother-in-law came over and interrupted.

'Listen, David, I've told you I'll look after them. She's my kid sister. They can come here, where they'll be with family.'

'No. If I bunked off, I'd spend night and day worrying about them. We've got to go on living exactly as we do right now. Nothing has happened yet, and there's nothing to panic about. I'm not a foreigner. I'm a citizen of France and no one can stop me living in it, here where I choose.'

'You bloody fool! You want to walk about wearing a yellow star?'

'You're the fool. This isn't Germany, it's France! We've taken in my people from Alsace. It's people like you, Georges, with crazy ideas about Resistance who will cause trouble. Your *Résistants* are all Bolsheviks or bandits. Worse! They're anarchists. They'll provoke the Boches into reprisals against us.'

In their anger, they'd forgotten about me. I tried to pay him for my coffee and go, but he didn't give me a chance.

'What about your business?'

'Well, what about it? The thing to do is to keep quiet for a bit, and the Germans will get bored and all want to go home.'

101

'Rubbish!'

'You talk a lot of crap!'

'I don't know why I bother talking to you. It's a waste of time!'

They'd clearly had this debate countless times but still enjoyed it.

I pushed past them and went to the lavabo. When I came back, they were still at it.

'... as for that traitor de Gaulle, it's all very well for him to bugger off to England and send us messages to join the Resistance. Why didn't he stay here and fight?'

I dropped some coins on the table and walked across to the station where the clerk sold me a ticket without question. The train puffed along steadily, whilst I sat hearing their comic, rather pathetic voices over and over again. For months afterwards, I dreamed about David and the wife and sons I'd never seen. Years later, I went back to Auxerre especially to look for him. His brother-in-law, the café patron, was still behind his bar, but rather less cheerful than he'd been in 1941. He told me the whole of his brother-in-law's family had been deported in 1942, and he supposed they'd died in a concentration camp.

'I tried to warn him, Monsieur, that he was in danger, great danger! I kept on telling him. But he was a stubborn, pig-headed Jew (I beg your pardon, Monsieur, I remember now, you're one yourself) and he simply wouldn't listen. We used to argue for hours about everything. And in the end, he became my best friend. I still miss him, and my sister, of course, but I was closer to him. It was our own town gendarmerie that came and took them away. And their children – my nephews – whom I loved, because we've none of our own! It was our people who took them and handed them over to the Boches. At night. Although I'd told him that it would happen, when it did I couldn't believe it!'

At Dijon I got out, went into a restaurant and ordered a first class meal of roast pork. To convince myself I wasn't a Jew!

102

Despite the war, this was still a gastronomic centre. The restaurant was full of fat farmers silently eating their way through several courses. From Dijon, getting a lift was more difficult, because there weren't many vehicles. I spent the next night in a field with only a raw turnip to eat, worrying about the curfew. Close to Switzerland there were more Germans about, some with bicycles and some with dogs. I felt hunted. Time after time, I told myself I was a Swiss citizen with nothing to worry about. Time after time, I braced myself to be stopped and questioned but never was.

It was evening on the third day when I got to Ferney-Voltaire, the little border village, named after the great cynic, where he'd lived and cultivated his garden in accordance with his own advice. In 1758, he'd been a refugee from the authorities in Paris. Just like me. For twenty years he'd been renowned as the great sage of Ferney, campaigning against bigotry, intolerance, and injustice, but well-placed to slip over the border if his enemies seemed to be closing in on him. Now it was my turn. For all I knew, my enemies were closing in on me.

There was one peaceful village street, and a *mairie* with an *urinoir*. There was also a statue of *Le Grand Penseur*, who stood in the middle of the road, with a look of encouragement on his face. The frontier post was at the end of the street. I walked slowly towards it, so as not to attract attention, and handed my passport to the French gendarme at the roadblock. He hardly glanced at it, grinned at me in a condescending way and waved me on to a second road-block, where the white cross on a red background was flying in the evening breeze to welcome me. I was nearing journey's end.

'Bonsoir, Monsieur.'

'Bonsoir, Monsieur.'

The young Swiss policeman in a green uniform with a comical hat riffled through the pages, but I was glad to see he hardly looked at the photograph.

Then he asked me to wait, and disappeared into his hut where

I could see him pointing out something to his colleague. Then he came back.

'Monsieur Hinziger...'

That was me, I remembered.

'I'm sorry to tell you that your passport has expired. The expiry date was the third of May last. I'm sorry we cannot admit you. You must get it renewed.'

'Renewed?'

'Yes, it is a simple procedure. You must take it to our Embassy in the country where you are residing, that is France, fill in the application form, and pay the renewal fee, which is five francs. I am sure you will have no problems. Good evening.'

'Are you saying I've got to go to Paris to get it renewed?'

'Naturally.'

'Can't I get it renewed in Geneva? That's much nearer.'

'That is not possible. As I have explained I cannot admit you with an expired passport.'

I stared at him speechless with anger, disappointment, hatred, humiliation. Why hadn't I looked more closely at the passport? Maybe I could have altered the date.

Too late now. His colleague – big, with stripes on his sleeve – came out of their hut, and both of them stood waiting for me to turn round and walk back into France. Which, slowly and reluctantly, I did. What else could I have done?

July 1941

In peacetime, Erich Reindorf had practiced as a corporate lawyer in Berlin. His profession had required a logical approach, attention to detail and ability to predict the course of events. He had thought carefully about Leconte's mission and he wasn't surprised that the courier should have been deceived about the true nature of it, nor that he had become puzzled and confused. Whoever had mounted the operation would have wanted to limit the numbers of individuals who knew its nature and purpose. Leconte had been an innocent bystander in a sophisticated game – more complex than the chess they'd played together. Reindorf found that he was getting confused himself. It was difficult to disentangle the layers of deception, or to be sure how much Leconte really knew. Only one thing was clear and certain: the Gestapo would decide – had already decided – that the secrecy of the mission was of overwhelming importance. Therefore, Leconte, the courier, would be regarded as an embarrassment and would need to be eliminated without delay. Reindorf had unhesitatingly decided he couldn't be a party to that. Beating an opponent at chess was acceptable, but murdering him was not.

When Reindorf got back to the Crillon after two days' leave, he wasn't surprised to be told that the prisoner Leconte had escaped. But he pretended to be furious, and told the guards that they would be court-martialled for their failure. Whilst deciding how to frame his detailed report, he was summoned to an urgent meeting with his Gestapo colleagues.

Before he could speak, the senior officer began, 'Major Reindorf, we regret having to impose this task on you as soon as you have returned from leave, but the matter is indeed urgent. It has been decided in Berlin that we don't need that French courier to take the Protocol back to England. The Führer has other means of communication. Take him out and dispose of him. In the country. An accident, of course!'

'Of course, sir.'

This was what he'd expected. What he hadn't expected was that this instruction should fit so neatly with Leconte's escape. He'd need to square the guards, but that wouldn't be difficult, because they would be delighted to escape punishment. However, it would be useful to trace Leconte, if only to make sure he didn't reappear at the Crillon, and that wasn't an investigation which could be delegated to subordinates. He decided that Leconte would certainly go to his wife's home and he thought that her name was Ann-Marie.

He telephoned the *Sûreté Nationale* and traced the address of Albert Leconte: 98 Boulvard Raspail, Apartment 3.

It all seemed too easy, and he was driven to the address in a few minutes. An elderly woman opened the door and he could hear a child yelling in the background. He saluted courteously.

'Madame Ann-Marie Leconte, *s'il vous plaît*.'

Albert's mother was startled to see on her doorstep an elegant German officer in black uniform with silver braiding. She hesitated. Could this be one of her daughter-in-law's lovers? She was too fearful to be rude to him.

'She is not at home at present.'

Reindorf put his foot in the door.

'Will she be returning shortly?'

'No. She isn't living at home, you see.'

'Where does she live?'

'At the Hôtel Victoire in the ninth district, I think.'

'The Hôtel Victoire?'

'Yes. It's where all the German officers are billeted.'

'Thank you very much, Madame.'

He got back in his car and told the driver where to go. In the Victoire lobby Monsieur Henri was talking to a couple of his German guests. There was a flurry of saluting.

'Madame Ann-Marie Leconte?' he enquired.

'I am sorry, no one of that name is registered at the hotel.'

'Where is she resident now?'

'I regret I am unable to assist you.'

106

Reindorf was already ready to try a bluff.

'You see, I have an important message for her. It concerns her husband, Albert Leconte.'

'If you care to leave a message here at the hotel, I'm sure she will call soon, and I will see that it reaches her.'

'I regret it is a message which can only be delivered personally. Perhaps I should notify the *Sûreté* and send them out with a warrant?'

'Wait another moment, please . . .' Ah yes! Madame Leconte. She left a forwarding address. It is La Chabanais, Place de la Madeleine.'

Reindorf got back in his car, wondering whether all his efforts would prove worthless. He didn't even know whether Leconte would be with her. Mostly, he left this sort of exercise to his assistants.

At La Chabanais, a uniformed maid opened the door, and declared, 'I regret, Monsieur, the establishment is not open to the military. I have available some addresses where you will be most welcome.'

'This is an official matter of importance. It concerns Madame Leconte.'

'One moment, please.'

A *sous-maîtresse* appeared.

'You wish to meet with Madame Leconte?'

'Yes.'

'You understand that she is not available. She is not officially registered as a member of this establishment. She is simply resident here.'

'This is an official matter. I require her to attend immediately for questioning.'

When Ann-Marie appeared, she wore a low cut blouse. She smiled at Reindorf very demurely.

'Good afternoon,' she said in German. 'How can I be of assistance to you?'

She looked at Reindorf with interest, regarding every senior

German officer as a potential suitor to whom she could show off her talents. Reindorf was disarmed by her attitude.

He took off his cap and said cautiously, 'It concerns your spouse, Albert Leconte. Where is he now, please?'

'Alas! I do not know.'

'When did you see him last?'

'It was in 1939, when he was called to the front.'

'When did you last hear of him?'

'I received an official notification that he was missing in action.'

'You understand, Madame, that it is important to be frank with me. If you are lying for some misguided reason I can have you sent to prison.'

'Why should I lie?' she answered staring at him, wide eyed. 'I once heard a rumour he was in England, but I didn't know whether to believe it.'

'How did you hear this "rumour"?'

'From one of his friends.'

'From whom, precisely.'

'I can't remember which one. He had many friends in Paris.'

'Didn't you want to find out more about your husband?'

'No. You see, he went off and deserted me, so that I regard myself as no longer married to him. He doesn't love me any more. I have been left alone.'

Reindorf believed she was lying but couldn't decide what lay behind her poise and charm. He considered himself an expert at cross-examination. He knew he should bully and threaten her, but her ripe and indolent posture disarmed him. The atmosphere of the salon where they were sitting had undermined his resolve. It smelled of lubricious activity. Womens' perfumes and body odours permeated the atmosphere. The walls were decorated with scenes of Oriental orgies. Upturned posteriors offered themselves generously to Arab princes, and, by implication, to visiting *Oberführers*. Ann-Marie seemed to belong to the world of the murals behind her; despite himself, Reindorf began to feel disturbed. Thoughts of pleasure were crowding out thoughts of duty. He tried to sound formal.

'It may be necessary for me to come and question you again. Please reflect carefully on what you have told me. If you have been misleading me, the consequences will be serious.'

He'd ended feebly, he thought.

'I shall be pleased to receive you again. Is your rank Hauptmann?'

'SS Oberführer Erich Reindorf.'

She succeeded in looking impressed.

'When will you come, Herr Oberführer?'

'Tomorrow ... possibly.'

'Come in the afternoon.'

'Very well.'

'Between five and seven. Those are the best times.'

'Very well. Au revoir, Madame Leconte!'

'Herr Oberführer.'

Afterwards he convinced himself it was essential to see her again in order to question her about Leconte. Anyway, there was no reason why duty and pleasure should conflict. On the contrary, they could sometimes be combined.

Ann-Marie had been wondering how to find a new protector. Monsieur Henri would visit her on Saturday night, but hadn't yet offered to pay the rent. So, when Reindorf left, both were pleased with the encounter.

July 1941

When I got back to the French checkpoint in Ferney-Voltaire, the policeman was laughing at me. I didn't feel much like laughing.

'What's the fucking joke?' I snarled.

This produced more laughter.

'They won't admit you into Geneva. Is that your big problem, Monsieur?'

'My passport is out of date.'

'That's really terrible!'

'He told me I'd have to go back to the Swiss Embassy in Paris to get it renewed.'

More laughter.

'What makes you think it's all so funny?'

'Well, Monsieur, because I'm a friendly, helpful policeman, I'll tell you the solution to your big problem. If you want to go to Geneva, don't worry about the check-point. You can take an easier route. Walk down to the end of this road.' He pointed. 'And on your right, you'll see a footpath across a field. Why not simply take that footpath? Everyone else does. They take it every morning to go to work in the city of Geneva, and in the evening to come home to Ferney-Voltaire. It takes half an hour and it's through some very agreeable countryside. That's the way of life in our village.'

I thanked him profusely, and followed his instructions, thinking that my escape from my enemies had not been achieved in the style of the gallant soldiers in my exciting childhood story books; it had instead been totally unheroic. I'd had no carefully prepared plan. I hadn't fought my way across barriers or jungles. When my path had been blocked, it had been at ticket offices, and was because some official was following his rules. When I'd moved on in my journey it was because someone had broken the rules to help me. Everything had been improvised. On reflection, it seemed my whole life had been like that, and I resolved to try to impose some order upon it. On further reflection, I began to think that there was no possible system for surmounting the hazards of life. You just had to take them as they came. If you made a careful plan it would probably go wrong. The events of our lives followed no logical sequence; to expect them to do so was naïve.

Whilst digesting these thoughts I met a friendly farmer and his dog. He told me his farm was half in one country and half in the other. Consequently, during the ploughing season he crossed and re-crossed the frontier sixty-eight times in the course of a morning's work!

Soon, I reached the neutral city of Geneva, where the British Consul's residence turned out to be rather like Lady Redesdale's house in Belgravia, with portraits of the British King George in the most unexpected places. Even in the lavabo! An official told me to 'make myself at home' whilst he got instructions from London and 'arranged transport'. Food and wine at the Consulate were excellent – as good as at the Crillon. Geneva seemed a prosperous and calm city; the shops were full of goods and the banks busy receiving both French and German customers depositing their savings. I felt a great sense of relief, forgot my problems, went for agreeable walks around the lake, admired the distant mountains, and ate lots of milk chocolate.

Not surprisingly, therefore, when early in the morning I got out of the RAF transport Hudson at Biggin Hill aerodrome in Kent, the world seemed depressing. I badly needed my steaming *café au lait* and Swiss croissants. Instead, I got some of that sweet, luke-warm brown stuff, the English called 'char'. I was stiff with cold and profoundly angry with Churchill and all things British. They'd double-crossed me. They'd not told me the true nature of my mission: Operation Determinate – whatever it had been. I'd spent the flight struggling to assemble what I'd learned in Paris. Firstly, the document I'd carried had not been destined for the Vichy authorities but for the Germans themselves. Secondly, when I'd recounted to the Gestapo the story I'd been told by Churchill, about the French territories declaring themselves for de Gaulle, they'd effectively called me a liar. Thirdly, they'd somehow been disappointed by it. Finally, Reindorf had somehow connected my mission with the German invasion of the Soviet Union and 'Peace in the West.' There was no doubt I'd been falsely briefed. Deliberately duped, tricked, deceived. The British had a large vocabulary for treachery, because they were regular and experienced practitioners of it.

Spears, smoking his eternal pipe, and two civilians in raincoats were on the tarmac to meet me.

'Hello, Leconte,' he said. 'How did you get on?'

'Well, sir...'

'Did you have a good trip?'

It was as though I were returning from a holiday weekend in the country. That was how the English behaved, I remembered. I was back in the land of the bland. His imperturbability really irritated me, but I managed a few conventional words as we walked towards a car.

'Is Colonel Palewski here?'

'He has been transferred to East African Command.'

Spears' attention seemed focused on the parcel I carried, which contained my dirty pants and socks and a packet of Toblerone.

We got into a waiting car and Spears said, 'I'll take that package, shall I?'

'Thank you very much.'

'Where are we going?'

'Chartwell.'

'Where is that?'

'Not far. The Prime Minister is to attend your de-briefing.'

I could see he was trying to feel the contents of the parcel on his knee, so I said, 'Just my dirty pants and socks!'

'Where is the Protocol?'

'Your friends never gave it back to me.'

'What? You haven't got it?'

Already I was being pushed onto the defensive. I remembered that famous British detective, Sherlock Holmes, and replied, 'Your deduction, my dear Spears, is perfectly correct!'

He went purple and began to stutter and puff up. I backed away into the corner of the seat, finding the hostility of his glare positively threatening. The rest of our journey passed in silence.

Churchill, on the other hand, was positively gracious when he received us at his country manor. He was wearing his battledress suit and smoking a particularly long cigar. We were ushered into his library, where there were drinks on the table, so that he could play the role of genial host. He got up and shook me warmly by the hand.

'Young man, welcome back to England. We are all greatly indebted to you. You have returned from a dangerous mission, sustaining fearful risks on behalf of the great cause for which we are all fighting. We shall recommend to your general that you be considered for a high gallantry award.'

This time I decided I wasn't going to be seduced by his charm.

'Now is your dawn after a long and dark night. This is the hour for de-briefing. Please look back over your heroic journey during the past month and recount to us in detail the course of events...'

So I told them about my landing in France, my stay at the Crillon, my escape through France to Ferney and thence to Geneva.

Then I said carefully, 'According to the terms of my briefing, I was to rendezvous with a Colonel de Moulin and exchange pass-words. He never appeared.'

Churchill laughed uneasily.

'And what you told me about the content of the protocol wasn't true.'

They stopped laughing, looked at one another, and then Churchill coughed.

Spears said coldly, 'It would appear, Leconte, that you failed to comply with your explicit orders which were that under no circumstances were you to open the top secret Protocol package, but to hand it, sealed, to General Weygand.'

'I didn't open it.'

'Then how do you know what it contained?'

113

'The Germans told me.'

This, of course wasn't strictly true. All that they had indirectly told me was what it didn't contain.

We glared at one another in silence.

At length, Churchill said in his oiliest tones, 'Now, now, young man, I can see why you are angry, but you must understand that if you had been correctly and fully briefed your knowledge would have made you hopelessly vulnerable. The secrecy of Operation Determinate is critical to Hitler and his Nazi hordes. It would have been necessary for him to secure your silence for ever. Your false briefing, which you naturally resent, was for your own protection.'

I started to think about this one.

'Let me offer you a glass of cognac from your own country. It will represent an agreeable reminder of your disagreeable experience there. Then I will arrange for you to be driven to London.'

Churchill shook me warmly by the hand, I gulped the cognac, and was shown into the hall, where I sat waiting. I suddenly had the thought that if my knowledge of Determinate – such as it was – had made me a threat to the Germans, wouldn't that also be true for the British? I'd been talking too much. Far too much for my own good. Maybe they were even now planning to dispose of me! I tried to listen at the door of the library, stuck my ear close to it, and heard Churchill saying: '... since they didn't send it back, signed and sealed, that gives us a perfect explanation for failing to comply with its terms.'

'Nevertheless, Prime Minister...'

I heard my name mentioned and what sounded like 'Mytchett Place'. Then a bell rang, signalling that the two big civilians were being summoned from somewhere back into the library. I decided they looked like policemen out of uniform.

They emerged, and said to me, 'We can go now.'

Like an idiot I followed them obediently to their car and got in the back with one on either side of me.

'I've forgotten my parcel with my socks in it,' I began.

The words were scarcely out of my mouth when I smelled chloroform and lost consciousness for what seemed an interminable period: months, years! When I recovered, I was lying in an uncomfortable bed staring through a barred window. The sun shone straight into my eyes, so I put my head under the blanket and fell asleep again. I didn't seem to have control of mind or body, and it was a relief to slip back into numbness. The next time I woke I felt very sick and vomited into a bucket by my bed. Sweat streamed from me and I had an uncontrollable bout of shaking. Once or twice I felt a stab like that of a needle, but didn't realize what it was. When I woke again I felt better, so I sat up and looked out of the window on to peaceful English countryside – parkland, with scattered trees and sheep grazing. My head ached, my mouth felt terribly dry but I tried to think. Where was I? *Who* was I? There was nothing in the room offering any clue. I wore a striped pyjama jacket and, feeling my face, realized I hadn't shaved for a while. Nor, I thought, had I eaten or drunk for days. There was a jug of water on the washstand. I took several mouthfuls, which made me vomit again. Soon, it seemed life had always been like this: sleeping, waking, drinking water, vomiting – a pattern of semi-consciousness which, gradually, I became able to accommodate.

I lost count of time and fell into fantastic dreams of childhood. On my fourth birthday in April 1917, Mama had baked a cake and had promised that Papa would be coming to my party, bringing toys. Papa was an infantry officer, fighting to defend France – against the Boches, of course. He was tall with a thick moustache. Last time he'd had leave from the front he'd shown me his pistol and binoculars and explained how to use them. He'd promised to bring me a battle souvenir: a German helmet with a spike on top. He'd already driven a nail into the wall over my bed, where he would hang this symbol of French pride in German defeat.

Alas! Papa failed to attend my party. Mama received a telegram which made her cry and cry and I couldn't comfort her.

'Your Papa isn't ever coming home again,' she told me, and started wearing a black dress which she'd never worn before. Later still, she showed me Papa's medals including the Légion d'Honneur and told me the story. My father had been serving under General Robert Nivelle and had led his company towards the German trenches wearing the pistol and binoculars that I'd admired so much. Enemy machine-guns had slaughtered the gallant attackers. This had been in 1917 at Chemin des Dames in the Aisne, the route originally built for the daughters of Louis XV. Nivelle had planned a six mile advance on the first day. Instead, some 600 metres were gained. At the end of the week there were 250,000 casualties. At the end of a fortnight all the ground gained had been lost.

Half the French army had mutinied. They were prepared to stand and defend their beloved land but not to advance. Forty ringleaders were tried and shot. My father's company had never mutinied. They'd followed their commander towards the enemy machine-guns, securing the privilege of death rather than dishonour. General Nivelle had refused to resign, but he hadn't been shot, merely replaced by a new Commander-in-Chief, a man of great nobility and dignity: Marshal Henri-Philippe Pétain. Pétain was already sixty-one, shrewd and wise. He'd toured the front, not to redress grievances, but appealing to patriotism and honour and restoring confidence. Papa had died gloriously, not far from Laon, where later – much later – I'd stood with de Gaulle on the ramparts, surveying the field of the 1940 battle. Some of all this I learned from Mama, some in history lessons at school.

All that was the childhood version. One day, when older and at the *lycée*, I opened Mama's desk drawer and looked at some of Papa's letters from the Front. One of them read: *You must have realized during my last leave that there is someone else in my life. Someone who has become very dear to me ... I can only hope you will understand and forgive...*

My father hadn't led his company into the face of enemy machine guns. He hadn't died gloriously at Chemin des Dames, and he hadn't been one of the quarter of a million casualties. He hadn't mutinied. He had stayed in his dug-out and missed the attack, because, he said, he had piles, which gave him intolerable discomfort. He hadn't come home on leave from the Front as promised. Instead, he'd gone off with a dancer at the *Folies Bergères*, whom he'd met on his last leave. After the war, they lived together happily in Neuilly. We never saw him again. What a shitbag!

Recalling all this seemed to bring me back to life. Gradually, my vomiting ceased and I started to want food. Once I got as far as the door and pulled at it, but it was locked. After some hours, it occurred to me I was in prison. The door had a covered peep hole. Once I caught an eye looking through and staggered across the room shouting, '*Allo! Allo! Au secours!*'

During my months in England my English had become quite fluent. Now it had gone from my grasp. I heard footsteps outside and the peep hole was opened.

A voice said, 'Ready for some grub, are we now?'

I stared uncomprehendingly, but nodded.

'What do you fancy then? Steak and kidney pud? Baked beans? Fish and chips?'

The words 'fish and chips' triggered a chord in my memory. Yes! Edna and Freda had given me some.

'Fish 'n' chips,' I repeated

'Not a chance, mate. I'll bring you some soup. Light diet, that's what you're on!'

Exhausted again, I got back into bed and pulled up the blanket. Next time I awoke, there was a dish of cold liquid put through the peep hole. I drank it, and collapsed again. Now in my dreams I'd left the *lycée* and was pursuing my engineering studies at the *Collège des Techniciens*. I'd made new friends and had an *entrée* in to Paris society. We'd begun to sample the life of Montparnasse, where students, intellectuals and poseurs met and sat talking all evening in smart cafés, the Dome or Rotonde where a glass of wine cost $2^1/2$ francs. The original party would break up, a new one form, and we'd go off together for a cheap meal, probably *riz espagnole*, which was popular. Then back to the Dome which stayed open all night. At dawn, if you had any money left, you went to Les Halles for a traditional *gratinée* – a thick soup with melted cheese on top – half a dozen oysters and Vin d'Alsace. In my half-sleep I salivated at the thought of those meals.

We were at the age when you discussed whether or not to be *engagé*. If you were on the Left, your hero was Andre Malraux, who was pre-occupied with the struggle against fascism and lived out his life as a novel with himself as hero. If you were on the Right, your hero was Maurras or Brasillach and you hated the Jews. My friend Daniel Cohen was *engagé*. He became a pacifist. That was, they believed, to avoid any further wars. Everyone should subscribe to ideals of peace and brotherhood in accordance with the principles adumbrated by Karl Marx. That was the way Russia was going: becoming a classless society, so that competition between social categories wouldn't need to occur.

For my part, I wasn't at all *engagé*. My concept of an ideal society was me and two lovely girls. My ideal position in society was horizontal. Girls were my hobby, even before I acquired any working knowledge of them. To secure my first practical experiences in the *bordel* in rue de Gaité I'd had to save up for months. Then I had a sequence of *petites amies*, without finding anyone who permanently attracted me. I liked fresh fields to conquer ... until I met Ann-Marie. She was younger, very bright and lively, recently arrived in Paris, with a luscious figure, popular with everyone. From our first meeting I felt a sense of danger. She wanted to secure me for herself, and she did so along traditional lines by telling me she had a bun in the oven and that I was the confectioner! The timing was perfect. Of course, there'd also been Céline, who was wonderful in bed, whilst Ann-Marie was rather systematic. But I couldn't do the honorable thing by both girls, and Ann-Marie had been quicker off the mark.

Dreaming about these girls made me feel more normal. This was my world; this was the reality with which I'd lost touch.

But in my current world – wherever that was – a routine began to establish itself. In the night my door opened and my slop bucket was taken out. Watery soup arrived regularly with sliced bread and a lump of margarine. I sluiced water over my hands and face, but wanted to bath, shave and dress. When I banged on the door, I got no answer. The house seemed very quiet but, once or twice, I heard a voice shouting in German, which was puzzling. I had a vague recollection of having been a prisoner of the Germans at some time in the past.

I tried to strengthen myself by walking round the room, but this left me very weak. My mind was also in a poor condition, and I suffered from loss of memory. I'd recalled the life of my childhood and youth and then the events of the day I'd landed in England, found Edna and Freda, ate their fish and chips, drank their gin and orange, and made love to them both. I could hear their voices saying: 'We're going to have a party and you're invited to it!'

All the detail of that day came back to me: the sound of dogfights overhead; the streets of Hastings with the milk bottles; smell of cooking fat; texture of their bodies where I'd held them. Subsequent events had been extinguished from recollection. A whole period had disappeared. How long had the gap been? A week? A year? What had I been doing? Was I going insane?

One day, the door opened and two men in white coats came in, together with a British army corporal.

One of them said slowly, 'Leconte, do you understand me?'

I nodded.

'I am Doctor McCartney, and this is my colleague, Doctor Lucas. You have been very ill and we have come to examine you.'

They produced stethoscopes and listened to my chest. They lifted my eyelids and peered into my eyes with a pencil light. They looked down my throat, tested my reflexes, and prepared to leave.

Before they got out, I managed to shout, mostly in French,

'Attention! What is my problem? Where am I? How long must I stay here? When do I get clothes, water to wash, food?'

They looked at one another.

'You are still very ill, and it is not safe for you to go out. You must stay in bed. But we will arrange for you to have ablution facilities. We will come and visit you in a week's time. Meanwhile you must rest...'

Whilst I struggled to understand this, they went out, slamming the door. Then a corporal came in with some old clothes, a clean bucket, a basin of hot water, a razor and a towel.

'There y'are! Just like the Ritz it is 'ere. You can posh yourself up, now.'

With my bread and margarine that evening, I got a spoonful of plum jam and a hard green apple. I ate every crumb. Obviously, I was being held prisoner. Not by the Germans, but by the British. And my knowledge of English was coming back to me.

Time passed slowly because I had nothing to do but think about the past, distant and recent! Then, one day, looking through the barred window at the view of the countryside, I turned sideways and saw a face at the adjacent window looking directly at me. It was a pale face, with a haunted look, low forehead and thick, black eyebrows. For some seconds we stared at one another and neither spoke.

Then my neighbour whispered in English, 'Who are you?'

I told him and asked the same question of him.

'Rudolf Hess, Deputy Führer of the German Reich. Here I am being held as prisoner by the British. I have come because I was invited by the Prime Minister, Winston Churchill. I have been guaranteed personal safety as an emissary to make peace between our countries. Carrying the flag of truce. Yet, they put me in prison.'

I found all this incredible.

'Why are you here?'

'I don't know.'

'You have been told you are going to be shot or hung?'

'No, have you?'

'Soon, that will happen. Churchill, he will shoot me, because I know too much.'

'What about?'

'Man is coming. Tomorrow we speak again.'

I spent the next morning at the window. When he appeared, I asked him, 'What is it you know? Why should they shoot you?'

'Maybe they shoot you too!'

'I don't know anything. I've lost my memory.'

'Of course, you have lost your memory. They tried with me but it does not work. Drugs into your arm. If you remember anything don't tell them.'

I realised that he was right. My arm had been sore. My loss of memory was explained, and I hadn't been going mad. I began to feel better.

When we next spoke, I asked him again what it was we both knew which made them want to silence us.

'I carried a message. You too, maybe?'

'Yes.'

'I brought a document from the leader of my country, Adolf Hitler, to Winston Churchill for signature. Maybe you took it back to my leader?'

'Maybe!'

'You don't know?'

'They didn't tell me it was addressed to Hitler!'

'Then you were deceived.'

'What was the message?'

'Man is coming. Tomorrow we speak again.'

I found it impossible to believe what he told me. I thought he must be mad, or an imposter. But perhaps it was all true. Perhaps we would both be shot or hung, or somehow permanently silenced.

As I got stronger, I began to hate the two corporals, Fred and Tiny, who brought me revolting food and only emptied the lavatory pail when they felt like it. They treated me like a naughty child. One of them was big and fat, the other small and wizened. Time and again I asked them.

'Why am I being kept here?' and 'When will I be released?' They never replied.

Vague memories of my imprisonment in the Hôtel Crillon began to come back to me. The food and the bathroom facilities there had been much better.

One day, I heard shouting and banging near my room. When it quietened down, I stuck my head out of the window and hummed a few bars of 'Lili Marlene', the only German song I knew.

'*Vor der kaserne, vor dem grossen Tor,*
Stand eine Laterne...'

In response, Hess appeared at the window, looking terrible. There were bruises on his face and blood on his clothes.

'What happened?' I whispered to him.

'I try to escape. They beat me up. I try again.'

The idea of escape hadn't really occurred to me until then. Suppose I got out of the house, where would I go? London? Paris? I seemed to have made enemies everywhere. I decided the only friends I'd ever made in England were Edna and Freda. I would go to them in Hastings, hide in their house, live on a regular diet of fish and chips and make love to them both. I began to plan how to escape. I would wait at the door, knock down the small one – Fred – as he came in, and run. I didn't know where. Fred was the more unpleasant of the two, although there wasn't much to choose between them. I had two possible weapons: the wash basin and my urine bucket. The former was more manageable. In the afternoon, when Fred was usually on duty, I took up position behind the door and waited.

There were steps in the corridor. Fred was doubtless bringing a plate of that disgusting soup. The bolts on the door were pulled back, the key turned, the door opened. I jumped forward, and slammed the basin as hard as I could, realizing I wasn't hitting Fred's head, but Tiny's. There was a great bang.

'You fucking French bastard!' he yelled.

He fell on the floor, dropping the keys, which I grabbed, and ran down a corridor towards a flight of stairs. There was a shout from the adjacent room – Hess's room. I stopped, fumbled with the keys and found one which opened his door. He emerged, looking like a great ape, and we ran together down the stairs, my head thumping from the unaccustomed exercise. Behind us, Tiny was groaning and cursing, and promising to kick the shit out of someone, presumably me. Ahead was the front door of the house which I pulled open. Hess and I nearly knocked one another over struggling to rush through it. Now we were in the grounds and I ran across the lawn – seen daily from my window – and dived into rhododendron bushes, tearing my hand on a sharp twig. For a few moments I lay still, recovering my breath.

When I peered through the leaves, Hess was apparently behaving like an idiot, which from my point of view was to prove ideal. He ran a few metres then stopped and stood in the drive, looking this way and that, appearing confused and dazed. In a few seconds, Tiny came blundering out of the door mouthing obscenities.

He saw Hess immediately and shouted, 'Come back, you fucking German bastard!'

Hess now started towards a distant gate, with Tiny staggering along in pursuit. Crouching low, I headed in the opposite direction towards the back of the big mansion house. The perimeter wall ran around a kitchen garden with a glasshouse and wheel-barrow which I tripped over. The wall was too high to climb and there was barbed wire on the top. Where now? Behind the green house, covered in weeds there was a wooden door set in the wall. It obviously hadn't been opened for years. Tugging at the rusty handle didn't budge it. I grabbed a rusty spade from the wheel barrow and struck at the middle of the door with what remaining strength I had. The rotten wood broke immediately, and I crawled through into a deserted country lane on the opposite side of which was a golden cornfield. In it, I collapsed, exhausted, bruised, sobbing, but free! I suddenly realized that this was my second escape from imprisonment; the thought generated a tremendous exhilaration.

It was dark when I emerged from the cornfield. Inside the house, the shouting had died away. Once there was the sound of a shot. I supposed they'd caught Hess and killed him. If it really was Hess, and not just a friendly lunatic with a wild imagination. Whoever he was, he'd provoked my escape, but now I didn't know where I was or where to go without papers or money. I crouched as I walked down the lane, shouldering my spade like a rifle, hoping to pass for a farm worker. The countryside was quiet, so they must have given up searching for me, at least until the morning. The lane turned away from the house and joined a road. As I stood on the corner, a farm truck appeared, loaded with cabbages, and stopped.

'Want a lift?'

'Yes.'

'Where you going, young-feller-me-lad?'

I didn't know how to answer, but I managed to say: 'To the city!'

'Well, you're a lucky one then, 'cos I'm going straight up to the big smoke. Taking this load to Covent Garden. Jump in!'

I had an overwhelming sense that all this had happened before. But where? When?

The journey took more than an hour, but I didn't have to say anything. The driver, an old farmer, gave me no chance. He droned on happily about the price of cabbages, having to drive straight back, his old missus leaving some stew in the oven for him, and lots more. I found it helpful to listen to him, re-tuning to the sound of English ... then I fell asleep. When the truck stopped, I woke up.

'Feel better now? Had a busy day, did you?'

Everyone in England seemed too pre-occupied with their own lives to ask any real question of anyone else. Or to wait for replies!

'We can get a cup of char and a wad at that stall.'

'I have no money.'

'No money! You poor little bugger! Come on, I'll stand you a round.'

The hot tea revived me. Porters unloaded his cabbages. As he climbed back into his truck, I thanked him. He laughed.

'So long, mate. Here's a bob for your supper. You're a foreigner, aint'cher? Not a German spy, I hope!'

I walked away from the vegetable market into London, where the noise was unbearable at first. The streets were crowded with Allied soldiers, sailors and airmen, mostly laughing and shouting. I looked at a street sign: 'Charing Cross Road', which meant nothing to me. Suddenly, there was a long wailing – an air raid siren. The street began to empty, and was soon lit up by anti-aircraft fire.

A man in a helmet grabbed my arm and shouted, 'Get off the street, if you don't want to get killed.'

I began to feel very weak. Food was what I needed. I pushed open the door of a café and found it was a 'Milk Bar', serving strange concoctions. A sign told me I was now in Leicester Square. Girls with electric torches stood on corners, illuminating their bodies as men approached.

'Only ten shillings, darling!' one of them said as I walked past.

'I have only one shilling.'

'Bloody cheek!'

The next girl said, 'Hello, stranger!'

Without thinking, I replied: '*Bonsoir, chérie!*'

'Are you French?'

'Yes, I am.'

'I like Frenchmen. Come back to my place for an hour.'

'I have only one shilling.'

She laughed at me.

'Well, come back, anyway. You look absolutely done in.'

Her room was up three flights of stairs, and I wasn't sure I'd make it. I collapsed on the floor of her untidy, attic room. She dragged me to a bed where I lay, struggling to think clearly.

'I am very sorry.'

'Don't worry, darling. Just drink this and lie back.'

'Thank you.'

'On the run, are you?'

'Yes.'

'Deserter, are you?'

I looked at her in the light. She had a snub nose, a wide mouth and a twinkle in her eye.

'Yes.'

'Well, you're safe enough here until morning.'

'Thank you.'

'Expect you'll pay me next year, sometime, never!'

'You are very good to me, and I repay you fully whenever I can do so.'

'Oho! Speechifying now, are we?'

That was how I met Lulu. She was the golden-hearted *poule* who exists in story-books but not in real life. Not in Paris life, anyway. So I began to love her, and she changed my life, although at the time I didn't – stupidly – realize that.

We were still cozily asleep when the door of her room silently opened. It had been the only night of my life spent in bed with a girl without making love to her. I'd failed not through lack of desire, but sheer physical exhaustion. I woke trying to remember who she was, who and where I was. I knew I wasn't still in prison. And I felt strong and confident, ready for the day ahead. In the open doorway stood a little dark dwarf with a big misshapen head and long arms. He looked like something out of a circus.

He stared at us, then said to me 'You pay now. Then fuck off!'

The girl stuck her head out from under the blanket and said, 'Fuck off yourself, Massini. You'll get your money later.'

He came further into the room, saying, 'You not hear what I say?'

'Leave him alone. He's French.'

He nodded and addressed me in French with a strong Corsican accent.

'You soldier? You deserter? You got money to pay?'

After my previous day's practise with the wash basin, and a good's night's sleep, I was surging with confidence and knew exactly what to do. I climbed out of bed and looked around for a weapon. Massini stood his ground. On the floor by the bedside was a china pot full of piss. In a single movement, I grabbed it and flung the piss in his face. Before he recovered, I smashed the pot down on his head, using the same over arm stroke I'd used for Tiny. Practice makes perfect, as the English say. And he was much shorter, so it was a simple shot. The pot smashed and pieces flew about the room. Massini dropped to the floor and lay there.

'You've killed him, you fool!' screamed Lulu.

Lying on the floor he looked even smaller. I tried to find his pulse and heart beat, but there was nothing there. I was pleased to note my hand was absolutely steady. I also felt in his breast pocket, and pulled out a wallet stuffed with notes – nearly a hundred pounds. There was a French passport, and two British Identity cards, one in the name of Georges Massini, and one in the name of George Mason. I divided the money into two wads and gave one of them to Lulu. Everything else I stuffed into my pocket.

'He is my favorite ponce, and I love him!'

'*Was!*'

'...and also hated him. My god! What a mess! What did you want to do that for? What's your name?'

'Albert. I usually kill people, I don't like!'

She couldn't quite decide if I was joking.

'I'm going to make a pot of tea.'

I remembered that, in England, it is usual after a crisis to drink tea as a restorative. Personally, I needed food. I looked at myself in the mirror to confirm who I was. My face was bearded and haggard but it had a new hopeful expression. Apparently, killing people first thing in the morning sets one up for the day.

'What are we going to do with him? You can't just leave him here with me.'

We gulped tea and smoked Massini's Capstan Full Strength whilst I tried to think.

'His brother will come to look for him. You've got to get rid of him.'

'How?'

'I don't know. Just do it.'

'How about an accident on the staircase?'

We took one leg each, dragged the little body to the top of the stairs and gave it a push. It slid only one step.

'Over the banister rail?'

With difficulty I hauled him up and dropped him. He landed two floors down with a surprising crash. There were yells from below and doors opened.

'I've got to go now, darling!' I said, and took the stairs two at a time, jumping over Massini's body and nearly colliding with a fat woman in a dressing gown. Even as I rushed past I could smell her nocturnal body odours. Outside in the street, I walked quickly away, lighting another Capstan Full Strength with Massini's gold cigarette-lighter. Where to go? I stopped a taxi, said 'Victoria station' and, in the buffet, ordered breakfast of bacon and eggs. I could afford the best of everything. But on the train I regretted running off and almost went back to Lulu. She'd shown me amazing kindness. Where did she live? How would I ever find her again?

The streets of Hastings helped restore me. Bits of broken past events were coming back to me. I'd arrived here, over a year ago, when there'd been aircraft in the sky and bombs on the ground. Today it was peaceful. I wandered away from the railway station through streets of red-brick houses to where I thought EDNA'S might be. The memory of their revolting fish and chips and their passionate kisses held great promise. Now, where houses had been, there stood burnt out shells or bare patches of ground.

When I thought I must be near I stopped an old woman with a shopping bag and said in my best English 'Pardon, please. Where is Edna's and Freda's fish and chip shop?'

'It's gorn. Copped it last winter!'

I didn't understand at first.

'Gone where?'

'Gorn to 'eaven or maybe the other place! Caught it fair and square, they did.' Seeing my blank stare, she added, 'It was in the winter blitz – a bomb. A big 'un. Blew the whole shop to smithereens, it did. Got to go all the way to the High Street now for fish and chips.'

'Edna and Freda?'

'They was there. Blown to smithereens too, they was.'

I struggled with the word 'smithereens'.

'Edna and Freda not here?'

'Gorn to 'eaven, I tells yer. Dead! Conked out! Got it?'

I got it. I stood for a long time looking at the weed covered site where their shop had been. I positioned myself where I'd looked through the window to the two girls serving. They'd winked and giggled and beckoned me in. They'd given me food and made me welcome. Everywhere in England, people had been generous to me.

I remembered making love to them both, urgent and passionate. That they were dead filled me with a sense of overwhelming loss. I remembered the extraordinary odour of their fish and chips. As a feeble gesture of homage, I lit a Capstan Full Strength and tossed the remainder of the pack onto the site.

Then I wandered back through the neighbouring streets, trying to sing 'Roll out the Barrel, we'll have a barrel of fun!'. I found my way to the railway station and sat for an hour on the platform waiting for a train. It seemed my remaining link with English life had been severed and I would find no clues to my missing past in Hastings. The train arrived and took me back to Victoria. I remembered that word had once seemed a good omen.

August 1941

Winston Churchill was at Ditchley Park dining with Jock Colville, his private secretary when he was told that Brigadier Robertson needed to see him as a matter of urgency. They had dined well, but the food, wine and congenial company had been insufficient to lift the Prime Minister from his depression. He'd been seized by what he called his 'Black Dog'. He suffered from it throughout his life, but this time it wasn't without cause. The news from the eastern front was depressing. Both in the north and in the south Stalin's armies seemed on the verge of collapse. At Minsk the Russians were encircled. On the 19th the Germans had captured 650,000 Russians at Kiev, and were sweeping forward towards Kurk, Belgorod and Kharkov on the Donetz river. In the north they were ten miles from Leningrad, advancing on the city itself. It had been reported that Hitler hated Leningrad – the birthplace of Bolshevism – and was determined to capture it. Churchill was beginning to think Hitler would soon smash the Russians and turn on Britain again.

Already, five hundred British civilians had been killed last month in German bomber raids. Churchill had just returned from meeting President Roosevelt at Placentia Bay, Newfoundland. His voyage on the *Prince of Wales*, and the meeting itself, had been stimulating, but now he felt only disappointment at what had been achieved. Not a single member of Roosevelt's entourage had shown any enthusiasm to join in the defence of civilization against the Nazi hordes. Afterwards, Roosevelt had told the American people the United States was not near to war, and his intention was to keep out.

Churchill had family problems too. His daughters really were tiresome 'gels', running around with unsuitable men, including actors, and getting their names in the daily papers. Sarah had appeared on the stage in the West End of London, and had been married to a Viennese Jew called Vic Oliver, a second rate comedian who played the fiddle. Not surprising their marriage was breaking up! And then there was his son and heir, Randolph, a ne'er-do-well by any standards: boorish, often drunk, regularly encumbered with gambling debts. Their mother was no help. He could never understand how he could have spawned such creatures. Perhaps, upon reflection, he hadn't!

But he'd been cheered by Colville's visit, the purpose of which had been to bring the Determinate Protocol signed by Adolf Hitler, Reichsführer. It had finally been transmitted back to London through diplomatic channels, delivered by the German to the British Ambassador in Lisbon, heavily sealed. It had been weeks in transit. Now Churchill re-read it with satisfaction, tempered by the thought that the armies of his new Russian ally were on the point of collapse. And good old Uncle Joe Stalin – as he'd now become – was demanding aid from Britain. The War Cabinet had agreed to send two hundred fighter aircraft. Now he wanted a million pairs of boots!

After dinner, there was port and brandy.

Churchill selected a cigar and pushed the box to Colville saying, 'Now, Jock, we come to a very important ceremony.'

'A brilliant idea, sir, brilliant!'

Churchill folded the stiff Protocol document lengthways four times, then stuck it between the bars of his glowing log fire. They used the flaming paper to light their cigars, and Churchill let the rest of the document burn away. He crumbled the ashes on to a tray.

'That's the last time we need to address that little matter.'

Within an hour, he was proved wrong.

Robertson, the officer in charge of MI5's Department B1, was announced and came in with a major in the Military Police.

'I apologize, Prime Minister, for interrupting you,' he said with unusual diffidence, 'but I thought it right to give you an immediate report on a most unfortunate series of events, as a result of which it may be necessary to summon a meeting of the Double Cross Committee. Matthews is here to explain in detail.

Churchill was ominously silent. Matthews began.

'I have to report, sir, a very unsatisfactory series of events at Camp Z. Due, clearly to lack of adequate supervision...'

'Get to the point, man!'

'Well, the fact is, Prime Minister, that Hess was caught trying to escape. He'd got out of his room and into the grounds before he was spotted. The orderlies chased after him and, in the ensuing struggle, he was unfortunately shot. Shot dead, that is. It is most regrettable.'

Churchill went over to the fireplace and stood with his back to the room, his arms clasped behind him. He was thinking. There was silence; his subordinates awaited a fearful outburst. Instead, he roared with laughter.

'Good God, man! There's nothing so terrible about that. Gets rid of the fellow for us without embarrassment. Shot trying to escape, eh? Can't be helped. Don't look so upset. Hess was expendable. We've been trying to destroy his memory. Now your stupid sentries have achieved what two psychologists and an eminent anaesthetist have been unable to do.'

'That's not all, Prime Minister. You remember the French courier, Leconte. He also has escaped.'

'Escaped? That is serious! How?'

'While the sentries were occupied in trying to capture Hess, Leconte got out. The house and grounds were carefully searched, but no trace of him was found.'

'Where could he go?'

'We don't know, sir. Naturally, we have considered where and to whom he might turn for refuge. He did not appear to have close associates or friends in this country. I have his file here. We have been through it carefully, but it offers no clues to his possible whereabouts. Amongst his former Free French colleagues, Colonel Palewski is, as you may know, abroad. The other possibility is General de Gaulle himself.'

'De Gaulle?'

The mention of the name was enough to arouse Churchill's anger.

'It would be typical of that ridiculous fellow to try to intervene.'

'As you know, the general is in Cairo at present. But I've arranged for his home to be watched.'

'Have the police been notified?'

'Yes, we have put out a signal that Leconte is a deserter.'

'Hmm! What was the situation before all this? How was his treatment going?'

'Very well, we believe. We had a full report from the medical supervision staff a few days ago. There is every reason to suppose the course has been successful.'

'They "suppose" that, do they?'

'Unfortunately, Prime Minister, the psychiatrists in charge had not completed all the scheduled tests before his unfortunate escape. But in their last written report they express total confidence. Here it is: "... for all these reasons, we are confident in this case that sustained memory loss will have occurred."'

'If they are correct, there is no great problem.'

'That is so, Prime Minister. It is merely that his release will have been effected earlier than planned.'

'Well then, what must we do?'

'There is in their report, one further aspect. They mention that the memory loss may not be permanent.'

'What does that imply?'

'Sir, at some time in the future, some event may trigger recollection of what has been erased. It is not possible to predict how or when this might occur. Perhaps within a few weeks, perhaps not for ten years.'

'Then it is important to recapture him at once.'

'Indeed, Prime Minister.'

'And then have him shot!'

Robertson was shocked at the bluntness of this.

'If we trace him, Prime Minister, we shall find some expedient for securing his silence,' he muttered.

'Well, get on with it, man! Don't just stand there. Send out your recce parties and report back to me. Personally.'

133

'Very good, Prime Minister.'

After they'd gone, Churchill turned to Colville.

'I think we shall need to find a substitute for Hess. Some appropriately talented actor will have to be recruited to play that rôle.'

'An actor?'

'Yes. It will provide an opportunity for a bravura performance!'

'On centre stage!'

'With a world audience!'

'But not a long run?'

'Who knows?'

July 1941

When I got back to London my memory slipped again. I thought about finding sanctuary with Lulu, but couldn't remember where she lived; anyway, wherever it was, it would be dangerous to go back there. I sat on a station bench, trying to organize my thoughts into orderly chains of reasoning. I'd been held in prison where I'd been systematically starved, drugged and disorientated. There was a fellow prisoner who claimed to be called 'Hess', with whom I seemed to have some connection. But I'd lost all earlier memory. Occasionally, I got glimpses into episodes in my life – jumbled events and people: flying; Paris; Ann-Marie, getting lifts from drivers in lorries. But my last coherent recollection after parting from Edna and Freda at Hastings station was travelling to London, the journey I'd just repeated. That event had occurred months ago. After I'd got to where I was now, what had I done? What had been my life since then?

Afterwards, I realized that being at Victoria station helped me. Looking around, I recalled escaping to London for a particular purpose: to join General de Gaulle. I'd met him once in France. He was a brigade commander and I was a raw reserve officer. If I continued to sit and ponder the events of my missing year, I'd go insane. The only possible course of action was to carry out my original plan: to join de Gaulle's Free French in London, be swept into the tumult of the battlefield and escape all the hostile forces who might be pursuing me.

I discovered that their headquarters was now at 4, Carlton Gardens SW1 and was directed there through St James's Park. The reception lobby was crowded with officers and other ranks, shouting at one another in French. Once again, I thought, it was like coming home.

A girl at the reception desk asked, 'What can I do for you, Monsieur?'

'I would like to see General de Gaulle.' She laughed. 'The General is in Cairo at present, but please state your business. If you have come to enlist, fill in one of these forms and I will arrange an interview with the recruiting officer.'

She handed me a form and I wrote in the appropriate spaces: 'Georges Massini' and '13 rue Bonaparte, Ajaccio, Corse'; 'age 26 years'; 'unmarried'; 'unemployed'.

After a few minutes I was summoned into a small office, where a youngish officer shook my hand impersonally and said, 'Bonjour, Monsieur.'

'Bonjour, Monsieur.'

He grabbed another printed form and started to fill it in.

'Name and army number?'

'Georges Massini, Number 1489292.'

'Real name?'

Without thinking, I replied, 'Albert Leconte.'

'Everyone has a pseudonym nowadays. Rank?'

'Lieutenant.'

'Don't suppose you've got a birth certificate or any identity papers?'

'No.'

'All right. You are welcome! Here is your enlistment card. Later you will get a pay book. Here is the address of the Reception Unit. It is in Aldershot in Hampshire. Do you know where that is?'

'I think so.'

'You know the British give their departments the most extraordinary names. There is one called Middlesex. Incredible, isn't it?'

'Absolutely.'

'Here is a travel warrant, which you will exchange for a railway ticket. And a movement order in duplicate. You will report to the officer whose name is entered in the first column and hand him the top copy. Is that clear?'

'Yes.'

'Do you need any money?'

'Yes.'

He fumbled in a drawer.

'Here is two shillings, which will buy you a meal. Please sign this receipt. When did you arrive?'

'Yesterday.'

'How did you get here?'

'By boat.'

'Where did you land?'

'Hastings.'

'Well done! Do you speak any English?'

'A little.'

'It is important to be polite to the English. They are our hosts.'

'Yes.'

We shook hands again and I went off to join the army. For the next two years I trained and retrained. I learned how to march, how to drill, how to bayonet an enemy infantryman. I learned how to drive a Sherman tank, a three-ton lorry, a fifteen-hundredweight truck, and a Humber scout car. I learned WT, Morse, hand signals; how to shoot a rifle, a Thomson sub-machine gun, a Bren, a Sten gun, a .45 Colt pistol and how to throw a hand grenade; how to load, traverse, aim and fire a six-pounder. How to kill a man by strangling him, knifing him, or hitting him on the head with a convenient heavy object (I already knew how to do that!). I learned how to climb a mountain, and how to ford a stream on a rope bridge. I learned how to cut barbed wire, how to capture a fortified strongpoint and how to swim ashore on a defended beach. I learned how to read a map and how to find my way without one. I learned how to lead men, how to salute superior officers, how to write a report and how to attend an O group. I learned to go without food and drink; and how to consume ravenously when it was available. I learned to live without girls, without leisure or comfort. I learned that a cigarette can be a sustaining substitute for food and drink, and that sleep is a precious commodity to be cherished.

I learned how to make new friends; how to do the *Palais* glide

137

(again), how to survive night bombing raids, V1s V2s and the terrible food and weather in England. Some of these skills I thought I already knew, but most of them I found I didn't. This education proved an absorbing process, leaving me little time to ponder the events of my forgotten year.

PART II

19 August 1944

Each morning it is my habit to sit at my familiar desk in the hall of my hotel welcoming arrivals and offering '*Bon voyage!*' to departures. Today, looking around with new eyes, I am ashamed how shabby my hotel has become during the last four years. During the Occupation, not a single item of furniture has been replaced. No rooms re-decorated, not even the carpet stains – wine, cognac and vomit – have been removed. I am becoming idle and sluggish. My hotel is without light or heat, because we have no gas and electricity. What food we have is cooked over ten-gallon petrol cans, in which we burn old newspapers screwed together for slow consumption. We are lucky to get café *nationale*, made from acorns or chicory. One month's ration is two eggs, 90 grams of cooking oil, and 60 grams of margarine. There is a good current joke about the meat ration. It is said to be so small it could be wrapped in a métro ticket. Not a used one, though, because then it might fall through the hole punched at the gate! Nowadays, the métro is closed from 11.00 a.m. to three in the afternoon and there are no buses. At night it shuts down at eleven and curfew begins at midnight. After that the streets are empty. There is nowhere to go, not even the night clubs, which used to be packed with German officers; they have now closed their shutters.

Mama has become disengaged from real life. Her safe, I know, is bulging! She is distrustful of banks, and of me. What is she saving for? I am trying to persuade her to disgorge some of our cash hoard, to buy some necessaries on the *marché noir*, and to permit me to continue to visit my little friend, Ann-Marie, at the Chabanais on Saturday evenings. She has become an important element in my life during the past three years, although I only spend one night a week with her. She listens patiently whilst I tell her the events of my life. Then I give her a full medical examination. I accept that she has other friends, but we have grown fond of each other with the passage of time and, perhaps, after the war ends, and after my mother dies, who knows...?

Normally, sitting at my familiar desk, a sense of *ennui* oppresses me, but I keep a book under the desk to occupy my time. I offer a courteous, if formal, smile, to all the world. Today is very different: the day when all my German guests are finally departing. Some have enjoyed *vacances d'été* lasting four years, and it is difficult to believe their decampment is at last taking place. I am scrutinizing each item of their baggage as it is loaded into trucks standing outside. As well as their military kitbags, most of them have suitcases full of 'souvenirs' acquired by barter or simple theft. My anxiety is to ensure that they don't 'liberate' the contents of my hotel – and as to whether the billeting officers will pay my guests' last month's bills before they, too, pull out. Everyone in Paris is calling it '*la grande fuite de Fritz*'.

Hopefully, the victorious Americans will soon arrive in the city to replace the Boches, as I can't afford to keep the hotel empty for long. It is rumoured they are at Rambouillet, only some fifty kilometres from Paris. Surely, the *Yanquis* will pay readily! Even privates are rich enough to wear collars and ties. This would be a good time to review the hotel room price list. But can I deliver a high enough standard of service to satisfy them? People say the Americans will demand baths every day – unheard of – and drink cocktails at *apéritif* time. The practice of mixing different drinks together in one glass seems extraordinary. But I hope their taste in girls will not be different from that of any other army. It has become a facility I am accustomed to supply, at short notice, in bulk, where necessary, night and day, in all shapes, colours and sizes.

Later, I strolled to the corner of rue Lafayette and watched the stream of traffic driving east: long, slow columns directed by the gendarmerie. Some rare specimens of the Occupying Power rolled past. There were at least two fat generals, driven by chauffeurs in open Mercedes. Both were accompanied by their lady friends wearing bright dresses, giving the impression of a summer vacation jaunt. There were long lines of half-tracks, armoured vehicles, ambulances and trucks carrying the spoils of war back to Germany: antique furniture, sculptures, rolls of tapestry, food, weapons, hospital equipment, anything of value. *Tout* Paris watched the German convoys, mostly from the safety of apartment windows.

Some cheered, waved lavatory brushes and shouted: 'What a load of shit flushing down the drain!'

My *veilleur de nuit*, old Monsieur Robert, appears, heading for my hotel. Last night, he'd not reported at his usual time. He talks too much, but he is a painstaking worker, and some exceptional event must have occurred to keep him from his duties.

'Bonsoir, Monsieur Henri. Please accept my apologies for absence last night. I am mortified by my failure.'

'Bonsoir, Monsieur Robert. But what was your problem?'

'The gendarmes caught me returning home late after a short trip to my cousin in the country for supplies.'

'What happened?'

'They took me to the *Feldgendarmerie*, where they confiscated my cabbages and made me spend the night cleaning their boots.'

'You were lucky. If the Resistance groups had been in action last night, you might have been shot this morning.'

'I know. Things are getting worse and worse. People are saying that in the fifth and sixth *arrondissements* the atmosphere is terrible. Yesterday, members of different Resistance movements were erecting barricades, but they seem to stop and argue all the time.'

'Really?'

'They find it necessary to punctuate their activity with dialectic

141

as to the moral and philosophical basis of their actions. The Communist *Franc Tireurs et Partisans* have acquired a store of explosives and weapons, but they are refusing to hand them out other than to comrades politically sound. That status is to be tested by debate and rhetoric, a time consuming activity. Have you heard that Colonel Rol, their commander, has expressed himself as ambitious to drive the enemy out of Paris, and to seize the city in the name of the Communist Party, and to fly the red flag over it? 'Paris,' he is reported to have said, 'is worth 200,000 dead.' That sounds a disagreeable prospect. The Gaullists, on the other hand are opposed to the popular insurrection. They naturally see it as a way of displacing them. What are your views, Monsieur Henri?'

'Less idealogical and more pragmatic, Monsieur Robert.'

'It is said that some "fifis" have taken terrible risks to get back into Paris, hiding by day, and driving through the nights. Now the Germans are too pre-occupied to worry about the Resistance, and this is a great opportunity to secure sweet revenge for the death, torture and humiliation inflicted on the citizens of our nation during the past four years.'

'Have you seen Jean-Pierre?'

'Yes. He is the leader of one group which has taken control of the métro station in Place St Michel. You know it is a key position on the Left Bank. They are wearing armbands with the letters FFI and a small *tricolor* and carrying sten guns which the British have dropped by parachute, and German rifles and pistols, which they wave about dangerously. One of Jean-Pierre's men was wounded in the foot when a falling sten fired a short burst. Yesterday, they captured two German sentries, one whilst he'd been asleep on duty, and had executed them immediately, shooting them in the back of the neck.'

'We are living in bad times, Monsieur Robert.'

'You are right, Monsieur Henri. Jean-Pierre came last night to meet me. He looked more adult than when I'd last seen him two years ago. According to him, the situation in Paris has become thoroughly confused, as control of the city key points changes hands. In the traditional revolutionary quarters barricades have been thrown up and bodies are piling on the ground. The German withdrawal is quite unco-ordinated and spasmodic. The communists have called for a general strike, but it isn't clear how far the order is being obeyed. Nor is it clear which strong points the Germans are manning, whether they will hold out to the end and then raze the city to the ground from the air, as they've threatened, and blow the bridges across the Seine. But I am detaining you...'

'*A toute à l'heure*, Monsieur Robert.'

'*Au revoir*, Monsieur Henri.'

Today, posters calling for *Mobilization Générale* have been stuck up all over Paris. Air raid sirens are now sounding at irregular intervals, so I have decided to take shelter in the crowded Bar Victoire. It is one of the days when no alcohol can be served. Despite that, there is a sense of excitement – rumour and counter-rumour are sweeping the customers.

'Have you heard, Monsieur Henri? General von Choltitz, the garrison Commander, has received new orders. To fight to the last man.'

'No, that's not true. They say he has already pulled out. His headquarters, the Hôtel Meurice, on rue de Rivoli is empty and free drinks are available at the bar.'

'On the contrary, the building is ablaze, and besieged by Resistance fighters.'

I listened without comment. Today's papers carry worse news. *Le Figaro* alleges that Hitler has given detailed orders to von Choltitz that Paris is to become a major battleground.

'*The defence of the Paris bridgehead is of decisive political and military importance... Paris is to fall into the hands of the enemy only as a field of ruins.*'

My conclusion is that since taking command of the city some ten days earlier von Choltitz has become uncertain how to act. It is rumoured that the Seine bridges and municipal buildings have been mined in preparation for wholesale demolition. Like him, my neighbours in the *quartier* have started to swim with the stream. Former collaborators, including many officers of the gendarmerie have hastily put on FFI armbands and then taken them off, as the wireless stations continue to give contradictory news, together with proclamations from opposed Resistance groups, evoking the spirit of 1789, and 1848, and declaring that each is in sole command of this particular revolution. The Resistance newspaper, *Combat*, has produced an eloquent editorial declaring that the nobility of man is such as to lift him above his capacity to destroy civilisation. I hope that this is correct, but also feel it important to complete my room re-pricing exercise.

Above the tumult, the sound of the Marseillaise continuously rings in our ears proclaiming that '*la jour de gloire est arrivée!*' Another more particularised lyric prophesy is: 'The Amis are coming!' I believe it is the close proximity of the Allied armoured columns that has provoked the Paris uprising, their object being to ensure that the city is to be liberated by the fifis – *Forces Francaises de l'interieur* – and that no one, certainly not the Americans, should be allowed to share the honour and glory of such a famous victory!

Postscript

We learned after the Liberation that the problem for von Choltitz was that, like many of his colleagues, he'd had an underlying distrust of Hitler as a vulgar little upstart. All his traditional military upbringing led him to carry out orders without question. But when he'd gone to see Hitler in his Wolf's Lair to receive the order to assume the Paris command, his class prejudices had been confirmed. The Führer had ranted and raved like a lunatic against his enemies, 'the generals'. After this experience, von Choltitz had begun to realize the war was lost. He also decided that if he were recorded for posterity as the destroyer of Paris, City of Light, he too would be lost. He couldn't disobey orders,

144

nor could he bring himself to carry them out. Somehow, he had to play out time until the Americans arrived. Then he could spend the rest of the war comfortably in a prison camp. When the popular uprising began, he thought he would have to retaliate, if necessary by destroying the city and massacring the population. Events were moving out of his control. With these thoughts in mind, he agreed to a temporary cease-fire, proposed by Nordling, the Swedish consul – a neutral, of course. But he insisted that he personally should not be a signatory to it.

We knew nothing of all this.

24 August 1944

As we approached Paris I began to envisage hand-to hand fighting though the streets of my home city, the Boches destroying it building by building. Paris would look like Warsaw, Leningrad, and Rotterdam. But there were happier fantasies. One night, when we were *laagered* in a small forest, I dreamed we'd already won the war. I'd been demobbed. Everyone else had been killed or wounded. Sitting in the Café des Sports with glasses in our hands, Sammy and I had rejoiced in survival. Peace had come at last. It was a bitter disappointment to wake at dawn and hear continuing distant gunfire. I lit a Capstan, and breathed smoke into the misty air.

Then I shook Sammy, still asleep next to me and told him, 'I just dreamed it was all over. That we were sitting in a bar having a vin blanc sec.'

He came to life slowly and reluctantly, as he always did.

'Is that why you woke me, you sod? That's nothing to boast about. I dream that dream every night.'

'It was on the Boulevard Raspail, and I was watching the girls.'

'Were there any good ones?'

'They were all worth a go.'

'Were you alone?'

'You were with me. Some of them were smiling at us.'

'Did you inspect their credentials?'

'Closely!'

'And?'

'And then I woke up with a gigantic erection.'

'Do you think we'll make it?'

'Make what?'

'Survive. Get to Paris. Get at all those lovely girls you've been dreaming about.'

'Who knows?'

'If we do, I'll buy you one.'

'I'll hold you to that.'

I began to brew up, lighting a small fire in a petrol can. For *petit déjeuner* we had hard tack biscuits and bully beef. We'd lived like this for nearly three months, sleeping on a groundsheet, with a helmet for a pillow, eating canned food, drinking tea. What a summer holiday! Operation Overlord seemed to have been going on for ever. I'd lost count of time. Cause and effect had ceased to have any relationship. We lived from day to day, hour to hour. All I knew was the last order from HQ: our small force was to move forward to reconnoitre the routes. De Gaulle's running battles with Churchill, Eisenhower and Montgomery left him little time to fight the Boches, but, in his mind, he'd allocated the honour of liberating the capital to us, his élite Second Armoured Division, which by then had reached *Rambouillet*, some fifty kilometres from Paris. He'd been lobbying the Americans for permission to advance without success. Now, behind their backs, he sent us forward.

So far, I'd been amongst the lucky ones. Not a scratch! We'd sustained heavy losses in men and vehicles, having been continuously engaged, since first landing at 7.30 a.m. on 6th June. Most of my friends, those with whom I'd trained over the last year, had been killed or wounded. Whose turn next? We'd driven off a rolling LCT straight onto Sword beach at *Lion-sur-Mer*, where the golden sands sloped gently into the sea and there was lots of space for children to make sandcastles. Now they were covered with anti-tank mines, designed to blow a track, leaving you immobilized and vulnerable. Shells exploded around us with great spouts of water and sand. Lumps of shrapnel bounced off my turret. The Sherman in front took a direct hit and burst into flames. Through my periscope I saw Raoul and his crew, with whom only yesterday I was sharing drinks and sandwiches, struggle to escape with their lives, as their Sherman brewed up. One of them made it into the sea. When I looked back there was no sign of Raoul, my best friend for two years, emerging from the turret and no way we could stop and help.

Somehow, we got through the mine-field and headed towards

a sea wall. Behind it was a line of small seafront hotels converted into German strong points and emplacements for anti-tank guns.

'Halt! Hull down position, behind the wall.' Then, to my gunner Sammy on the intercom I said, 'Traverse right... Steady.... On! ... Hotel building ... two rounds... HE. Fire!'

He rotated the turret. Through my periscope I could see a faded sign on the building I'd selected as my first target: 'Plaisance Hotel ** Vue de Mer'. In the ground floor salon, however, *petit déjeuner* was not presently being served! An 88mm anti-tank gun mounted there was being reloaded and the crew was trying to revolve the barrel towards Dolly, my Sherman. We got our shot in first. Sammy's aim was good – he could hardly miss at twenty metres. His first shell hit the upper wall, and the roof of the building collapsed in a cloud of smoke and dust. Boche infantry scurried out, and were mostly cut down by machine-gun fire in the street as they ran for cover. We were so close I could see they were very young, only children. They were shouting to one another, but not in German. It sounded more like Russian. After we got through the first line of defence two more Shermans in my troop were knocked out by 88s located in the ruins of the Hôtel Moderne. The muzzle velocity of this weapon was so high that even the thickest armour was pierced. And the shell landed before the crack of the gun was heard. Having lost three out of the five under my command, worrying whether my friends had got out and survived, and mourning their deaths, I began to take 'Dolly' forward more cautiously, along the central boulevard of the town, sheltering behind buildings or whatever cover we could find. A street sign read 'Boulevard Calvados' – a taste of that would be welcome! As we advanced we machine-gunned German infantry and vehicles. At each forward movement, my back-up, Jean-Claude in 'Benny', gave covering fire.

Slowly, our regimental bridgehead expanded inland, but we were repeatedly halted by a series of German strong points. Gradually, we learned our lessons. Instead of rushing forward towards certain death and destruction, we waited whilst Jean-

Claude radioed to base for air-strike support. Within twenty minutes British Typhoon fighter bombers, swooping low, knocked out the enemy position with rockets and cannon fire, so allowing my troop, or what was left of it, to continue on the road towards Caen. But progress was painfully slow, much slower than had been predicted. Montgomery's strategy had been over-ambitious. His master plan to capture that town by the evening of D-day had been a costly failure. Back in his caravan at HQ, losses of men didn't mean much to him, just statistics.

I remembered that the beach where we'd disembarked had been not far from the resort of Cabourg where, in my childhood, I'd once spent an agreeable summer vacation with my parents. We'd stayed at the Grand Hotel, favoured by Proust, and I'd built sandcastles on the beach outside. In the evening I'd listened with my mother to the orchestra playing selections from Meyerbeer and Gounod. But on this day, I'd been far too busy to summon up remembrance of things past in sessions of sweet, silent thought. There was no time to reflect that we were fighting to liberate *la belle France* – or to reflect at all! We'd listened to de Gaulle's wireless appeal to my compatriots on 16 June: '*The battle of France has begun... Behind the terribly heavy cloud of our blood and our tears, here is the sun of our grandeur shining out again...*'

Our reaction was to sneer with contempt at this absurd sentimentalism.

'Your tears – our blood!' we'd shouted back at him.

Then we sang a song. Its title, and the only lyrics, were: 'What a big, stupid prick!' We repeated this one line over and over again with a sense of satisfaction.

No singing today. Survival in battle required all one's attention. You had to strain to see every detail of the outside world through the periscope. For those who failed to look, death lay in wait at every cross-roads and around every corner. This was what we'd been preparing for throughout the three years since I'd rejoined and been posted to the 601st Tank Regiment, to be trained as a troop commander. Retrained, it seemed, because the technique of armoured warfare had developed since the Battle of the Marne in 1940. I'd changed too. Instead of being constantly gripped by sickening fear, I was gratifyingly calm – pre-occupied with the tactics of the battlefield, calculating and recalculating the odds of life and death – as we bumped and swerved along. Sweat poured from me, but I'd learned to keep my head down. The hedgerows formed natural lines of defence, so that the *bocage* country was lethal for tank commanders who stuck their heads out of turrets. I now felt that my 1940 battle experiences had slipped into history. As for the missing year, the gap in my life, I'd convinced myself that it had been a memory loss caused by a battle wound. So I applied for a wound stripe, gold braid worn on my sleeve as a symbol of experience mysteriously lost.

This had secured some respect, particularly from the British. For nearly a year, I'd been seconded to the British army for training and liaison. That had been an extraordinary experience. I lived with them, worked with them, talked, got drunk, quarrelled and made friends with them. Then I'd been posted back to the Free French, and couldn't recall any of their names, except that they'd all been called 'Tiny' or 'Jock' or 'Paddy' or 'Lofty'. They'd all had girls waiting for them at home. They composed long, emotional letters to them, writing SWALK on the back of the envelope. This, I learned, meant 'Sealed with a Loving Kiss.' If you were expecting to go home on leave, you wrote 'BURMA' which meant 'Be Undressed and Ready My Angel!' When these jokes were explained to me, I laughed, then realised I'd learned to speak English fluently.

As everyone else was writing, I wrote a letter to Ann-Marie, asking about the baby. Was it a boy or a girl, I asked, because I couldn't remember? In a vague way, I wanted to see them both again. I was convinced he was a boy, and that he looked like me. I ended the letter, 'Your loving husband.' But my wife and my marriage seemed to belong to another lost world. There was no way of sending mail to Occupied France, so I had to tear it up.

My comrades in the Second Armoured Division were a curious miscellany. We'd all escaped from somewhere to join that idiot de Gaulle, but by a variety of routes. Sammy had spent eighteen months in a Boche prisoner of war camp. Some, whose homes had been in the North African colonies, had never set foot in metropolitan France before and barely spoke French. Most of us had been separated from families and friends for many years. At the time, we knew nothing of Eisenhower's strategy to by-pass Paris in the course of the strike eastward. He and his generals reasoned that to take Paris would delay the pursuit of the defeated German army across northern France. But the premature insurrection in the city forced a change of plan. Eisenhower feared that failure to support the Parisian revolution might result in a terrible massacre. Maybe he was right. Anyway, the objective of liberating Paris, *La Ville Lumière*, gave us renewed hope. On 22 August, General Leclerc was still lobbying General Omar Bradley, backed up now by an F. F. I. officer, who reported that von Choltitz was ready to surrender. Finally, Leclerc's persistence paid off. Tired and bored by the goddam, argumentative French, Bradley gave way. Leclerc got the order he wanted: *'Mouvement immédiat sur Paris'* by the 2ème D. B. It was the first of a series of famous French victories.

By the 24th we'd fought our way to the suburb of Fresnes, from where we could see the Eiffel Tower. But resistance continued. The Boche garrison held out in the prison, for a whole day, and my troop was again reduced in strength to three Shermans and eleven support vehicles.

After I'd reported my losses, I heard my colonel on the R/T giving the order: 'Hello, Baker Troop, pull back now. I repeat, pull back now. Over!'

'Hello, formation leader. Permission to push on? Over!'

'Hello, Baker Troop, permission refused. Your unit is no longer viable. Over and Out.'

Bitterly disappointed, but recognizing the dangers of advancing without back-up, we turned around with difficulty and headed back along the road we'd come. Before we'd gone more than a few kilometres, wc saw a Chrysler staff-car flying the general's flag, halted by the roadside. It was our general, Philippe Leclerc himself. An aide flagged us down.

'Who are you?' he demanded.

'Leconte, sir: B Troop, 501st.'

'In God's name, man, what do you think you're doing? Why are you retreating?'

'Those are my orders, general – to fall back and wait for infantry support.'

'Countermanded. Do you understand me? Countermanded! Get to Paris. Get there with all speed. Get there first! Get there now! Before the Americans! Go, man, go!'

We reversed direction again, cursing but happy, and drove blindly through the night, without food or drink, uncertain as to whether we'd find the city burning or in a state of siege, and whether we'd have enough fuel to get ourselves there. At dawn, after an exile of half a lifetime, I led the convoy into my home city via Porte d'Orléans. We halted in the square, later to be named '*Place du 25 August 1944*'. It should have been an emotional homecoming, but by now I was too exhausted to cheer or cry with happiness, or to think about anything other than how to stay awake. And alive! Sentiment was a luxury I could no longer afford.

It was a bright summer's day, but the citizens of Paris had been busy building barricades, followed by a disturbed night. Most of them were sleeping late this morning. Because of my US style equipment and the white star on Dolly, the first Parisians I met mistook me for an Amis, and shouted to me in broken English: 'Welcome to Paris!'

When this misunderstanding had been corrected, we began to receive a tumultuous welcome. Men and women tried to climb onto 'Dolly', offering us champagne and kisses. Sammy found it impossible to move forward because of the crowd. Dazed and confused, I accepted some of both, until I finally fell asleep for ten minutes standing in my turret.

Jean-Claude's voice forced me awake.

'Wake up, Albert, you dozy bastard, there's more to do yet. The war's not over, you know. I've just been told there's fighting in Concorde. The SS are holding out in their HQ. It's the Hôtel Crillon. The fifis are surrounding them, but they've got no fire power'.

'OK, but I'm down to two rounds of HE.'

'Take some of mine. I'll send Andre. Mind how you go. The Boches are still around everywhere; I've just been told some of them are crazy as shit. And the SS are suicidal apparently.'

Jean-Claude headed for the Meurice and von Choltitz's headquarters. I climbed wearily into my turret and gave the order to move off. Sammy, my driver, who was from Marseilles, was making his first visit to Paris. I had to direct him towards Denfert Rochereau, and instruct him to turn left along Boulevard Raspail. The *tricolor* was beginning to appear on buildings. We drove past the Montparnasse cemetry, where I'd played as a boy, then past my own apartment block, no. 98. I struggled to look in the windows, my mind whirling chaotically into the past. Was my wife there, I wondered? I hadn't had much time recently to think about Ann-Marie. And my son? I knew I had a son, but what was he called? On the opposite side of the Boulevard, I could see my favourite Café des Sports, already open, bright in the morning sun. The chairs were all set out in their usual places, and one or two customers were reading the newspapers. Occupation, barricades, death, liberation, come what may, Parisian café life went on as usual. I'd first met Ann-Marie in that café. Where was she now? And Daniel, and Gaston, the waiter? Would life in Paris be ever again like it had been five years ago, carefree and secure?

I turned left in Boulevard St Germain, and was fired on from the Ministry of War building on the left. A sniper's bullet whined past my head. I got down quickly and closed the turret hatch to cross the Seine over Pont de la Concorde. Now I was in the square itself. A crowd had gathered in front of the Crillon and the Ministry of Marine, and we had to slow down and then halt to avoid crushing pedestrians. Red and black swastikas still hung outside the Crillon. It appeared an extraordinarily familiar scene, but I couldn't think why. I opened the turret and stood looking across the square and up the Champs Elysées, which was deserted, so immersed in the past that I could hardly drag myself back into the present.

Then I heard the crackle of Pierre's voice on the intercom. 'Where now Commander?'

I couldn't spend any longer chasing ghosts of history. Behind a barricade of wrecked vehicles, torn down railings, and broken furniture, a group of fifis were firing rifles and pistols into the Crillon windows, without much effect, so far as I could see. Through a loud hailer, someone shouted: 'Surrender, you German bastards, or we'll set fire to the building and fry you alive.'

The response was a burst of automatic fire from the roof. It was aimed at civilian onlookers, who all ran or ducked for shelter. One fifi, a young man with a beard and glasses, zig-zagged out from cover right up to the hotel, apparently intending to throw a Molotov cocktail through a ground floor window. The roof top machine gun got him, and he fell and rolled over several times before lying still. Provoked by what seemed an absurd waste of a life, I rapidly closed the turret, drove Dolly up to the hotel entrance, and into firing position. The roof top machine gunner gave me a long burst, but he had no power to penetrate Dolly's armour. I used one of my few remaining HE rounds to blow out the main entrance door in a cloud of smoke and dust. Another round, fired at point blank range, exploded within the main hall of the hotel; it was followed by a secondary explosion and a terrible crashing and screaming from inside.

There was silence, followed by a shout: 'Enough! We're coming out.'

A line of Germans appeared through the smoke, the first few slowly and tentatively, waving white towels. The others emerged with more confidence. They were all holding their hands up. Some were stumbling, others bleeding, one half carrying, half dragging a wounded man. They were mostly other ranks, but amongst them I could see the black and silver uniforms of SS officers, some apparently of senior rank. There were about twenty in all. The fifis waited until they stopped coming, then they broke cover, cheered and rushed forward, shouting obscenities. They immediately began to prod and hustle the Germans, pushing them and hitting them with their rifle butts until they were all grouped standing against the side wall of the Crillon by the service entrance in rue Boissy d'Anglas. My God! I suddenly remembered that was the door through which I'd once escaped from the hotel to visit my mother and Ethienne. Yes, 'Ethienne' – that was my son's name.

For a few seconds the demanding present was muddled hopelessly with the past, but when I recovered I saw that the fifis had stepped back a few paces and were beginning to line up and cock their rifles. I realised they were going to shoot them down in cold blood. I stuck my head out of the turret and fired my pistol into the air to attract their attention.

'Stop that at once!' I shouted. 'No reprisals. Those are my prisoners, and I order you to leave them alone.'

I told Sammy to roll slowly forward, so as to position Dolly between the fifis and the Germans. One of them, a big guy with an arm band, and a sten sun shouted back to me in English.

'Fuck off, you yankee shitbag! Zis is nothing to do with you.'

I replied in French.

'Oh, yes it is! And fuck off yourself, you gangrenous half-baked fuck-pig!'

This provoked a roar, half of laughter, and half surprise. They stopped cocking their rifles and came running over to offer me a hero's welcome. In the excitement of the moment the Germans were forgotten, but they were too broken and exhausted to think of escape. Some gendarmes who'd arrived on the scene began to take charge of them.

155

We got down to see if we could help. There was one badly wounded senior SS officer lying against the wall. He'd been dragged out of the building, because his right leg was almost torn off below the knee. Someone had used one of the white surrender towels to make a crude tourniquet, but blood was still pumping out on to the pavement. His teeth were gritted and his face was white and twisted in pain. I had morphine in my first aid kit, and sent Sammy to get it. Then I tried to loosen the German's collar; as I bent over, I looked him squarely in the face. He was peculiarly familiar, incredibly familiar! Somewhere, sometime I'd known this man. Where and how? I struggled to organize the flickering, elusive memories reawakened as I'd driven towards Hôtel Crillon. Suddenly I realised that the German dying in agony on the pavement was Erich Reindorf, the SS Oberführer, who had been my escort at the Crillon when, a long time ago, I had been imprisoned there. Reindorf! No longer laughing at me and telling me to protect my queen. I bent over him and said the first words which came into my head:

'Major Reindorf. It's me, Leconte. Do you remember me? Hold on, I'm getting you some morphine.'

Reindorf opened his eyes and stared at me with dawning recognition.

'Leconte?' he muttered.

'We played chess together. Three years ago. You always captured my queen. Do you remember?'

I tried to tighten the cloth around his leg. He was now lying in a pool of blood.

As I jabbed the morphine needle into his arm, he said, 'Yes, I captured your queen. Ann-Marie – she's there.'

'What?'

'Ann-Marie ... she's there.'

'Where?'

As the morphine took effect, his head rolled and his eyes closed. I shook him.

'Where is Ann-Marie?' I shouted. 'Where is she?'

There was no response. As I bent over him I was vaguely aware of someone approaching me from behind. Then I felt an explosion at the back of my head, lost consciousness and collapsed on to the pavement next to Reindorf's corpse.

'You missed all the fun, Albert,' Jean-Claude told me laer. 'It was my best day since joining the army.'

Whilst I was heading for the Crillon, he and the rest of the troop had roared down rue de Rivoli towards the Hôtel Meurice. Sporadic street battles continued. Resistance fighters now held the Left Bank, but the Germans still controlled some important administrative buildings. By midday, their headquarters at the Meurice were surrounded. In the afternoon, they were stormed. When von Choltitz was led out into rue de Rivoli the crowd shouted, '*Voila le générale boche!*' and spat on him. A great wad of spit landed on his cheek just below his monocle. A fifi tore his valise from the hands of his orderly and ripped it open. The general's red striped trousers fell out, and the mob ripped them to pieces. Von Choltitz wiped his face, thinking he was about to bc given the same treatment.

Then Leclerc and his headquarters staff arrived, approaching Paris from the South West. He based himself at the préfecture de police, the symbol of authority in the capital, and an appropriate location to accept a German surrender. Von Choltitz was vastly relieved to be hustled through the hostile crowds, now envisaging a comfortable life as a prisoner of war, instead of a court martial and sentence of death by hanging. Hitler had threatened that all generals who failed in their allotted tasks would suffer ingenious tortures, followed by 'a long bounce at the end of the hangman's noose!'

Instead, he was taken to Leclerc at the préfecture who greeted him: '*Sind Sie General von Choltitz? Ich bin Général Leclerc!*'

They exchanged smart salutes and signed the document recording the surrender of the German garrison. Leclerc's failure to make allusion to the government of Général de Gaulle was later a topic for acrimonious dispute. Allied troops swarmed through the city greeted by welcoming crowds. Girls offered themselves without charge to anyone wearing uniform. Now that the battle was nearly over, de Gaulle chose to make a theatrical entry. On the following day, he and Leclerc, Rol, Koenig and the other Resistance heroes strutted down the Champs Elysées to the roaring applause of even bigger crowds. De Gaulle was in the lead.

Whenever any other marcher got alongside him, he would tell them: 'A little to the rear, if you please!'

It was then he made his famous speech: 'Paris outraged! Paris broken! Paris martyrised! But Paris liberated! Liberated by itself, liberated by its people with the help of the armies of France... of France alone...!'

His noble rallying call caused bitter disagreement and conflict. Wild shooting swept through Nôtre Dame as a Thanksgiving Service began. De Gaulle walked erect down the aisle, unmoved and unyielding. But the service had to be terminated after the Magnificat. It was the communists, not the Germans who were venting their anger. For them, it did not seem a famous victory. For everyone else, Paris had been liberated – and by French forces. The years of humiliation were over. Honour had been restored. Vive la France! Vive de Gaulle!

To my chagrin, I missed these glorious celebrations. I lay immobile for nearly 24 hours, suffering from extreme concussion. I never knew who'd hit me on the back of the head as I bent over Reindorf, probably a fifi not a Boche, outraged that anyone should ever want to save anyone else's life! When I recovered consciousness, I found myself in a hospital ward, beds stretching into the distance. My fellow patients, bandaged, but apparently with minor wounds, were smoking, drinking wine and boasting of their heroism during the liberation battles. Particularly the number of Boches they'd personally executed. And demonstrating precisely how! Nurses ran around clucking and flapping and trying to persuade them to get back into bed. The noise and excitement was stupefying.

Amidst all this I lay sipping a glass of water. My mind seemed detached from my body – clearer than it had been for months, as if recovering from a long and crippling illness. I remembered the detail of the scene at the Crillon, but also, in a sudden extraordinary burst, my memory opened and I recalled all the events of my lost year: my secret mission to Paris in 1941, imprisonment at the Crillon, escape, the walk up Boulevard Raspail, calling on my mother, meeting my son, Ethienne, seeing Daniel at the Café des Sports. Then it all unrolled jerkily and out of sequence, like a silent film: meeting de Gaulle and working under him, Palewski, his mistress Nancy, Operation Menace, Operation Determinate, Churchill, Spears. And the duplicity, trickery, deception of the British. I remembered being put in prison where I'd met a man who'd claimed to be Rudolf Hess locked up next door to me. I reflected on how naive I'd been at that time. I lay trying to understand these events and their implications. Gradually, I pieced together the course of my life during 1941, in correct sequence. What continued to elude me were the motives and consequences; they were not what they had seemed. I had undoubtedly been used as a credulous dupe. I remembered my briefing for Operation Determinate, my return to England, my 'illness', my second escape.

I stared unseeing into the distance, hearing nothing of the babble of voices around me. Undoubtedly, my memory loss had been induced by drugs: Churchill had been keeping me locked away to secure my silence. I hadn't expected a medal from the British, as Reindorf had promised – nor to be given amnesia because they hadn't trusted me to keep quiet about Operation Determinate. Instead of being decorated for my courage, I'd lost a whole year of my life. Instead of being treated as a hero, I'd had to hide like a criminal.

A nurse brought me food, which I ate mechanically. Even now, I couldn't wrap my mind around the fact that Determinate had been a deliberate fraud – on both sides, German and British. That Churchill was personally implicated, I half grasped, but I still didn't comprehend the depths of his duplicity. There had been a secret bargain between Churchill and Hitler! What exactly had it been? The true purpose of Operation Determinate still eluded me.

I felt that if I could sit calmly and reflect, some important concealed truth would emerge. But I was now too impatient to do that. Instead, I got out of bed, head spinning and began to drag on my filthy battledress. My trousers were stained with Reindorf's blood. My only possession was my first aid haversack, which Sammy had handed me as I bent over him. My last memory was of giving Reindorf morphine. I hoped the poor bastard had died peacefully. What had he been muttering about 'my queen'? Surely he'd mentioned Ann-Marie. I must have told him her name.

The hospital ward had become a tumult of shouting and fighting. *Quelle pagaille!* I'd ceased to care. Dirty and unshaven, and in an effort to get back to normality, I searched for a tap to wash myself. Being in hospital was like being back in prison again, and, from prison, for a third time, I had to escape. As I walked shakily down the ward, a naked crazy soldier barred my path.

'Why are you retreating? Stand and fight like a brave warrior of France!' he shouted.

What an idiot! I pushed him out of the way and he fell to the floor, cracking his skull on a bedstead. His comrades began to crowd around me so, stepping over him, I headed for the door. From there on, the way was clear. No one challenged me as I walked down the corridors of Hôpital St Vincent de Paul and out of the main entrance in Avenue Denfert Rochereau, near the Place, through which I'd entered Paris in Dolly, three days earlier ... and within walking distance of 98, Boulevard Raspail. By comparison with the hospital ward, the streets of Paris seemed a haven of peace. Newspaper placards announced: 'Le Retour Des Beaux Jours!'

I hoped they were right.

When my mother opened the door of our apartment, I hardly

knew her. She seemed to have shrunk to half her size. Her face was grey, her hair white. She gave no sign of recognition on seeing me, but simply stared.

'Mama, it's me, Albert. Don't you know me?'

'Albert?'

'Yes, let me in. It's me – Albert.'

'No, you're not Albert. My son, Albert, is dead.'

'Mama, look at me. I'm alive.'

I tried to embrace her, but she pushed me back. I managed to get into the apartment and smelled its familiar odours of stale cooking.

'Albert was killed. Years ago!'

'Mama, please listen to me. I'm not dead. I'm here with you. I'm alive and well. Where is my son, Ethienne?'

'Ethienne's here. But he is ill, very ill. He is near to death.'

'What? Is that true? It can't be. What's the matter with him?'

'It's scarlet fever. I have been doing all I can. I think you *are* Albert! But you look so old and thin.'

Mama suddenly burst into tears, and so, almost, did I. I put my arms around her, kissed her, and tried to comfort her. She took me by the hand and led me into the bedroom, where a tiny child whose face was covered in bright red spots lay shivering in a cot. He looked at me as I came in, but gave no sign of recognition. I could hardly believe this was the fat, cheerful baby I'd met briefly three years ago. I bent over him, and stroked his hot face. He'd recently been vomiting.

'What does the doctor say? Shouldn't he be in hospital?'

'There are no spaces.'

'Has a doctor been to see him?'

'Three days ago. They are very busy.'

'Is he taking medicines?'

'There aren't any. And there is no food. No eggs, no bread, no butter; nothing I can give him, nothing!'

She collapsed into sobbing, and I tried to comfort her. Suddenly, I realised how much I'd been looking forward to seeing my son.

161

I'd spent about three minutes in his company some three years ago, and in the intervening time had hardly been conscious of his existence. But now I felt automatically drawn to him, and couldn't believe he was gravely ill. I took my mother's hand and sat with her on the sofa.

'Tell me what has been happening, Mama.'

'It's the scarlatina,' she repeated. 'I'm doing all I can for him.'

'I know.'

'There aren't any medicines, you see.'

'I see.'

'There hasn't been any heat or light. I couldn't even make him a hot drink. And there's no food,' she repeated. 'No eggs, no butter, no bread. There's nothing to give him, nothing ... nothing.'

She collapsed into sobbing again, and I tried again to comfort her.

'Have you been with him all the time?'

'Of course! I hold his hand and tell him his Mama and Papa will come and look after him.'

'Ann-Marie? Did she come?'

'Not that bitch. I've never set eyes on her since she walked out of here, and never hope to. Her son suffering with a terrible fever and dying, the poor little one, and she can't come to him.'

'I should have been here.'

'Yes, Albert, you should.'

'I'm here now, Mama, and I'm going to look after both of you. I'll get some medicine for him, and some food.'

I talked to her for a while, until she was calmer. Then I got some sulphonamide tablets out of my first aid kit, crushed and fed them to Ethienne on a spoon. Within a few moments he fell asleep. Then I went to my old room, took off my filthy clothes, lay on the bed and closed my eyes for a few seconds. I too badly wanted to sleep. My head had become very painful, but there was no time to think about that. There was a lot to be done, and it had to be done quickly.

That day was the final day of the liberation of Paris. It was also the *jour de fête de Saint Louis*. Louis IX of France, a noble king, great Crusader and moralist, reformer of legal and parliamentary systems, canonised for piety, in whose reign was built La Sainte-Chapelle and the Sorbonne. It was a fine midsummer day, designed for celebration of victory and rejoicing for peace after long years of war. Tomorrow there would be mourning for dead comrades. But today the citizens of Paris prepared themselves for singing, dancing, and sexual activity. From secret hiding places in their cellars they brought up bottles of vintage wine, treasured for this occasion, and prepared to share them with their liberators. All the girls of Paris, in gratitude for deliverance, made ready to distribute personal favours with abandon.

For the second day, I was excluded from these celebrations. My time was divided between caring for my sick son and trying to come to terms with my past failures.

August 1944

I woke at dawn and looked out over the Seine. Had I not still been wracked by shame, it might have seemed a beautiful morning. And all my body was bruised and sore, and covered in filth. My first thought was that the black demon is now riding permanently on my back and I cannot escape him. He has brought me misfortune, sorrow and despair. Having worked desperately hard to get my life into order over the last two or three years, the Fates might have allowed me a little luck. Not at all! Yesterday, those bastards destroyed the life I'd so painstakingly organised for myself. And the God, to whom I'd once devotedly prayed? Where was He when I needed Him? At my side giving me comfort? Helping me fight my battle to survive? Why, I kept asking myself had I been singled out for such punishment? What had been my sin? What had I to repent?

For me, the Day of Liberation was not one to celebrate. On the contrary, it was the Day of the Apocalypse, when my happy and familiar world was brought to a terrifying end. It was the day when I lost my home, my pride, my treasures. The bridal suite at the Crillon had become my familiar nest. I'd come to regard the Louis Seize desk, the crimson velvet sofa and the tasselled plush curtains with affection. As if they were my personal property. Now, hiding under the bed in the gold and cream bedroom, listening to the bursts of machine gun fire, I shuddered in terror. Then I heard two explosions in quick succession in the hall several floors below. I should have got out of the Crillon much earlier, but I'd been reluctant to leave my comfortable suite and all my possessions. During the winter, Erich had given me a valuable mink coat, now in my wardrobe. I loved that coat, and was determined not to lose it.

Erich had declined to leave Paris with his colleagues; he had stayed to command the rearguard. He also had responsibility for maintaining communications with his Berlin masters. With his usual cynical grin, he'd said: 'No doubt, the victors, whoever they are, will execute us – either at once, or after a show trial. Being in the dock will be a new role for me. It will enlarge my legal experience.'

'Why don't we both just go?'

'Duty, my pet. Duty.'

I hadn't expected to be parted for long, when he went downstairs in the morning. Our adieus had been brief, but he'd told me he'd loved me.

'If I get killed today, don't grieve. Be happy with someone, perhaps – your husband, after the war.'

'No chance of that!'

'Well, your friend Henri.'

Erich loved to tease me about my lovers. He seemed to be without jealousy. I'd held him close and told him that I wanted our life together to go on for ever and ever. And I'd cried a little. Now, once again, I had nowhere to go. The Chabanais was closed for the liberation, as if it were a *jour de fête*. That left the Victoire, but Henri hadn't offered me refuge and I couldn't contact him. The telephone lines had been cut. He was expecting the *Yanquis* to move in any day now. Then he'd make his fortune. And the thought of his terrible old mother deterred me. Once, no, twice before I'd gone to the Victoire in an emergency. How often could I do that?

I knew the staff at the Crillon would kill me given the chance. They hated me as a *collaboratrice*, or because I hadn't always been polite to them. There was one old chambermaid who was a thief and very unsympathetic. I checked again that the door was securely bolted and, carefully edging forward, looked out of the window into the Place below, where I could see the Germans from Erich's headquarters. They were surrendering. Under cover of their white towels they were walking or limping towards an American tank. Great fighters they'd proved to be! The smoke and the angle of my window prevented me from identifying anyone. Was Erich amongst them? I wondered. He wasn't a man who would readily surrender.

A terrible banging outside dragged me away from the window. I guessed the Americans had stormed the building and had arrived at the door of my suite. For a few seconds I thought of hiding in the wardrobe, or trying to climb down from the window, but I hadn't the courage. The only course was to brazen it out.

I shouted authoritatively, 'What do you want?'

'Open the door or we'll shoot our way in.'

I opened the door, and tried to stare them down. They weren't *Yanquis*; they were partisans – fifis, they were now called. Most of them were last minute converts to the resistance, nicknamed *résistants du mois d'août*, or RMAs.

'Who are you, and what do you want?' I said as severely as I could.

There was a burst of firing outside the hotel, which distracted them; for a moment, I thought I might get away with it. There were only two of them, armed with German sub-machine guns. Neither was young, and one was wounded and bleeding. They pushed past me and ran across to the window, which they'd selected as a vantage point. Realising they were badly placed, they turned away and looked at me properly for the first time.

'She must be that filthy whore living in luxury here with the Boche general,' said one.

'Let's shoot the bitch now, said the other.'

He suddenly hit me across the face.

'No, wait, Jean. That's too easy.'

'You're right. Let's take her down to the street.'

Prodding me with their gun-barrels, they pushed me down through the still smouldering hall of the Crillon. I was too frightened to protest. An ammunition box had exploded, and bodies, or parts of bodies, lay amongst the rubble of bricks and plaster. Broken glass crunched underfoot. I didn't resist. How could I? Shame and fear kept my head down, whilst my captors argued about whether to shoot me against the wall of the Crillon. Two women approached and spat in my face; another kicked me on the shin. I might have hit them back, had the fifis not grabbed me and hustled me into the back of a truck.

Sitting there, riding through the streets of Paris, I thought over my life with Erich. I had achieved a degree of stability I'd never known with any other lover. Most of his work day, Erich was at home, because the Crillon was his HQ and his office. So I was never lonely. I sat by his side on important official occasions, in his box at the Comédie-Française and at Longchamps. The General himself greeted me with respect. The Crillon was an ideal home: no domestic responsibilities, and good service. I acted as interpreter for Erich in some of his interrogations, which made me feel useful.

But we were together for only six nights of the week. When he'd invited me to come and live permanently at the Crillon, I'd hesitated.

'No, I'm desolated Erich. I'd like to be with you because I love you very much, but I can't leave here.'

'Why not, pray? Why live in a squalid brothel when you're offered a room in a five star hotel, one of the most famous in the world?'

'I have to tell you, I suppose?'

'Yes, tell me.'

'Well, I think you know already that there is another man in my life. I owe him a great deal. We have a special relationship.'

I paused.

'And?'

'He comes to see me here.'

'I've never met him.'

'No ... well, he comes only once a week'

'So?'

'I don't want to abandon him.'

'When exactly does he come?'

'Only on Saturday nights. But he stays.'

Erich laughed at my embarrassment.

'That's no problem, my pet. I will give you a gilt-edged *laissez passer* for each and every Saturday. We'll have a six day a week marriage and, on the seventh day, like the Lord above, we'll both be released from our labours – the labours of love. You will be free to return here, and I'll be free to dream of my wife and family in Berlin. It will be good for us both. On Sundays we'll meet refreshed.'

'Do you seriously mean that?'

'Of course. Why not?'

So I moved in. I formed the habit of packing an overnight bag on Saturday afteroons, usually adding a bottle of burgundy and one or two delicacies. Then I would walk up Rue Royale to Place Madeleine. La Chabanais was only a few minutes from Hôtel Crillon. There I gossiped with acquaintances amongst the staff, who envied and adored me. Henri usually arrived in the early evening for his glass of wine, and we passed an agreeable night together. He left early in the mornings to get back to the Victoire to serve breakfast. I normally returned 'home' for lunch with Erich.

I admired Erich's wisdom and sophistication. With him there were none of the pretences I'd needed for earlier lovers. He didn't need looking after like Albert. And he was never dull or boring. He talked to me about his ideas and his work, making it all seem rich and interesting. Above all, he had the capacity for seeing the comic aspects of life, his own and others, which endeared him to me. His irony and detachment made me forget his nationality. That he was German no longer mattered. Whether he gave me money wasn't important. He was who he was. We learned each others' languages. He taught me to play chess, telling me the game was a good introduction to the battle of real life. It offered, he said, conflicting situations: victories and defeats; crises and failures; reason and emotion: beginning and endings. I made good progress, although I could never beat him. He admitted to me he was more confident about the outcome of a particular chess match than he was about the outcome of the war. For him, that too was a sophisticated game.

There was rarely a cross word between us. We became friends as well as lovers, and I felt accepted by Erich's colleagues, settled in my life style, and that things had become good for me at last. I used to make comparisons between Erich and Henri, and I loved both of them for their strength and wisdom. With Erich I got really close, but never with Henri. When we made love, we were always acting out the roles of characters in a one act play. Doctors and patients, nurses and doctors, were Henri's favourites, but also teachers and pupils, emperors and handmaidens, strangers on a train. I never felt I was making love to the real Henri – frustrating, but also, I had to admit, exciting. So impersonal was our lovemaking I never felt unfaithful to Erich.

I thought a little about some of my earlier lovers. Daniel, who was, I supposed the father of Ethienne. He had been good to me. Albert, my husband, now seemed a figure from my childhood and a child himself. Then there'd been Max, whom I'd loved, and Hans-Otto, whom I'd hated, and Jean-Pierre, whom I'd loved. They'd all promised to look after me, but none of them had been faithful. Had I loved Albert? It all seemed so long ago, I honestly couldn't remember.

The truck stopped. We'd got to the fifi headquarters in Place du Châtelet, where I was pushed in with a group of other girls, all of us accused of *collaboration horizontale*. Some of us were tearful, some vehemently denying the charge and shrieking back angrily at their accusers. Some had already had their heads shaved, some were naked to the waist, with a swastika painted in red across their breasts. Some wore a cardboard sign reading: 'I have been sleeping with the Boches.' Two fifis pushed me into a chair, and crudely cut my lovely blonde hair with a kitchen knife so that wild tufts remained. Then all of us were forced to parade around the square, so that passers by could jeer and spit at us. One girl carried her little baby throughout.

I didn't scream or sob, but submitted dumbly. I'd reached the stage of concluding that it was my destiny to be brutalised by men one way or another. There was no sense in resenting it, in feeling guilt or anger. At the age of seventeen, when Albert had left me, I'd been ready to fight back. Now, four years later, I was becoming resigned to cruelty as part of my ordained way of life. When the fifis got tired of their parade, they set us to scrub the floors of their rooms, and the streets, on our knees with cold water, whilst they guarded us, giving us an occasional kick in the backside as they walked past. But after dusk, when the celebrations began, they soon found better things to do, and I was able to slink away into the night. Not all the girls had been silenced. I could hear one of them repeatedly shouting: 'Listen to me, you bastards. I may have given my cunt to the Germans, but I've always given my heart to France. Always! Always!'

Sick with weariness and humiliation, I crept down to the bank of the Seine and vomited into the river. I wondered whether Erich, like me, was still alive, or already dead. Then I lay down under a tree and watched the flowing river. Gradually, the distant music, shouting and shooting all ceased. Finally, Paris slept … and so did I.

26th August 1944 and afterwards

In the middle of the night, I suddenly woke. Air raid sirens were screeched and I could hear bombs exploding. It was Hitler's attempt at revenge: he'd ordered the Luftwaffe to destroy Paris. The long night of dancing, singing and love-making was interrupted, and the general sense of joy and release changed to fury and hate. The war wasn't over yet! I tried to go back to sleep, thinking confusedly that I had to see Ann-Marie again. She'd deserted our son – but so had I.

At seven o'clock, my mother brought me coffee.

'It's nice to have you home, Albert.'

'It's nice for me too, Mama, but I can't stay long, because I have to re-join my regiment. But first I have to see Ann-Marie. Where is she now?'

'Gone to Germany with her general, I expect.'

'Her general?'

'They say she was keeping company with a terrible SS general called Rendorf or Rindorf.'

'Reindorf!'

At the time it seemed an extraordinary coincidence that Reindorf and Ann-Marie should have been lovers. I didn't know I'd been the agent for bringing them together. Now I remembered that as he lay bleeding outside the Crillon he'd muttered, 'I've captured your queen.'

I had to find out whether he was dead or alive so I gulped my coffee and set off for Place de la Concorde.

Today, the hate generated in the night was directed against prisoners. Already, Montparnasse police station had been stormed by a mob, who'd dragged outside two German corporals and beat them slowly to death. The fifi sentry at the Crillon explained to me that the hotel had been the SS HQ, and been blown up by the *Yanquis*.

'Really!'

Some of the irony in my tone got through to him. I showed him my army pass-book and he gave me a sketchy salute.

'Listen! The German general who was wounded here yesterday. What happened to him?'

'Don't you read the papers? Died of his wounds. Good thing too, in my opinion.'

I walked away. I'd killed Reindorf. Another death on my hands! I began to recollect the events of 1941 with nightmare clarity. I'd gone then to the Hôtel Victoire. Now I retraced my steps, pushed the hotel door open, with an intense sensation of déjà-vu. The fellow who had given me the passport was still behind his desk in the hall. Had he been standing there for the whole three years?

'Bonjour, Monsieur. Thank you for the passport. It was indispensable. I'm sorry to be unable to return it.'

'Bonjour, Monsieur!'

'My name is Albert Leconte. I came to see you three years ago. I was looking for my wife. Now I'm looking for her again.'

'Yes, I remember.'

'Can you tell me where she is?'

'May I be permitted to ask why you want to see her?'

'I want to talk to her: to decide whether ... we're to be together or not.'

'I see.'

'Well?'

'You've been away from Paris?'

'Yes.'

He addressed me as if I were a client booking in at his hotel.

'You wish me to be frank with you?'

'Of course.'

'I have to tell you that for a long time – years now – your wife has been the *petite amie* of a German general, SS Brigadeführer Erich Reindorf.'

'So I have already been told.'

'Then perhaps you also know that they were living together at the Crillon through the dark years of the Occupation. Your wife became quite a well known personage.'

'I didn't know that.'

'Two days ago there was fighting at the Crillon; it was stormed and captured. Reindorf was severely wounded and, according to today's *Figaro*, has died of his wounds. It is reasonable to suppose that your spouse, Ann-Marie, was with him too. But' – he hesitated – 'her body has not yet been found.'

He showed me the newspaper with the familiar headline:

Paris outragé! Paris brisé! Paris martyrisé! Mais Paris libéré!

'Is it known she was killed?'

'It is not certain, but it seems likely as the hotel was shelled and stormed.'

I turned to go: 'If you see her, tell her I was asking for her. Tell her to come home.'

'I will, Monsieur, but I think it unlikely you or I will ever see her again. Your wife was a beautiful girl whom everyone in Paris admired.'

I stood outside, angry and stunned. The two shells I'd fired had apparently killed Reindorf and Ann-Marie. Each attempt I made to release myself from my web of guilt enmeshed me further. I'd been killing people since last June but at least they weren't known to me. All I could think of was seeking out my political masters and telling them they'd recruited me into becoming a murderer.

At General de Gaulle's HQ, 14 rue St Dominique, part of the War Ministry, I walked in without being challenged and said to an officer at the desk: 'I wish to see the General. It's Leconte from his London office. Official and urgent!'

He didn't look up.

'The General is heavily engaged. I will send your name in when I can.'

I waited, feeling foolish, my bad temper ebbing away. I'd been crazy to come here. Before I could go, I felt a tug at my arm. It was Colonel Gaston Palewski, whom I hadn't seen since 1941. He looked like a fat and successful banker.

'Leconte! What in God's name are you doing here?'

'Trying to see the General.'

'My dear fellow, why should you wish to do such a bizarre thing?'

He was just as upper-class English as he'd been four years ago.

'I've recovered my memory. And I'm very angry.'

'Are you, indeed? Sit down and tell me about it.'

I knew I should resist his charm.

'Listen to me, Leconte. I am the General's *chef de cabinet* again. Exactly as I was when we first met. When was it...?'

'June, 1940.'

'Yes.'

'You remember I helped you then, and I can do so again. 'GPRF', they call me. *Gaston Palewski, Régent de France.*'

I poured out my story to him: how Churchill had deceived me; how I'd been imprisoned and my memory destroyed; now I was going to expose them.

When I'd finished, he said slowly: 'Listen to me, Leconte. Suppose all you've said is true. There's nothing to be gained by public denunciation. It will rebound on you. Churchill and de Gaulle are now both great war leaders – heroes! Soon the war will be over, and you'll be able to come home and rebuild your life. Where is your unit?'

'Somewhere here in Paris.'

'This is my advice to you ... no, these are my orders to you: Find it. Report back. You too are a war hero. What you have done will not be forgotten, I promise you that. I will arrange for you to be promoted and decorated. You will work here with me in Paris. We worked together in London four years ago and we can work together again now. I need your help. I will find you a lovely girl to satisfy all your needs. You have made me late for an important meeting, but come back tomorrow. I have a lot to say to you, *mon Colonel!* You are now Colonel Leconte!'

He put his arm round my shoulder as he used to do in London, steered me out of the office, and climbed into a Studebaker

174

saloon with an American army sergeant at the wheel. I watched him go, all my hate and anger replaced by a sense of pride in my achievements and reciprocation of his apparent loyalty and warm friendship.

Next morning I felt relaxed and composed. Ethienne was better too. He sat up and smiled tentatively at me. I put on my battledress, which Mama had cleaned and pressed, and decided to sneak back into the hospital and get more medicines for him. On the way I permitted myself a sentimental journey to the Café des Sports. Through opened windows Maurice Chevalier could be heard singing the patriotic 'Fleurs de Paris!'. He was putting all his spurious charm into it, to compensate for having performed on the German controlled radio throughout the Occupation. Outside the café a group of fifis with armbands were sitting with glasses of wine and cigarettes. One of them was my old friend, Daniel, thin, balding, with a straggly beard.

'My God! It's good to see you again!'

He introduced his colleagues, who grinned and shook hands. The old waiter, Gaston, appeared and made a formal speech, welcoming us back and offering us a glass of *rouge*.

'Have you seen Ann-Marie lately?' I asked Daniel impatiently.

'No, not for years. How is she?'

'I don't know.'

'It must be two or three years since I saw her. She told me you'd quarrelled and she was depressed. I had to get out of us Paris because they were rounding us all up – the Jews.' He paused. 'Albert, did you know Ann-Marie had a German lover?'

'Yes. He was called Erich Reindorf.'

One of the others, who'd been listening, said, 'Reindorf was a *vraie vache*. Clever as a monkey! Head of the SS in Paris. Responsible for countless atrocities. Happily, he was killed at the Crillon when it was stormed three days ago.'

'Anyway, it's great to see you again. How long will your unit stay in Paris?'

'I don't know. What are you going to do, Daniel?'

'I don't know either. I haven't had a chance to think about it. Survive a little longer – that's my ambition!'

One of the fifis raised his glass, '*A la tienne!*'

'Here's to survival!'

We clinked glasses and drank. On the boulevard directly opposite an old black Citroen suddenly came to a standstill with a screech of brakes. As a sten gun was poked out of a rear window, I was first to react, diving under the table, banging my head and almost knocking myself unconscious. The gunman fired a long burst, the bullets clanging and ricocheting off the old iron table and spraying the pavement with glass. Then, with another screech, the Citroen raced off up the boulevard.

I was too stunned to think or speak. Daniel had a bullet in his arm but one of his friends was lying in his chair in a position indicating that the toast to survival was the last time he'd raise a glass to his lips.

'*Les salauds!* They've killed David. *Les salauds!*'

'Daniel! Who were they?'

'How do I know? Fascists? *Miliciens?* Someone with a grudge. Get out of the way! I've got to get a doctor.'

Gaston appeared and gave me a mouthful of precious cognac. My composure had been totally destroyed. I slumped into a chair as I realised I'd seen that black Citroen parked outside Mama's apartment when I'd come out. I had been their target. On the previous day I'd told Palewski that trying to silence me with drugs had failed, and now they were trying to complete the job with bullets. Palewski had been a party to Operation Determinate; he had summoned me to my first briefing with Churchill; he and Spears had plotted the whole thing. Yesterday I'd poured out the story to him, and today he'd arranged to assassinate me. And he'd try again. His apparent warmth and his friendship were false and dangerous – almost fatal!

It was already noon. Palewski had invited me to come back to his office at lunchtime. What should I do? Confront him? Make a run for somewhere safe? Go back and find my regiment?

I walked unsteadily down the boulevard to rue St Dominique and found the same harried young officer sitting at his loaded desk in the ante-room.

'I'm Leconte. I have a meeting with Colonel Palewski.'

'Ah, yes, Leconte. He left this letter for you.'

I opened it.

My Dear Leconte,

I hope that life today seems sweeter than yesterday. Please accept my sincere apologies for failing to keep our lunchtime appointment. Come back at 1600 hours. In the meantime, please take note: I have secured your immediate promotion and transfer to my staff. Claude will make any arrangements you require.

A bientôt,

Gaston Palewski

I'd been crazy to confide in him. Now another trap was being set for me. But this time I'd get away. Rejoining my regiment would be fatal. That would be where they'd go first.

'Are you Claude?' I asked the officer on the desk.

'Captain Claude Guy, *aide de campe.*'

'I want to you to make out a travel pass.'

'Where to?'

'London.'

'On what authority?'

I shoved Palewski's letter under his nose. Reluctantly, he produced a blank pass form, signed and stamped it.

'I don't know how you'll get there. Any message for the Colonel?'

'No.'

I was anxious that Palewski might return to the office at any moment. I grabbed the leave pass and bolted.

As my train from Paris pulled into Victoria, I remembered my excitement when I'd first arrived at the station. In 1940, the word 'Victoria' had sounded very encouraging. I'd been sustained by hope and the promise of victory. Now, in 1944, I was a fugitive once again. I looked around carefully on the platform, but no one seemed to be following, or waiting to assassinate me. My hospital train was full of walking wounded of all Allied nationalities. At the barrier, Red Cross girls offered NAAFI tea and sandwiches, and guidance about travel arrangements. I munched a thick wedge and drank a mug of hot, sweet, brown liquid. There was no doubt I was back in England – always a hospitable country. Its cities had been blitzed, its leaders corrupted, but its people seemed untouched by the war. They would go on pouring out their tea, and eating their extraordinary food until the last trumpet sounded. Today, as always in London, it was raining.

My first call was at Coutts bank in the Strand, where I was relieved to find that my command of English had returned. A frock-coated cashier graciously allowed me to withdraw twenty pounds from my own account, untouched since D Day. I walked a hundred metres and booked a room for the night at the Savoy hotel, where the head porter bowed me in even though I had no luggage. Then I went shopping. My Free French battledress uniform and my pound notes seemed acceptable substitutes for clothing coupons, and I was able to buy a suit, a shirt, a tie and a pair of shoes, at the Civil Service Stores. I resisted the temptation to look at the Free French headquarters in Carleton House Terrace, where I might be recognised. Instead, I went back to the Savoy, changed into my new clothes, and lay on the bed to consider my predicament.

They would try again to kill me, or put me in prison. My only recourse was to hide myself in the heart of the city, if possible with a *petite amie* for company. For the British, Paris represented a city of sexual licence. I felt the same about London. Four years ago (it seemed like a lifetime) I'd met a lovely girl in the French pub. By now she could be married with two children, but I set off to find it, a familiar rendezvous when I'd been in London. The patron, Gaston Berlemont, was able to produce Algerian *vin rouge* for his compatriots, from some unknown

178

source, when other pubs had only weak draught beer. He was an expansive type with a cultivated moustache and a knowing manner.

I stood at the bar, gulped my wine and looked around. Gaston claimed my acquaintance, as he did with everyone.

'How are you, *mon capitaine?* Have you been released?

'Not exactly.'

'Looking for a nice girl, this evening?'

'Maybe.'

'There's a useful pair over at that table in the corner. The dark one is called Germaine, and she comes from somewhere in Normandy. The other one is English.'

'Thanks for the introduction.'

'Not at all.'

I wasn't attracted to Germaine, who was obviously a *pouliche*, and probably a homosexual one. But the English girl was different. She had a snub nose, a wide mouth and a twinkle in her eye.

I smiled at her and said,

'Hello, my darling. You want to have a little drink with me?'

Germaine gave her a nudge, got up and left. The other came over to the bar, smiling.

'Why are you all alone, *ma petite*, in Soho, when you could be in Mayfair?' I asked.

It was then I realised she was the girl I'd been looking for! She looked a little older, but not much. At first she gave no sign of recognition.

'No one's asked me, darling.'

'Then I will ask you. We will go to a chic party and dance the night away. Just you and I, and as the dawn breaks...'

'Are you French?'

'Of course.'

Then she stared at me and changed colour.

'My God! I remember you. It was years ago. Your name is Albert!'

'And yours is Lulu.'

'Why did you run away from me?'

'I had a date with a friend.'

'You left me in a load of trouble.'

'What happened?'

'The police came and asked lots of questions. But they didn't really care who'd duffed him.'

'So what was your problem?'

'His brother. He told me he'd kill you if he found you.'

I looked around nervously. 'Is he here?'

'Don't get excited, darling. He was sent down for seven years.'

'When I see a beautiful girl I get excited. So excited I call out to her. I buy her wine and take her dancing.'

'Don't know whether I should go with you, darling.'

'Why not, please?'

'Last time we met, you caused a lot of trouble.'

She asked whether I'd been wounded in the war. That was because I was very pale and thin, and had a big bruise on my forehead. But she liked me, she said, because I made a lot of jokes, and was generous with money. I took her to a dance hall in Shaftesbury Avenue. We were almost the only couple not in uniform.

Several officers asked her for dances, but she refused, saying, 'I can't – I'm sorry, but I've got to stay with my foreign friend or he'll get lost and upset.'

This made us both laugh and, whilst she was still laughing, I kissed her. After the last waltz I took her back to my room in the Savoy hotel, which impressed her enormously. Although three years had passed since I'd met her in Leicester Square, she seemed unchanged. I was curious to know how she'd become a whore.

'Now let us be serious. Let us tell each other the stories of our lives,' I said. 'You must begin.'

'Not much to tell, darling. I grew up in Liverpool and came to London to get a job. My Mum told me I was too young to go off on my own and that I'd get into bad company. I laughed

180

at her and told her that I had to learn to look after myself, that everyone was in the army, and that the least I could do was to get a decent job.'

'Go on.'

'And I said that when the war was over, and Jack was demobbed, we'd get married.'

'Who was Jack?'

'My fiancé. He'd been my steady boyfriend from childhood until he joined the RAF in 1940. Each week we'd exchanged long love letters, with kisses, saying how much we missed each...'

'Go on!'

'...how much we missed each other and it wasn't long now – was it – until his next leave. Then, suddenly, he told me he'd fallen in love with a beautiful girl in Edinburgh. He was very sorry, but he'd been swept off his feet. I read and re-read his letter to make sure it wasn't just a bad dream. Then I sat absolutely bloody stunned, listening to the radio playing 'How sweet you are!' and 'Hey, good looking!' Then I cried for an hour...'

'My poor Lulu!'

'My name was Betty then...'

'Go on.'

'Well, a few weeks later, I got an official letter of condolence. He'd had an accident on a training flight and been killed. Serves him right, I couldn't help thinking, but afterwards I felt guilty about having thought that, and I went a bit crazy, and gave up my job and lost all my friends. I spent days crying and looking out of the window. Then one night I recovered a bit, and went out to the Milk Cow in Leicester Square to find another man. There I met Germaine – she's French and very high class; she taught me to earn my living on the game...'

I pressed her to tell me more and reluctantly she went on.

Germaine had come and sat at her table uninvited saying, 'Hello, my darling. What is your name?'

'Betty.'

'You have a terrible English name. You should change it.'

After they'd talked and Betty had told Germaine about Jack, they went to the French pub for a gin and orange. Germaine introduced Betty to the proprietor and that was how she'd got into her present way of life.

'We became so popular that those Massinis began to claim a share. Now that's enough about me. You tell me your story, Albert.'

'My story is even more complicated than yours. I don't know where to begin. Well, I am from Paris. I am an officer in the Free French forces, and I have been serving in France, fighting the Germans. Now that Paris has been liberated, I have come back to London to work in my headquarters here.'

'Are you a Captain?'

'No, I am a Colonel.'

'I don't believe you! You aren't old enough.'

'I am very old and very wise.'

To demonstrate my skills I undressed her and made love to her very passionately and affectionately. I'd been so deprived for the last six months that I was ready to continue day and night. Our relationship was an outstanding success from the outset. Her wide experience hadn't dulled her appetite for sex; indeed, it seemed to have increased it. I wasn't resentful or jealous about her past sexual experiences because she seemed so untouched by them. Nor was I repelled by the fact she'd sold herself for cash, as I had been by the similar history of my wife, Ann-Marie. Perhaps that was because Lulu wasn't my wife. Or perhaps it was that she hadn't sold herself for German cash. But I decided from now on she would become 'Betty' again, and that was how I began to think of her.

That night was the beginning of our life together. The next day, we met again in the French pub. There were little round tables in the private bar where lovers could sit, talk, and hold hands under the table. We talked and talked about everything. We became friends. I told her about my early life in Paris and about the war in Normandy; talking helped release my tensions.

She was a good listener. But I didn't tell her about Ann-Marie, nor Operation Determinate, nor that I was a fugitive in hiding.

We both had our problems. I began to worry what I'd do when my balance at Coutts was exhausted. Betty's anxiety was about her friend, Germaine, the girl who'd helped her become a prostitute and who'd been with her when we'd met in the French pub. I never met Germaine, and never wanted to, but I knew she was terribly jealous of our relationship. Later, after I had been arrested as a deserter, and sent to prison, I believed it was Palewski and Churchill, who had caught up with me again. But Betty found out that I was wrong.

What happened at the time was inexplicable: we were sleeping peacefully in my hotel room, when there was a tremendous banging on the door. Betty opened it, and two big policemen pushed past her, grabbed me by the elbows and told me I was under arrest, and that anything I said would be used in evidence. They hardly gave me time to put my trousers on before dragging me down to a police van, and subsequently shoving me into a cell at their police station. I wasn't able to say anything to Betty, who stood there stunned and helpless.

September 1944

Yesterday evening, Monsieur Robert appeared early, looking pleased with life and anxious to discuss the week's current ideologies.

'Monsieur Henri! Have you seen today's *Figaro*? It contains a newly published Manifesto by Members of the National Committee of French Writers and signed by members of the French Academy: Georges Duhamel, Francois Mauriac, Camus, Eluard and Sartre.

He pushed the paper under my nose, which irritated me.

'Look! It concludes with this stirring message.'

I read the article's closing sentence: *Let us remain united for the resurrection of France and the fair punishment of imposters and traitors!*

'Alas, Monsieur Robert, I have to confess my lack of commitment to great issues. I am *dégagé*. As an hotelier, I cannot choose whom I receive as guests. I am obliged to maintain a neutral view of their behaviour. Whatever their nationalities, follies and absurdities, it is for me to nod and smile graciously. So also in the larger world.'

'But Monsieur Henri, these are issues which affect us all.'

'So you say, Monsieur Robert. In my view, great leaders promoting great causes come and go with remarkable speed. Just like my guests. Here today, gone tomorrow. When they are in power their ideas circulate; when they've gone, we forget about them. They may reappear. They may not.'

'You are a great pragmatist, Monsieur Henri, but you cannot turn your back on history.'

'And I'm not in favour of punishing "traitors". The patriots of today were traitors yesterday and vice versa.'

'Monsieur Henri!'

'Look at this fellow de Gaulle. Last week he was a traitor, a pretender to the throne, a refugee in exile, with a price on his head. Today he is a great hero and a great leader. When he appears in procession, we all cheer!'

'Monsieur Henri, you are a cynic as well as a pragmatist.'

Maybe Robert is right, but the life of an hôtelier destroys one's capacities to believe in causes. That is one reason why I'd like to give it up. The only real issue is whether clients will pay their bills, but I must say my new *Yanquis* clients seem very promising in that respect. But they are like all the armies of the world. Drink and fornication are their only off-duty activities. They are now liberating the brothels and wine cellars of Paris. You might think the war was over.

The possibility of abandoning my life as an hôtelier and pursuing my true vocation seemed to come closer this week. My mother was taken grievously ill. When I found her slumped at her desk, she appeared to be counting the week's takings, but actually she was in a state of collapse.

Not realising this, I said, 'If it has been a good week, Mama, I should be grateful for an advance of ten thousand.'

There was no reply.

Seeing her contorted features, I shouted, 'Mama! Mama! It's your son, Henri!'

Still no reply. A heart attack, I thought, from which it seemed she might not recover. She was carried to her room and confined to bed. During her illness, I naturally took the opportunity to possess myself of her keys. Last night, I opened the safe in her office and was amazed at the total amount of money she'd squirreled away over the years. Nearly ten million francs! Of *my* money! Well, I suppose 'our money'. I immediately began to make enquiries about buying a *chaumière* in the country, perhaps in the valley of the Loire, and made an appointment with an agent to find a possible purchaser for the Victoire. If Mama recovers, I thought, I will present her with a *fait accompli*. Moving to the country would be beneficial for her health. Naturally, I was anxious about her and looked forward to her full recovery. On the other hand, I had to confess to myself that her death would solve various problems. She did not enjoy life as a widow with an unsatisfactory son, and had no interests in life other than counting money. Death would be no great deprivation for her.

On Saturday, I went to visit Ann-Marie, who is now permanently installed at the Chabanais. She was sitting immobile at the window, staring out into the street below. I could see that she was reliving what had been a terrible experience for her. But I think she's slowly recovering from it. Her fine blonde hair is beginning to grow again, and her bruises are fading. But it's difficult to engage her attention and my plans don't seem to interest her.

'If I am able to move to the country,' I told her, 'I would like you to accompany me. It would be the start of a new life for us together. Would you like that?'

'I don't know.'

'We will find a little cottage and live simply but happily. I haven't quite decided where to go – perhaps the city of Tours which is my birthplace. The countryside is attractive and good French is spoken in that area. Around the river banks there are medicinal herbs growing in abundance. What is your preference?'

'I don't know.'

She has lost all her vivacity, but that is understandable. I have thought of inviting her to move in with me at the Victoire but there are two problems. Firstly, my mother may recover, and she would never tolerate Ann-Marie's presence. She is jealous of any friend of mine but would absolutely condemn Ann-Marie as a *collaboratrice horizontale*. Then where would be terrible scenes – shouting and screaming – which I deplore. It is bad for the reputation of the hotel. Secondly there are the *Yanquis*. So I have decided to leave her at the Chabanais for the present. She is comfortable there and not too many demands are made on her.

In order to help her recovery, I have encouraged her to tell me her life story. As you might expect, she is torn with guilt. After many hesitations and false starts, some of her history emerged. She told me about her husband, and how he had left her not once, but twice. And she'd been pregnant.

'Did you know, Henri, I have a son, Etienne, now aged four? I haven't seen him since he was a baby. He has been ill with scarlet fever – at death's door. But someone got him some drugs and his grandmother says he's getting better. I should have been with him. Why wasn't I?'

'It's the war that has disturbed all our lives.'

'Not yours.'

That was true, but the irony is I would like my life to have been changed and am now struggling without much success to change it.

She told me that Ethienne had been living with her mother-in-law, but now another, his father, not Albert, is going to take care of him.

'You have nothing to reproach yourself for. You are very lucky. I would like to have a son.'

'I don't want children.'

I'd never thought of having children before, but suddenly the idea attracted me. Perhaps when we are settled in the country, far from the horrors she has endured in Paris, she might feel differently. After all, she is very young and I am confident a diet of fresh country food would aid her return to normality.

'Do you think you are ready for a full medical examination?' I asked.

'Go away!'

What she really said was 'Fuck off!' She can be very brutal, but that is understandable. At first I thought her rejection presented no problem because I was in funds and the personnel at the Chabanais had recently been reinforced with some new recruits. But then I began to imagine a life with Ann-Marie, intimate and caring, perhaps with a child to bring us even closer. Even if she didn't want to move to the country, I decided that when the *Yanquis* had gone, and if my mother didn't recover, I would certainly take her back to the Victoire, where we'd live together and perhaps even marry. I would make her into a partner in every sense of the word; she would help me to manage the enterprise.

When I returned to my hotel I found my mother was conscious and asking for me. To be precise she was asking me where her keys had gone. She thought someone had taken them, but I assured her this was not so and that they were exactly where she'd left them. She seems to have made a rapid recovery from her attack. Obviously, my diagnosis was wrong and it was merely of a gastric nature. All the plans I'd been so hopefully and busily making during her illness now seem unlikely to come to fruition – at least, not for the present. I am deeply disappointed, but console myself with the thought that Ann-Marie is young and there is still time for us to make our lives together. When I see her again, next Saturday, I will tell her that.

4 May 1945

At 11.00 a.m. the Double Cross Committee began its monthly meeting. Over the years it had changed its title and had now become the 'Joint Tactical Planning (Provisional) Group.' Its function had remained the same and if the members had changed that would have been hardly discernible to an outsider. Colonels, Group Captains and civilians from Intelligence Services sat around the same table in the Basement War Room, puffing their pipes, and chatting about mutual friends and colleagues. A mood of self-congratulation had been created by news of Hitler's death in the Berlin bunker on 1st May. The war in Europe had been won; it was time for celebratory drinks and awards for conspicuous gallantry. No-one was now expected to dream up new dirty tricks. Many committee members were university dons recruited for the duration. Some were beginning to think of resuming their normal lives amongst the dreaming spires, and one or two even worked on their own private research whilst the meeting was in progress.

After approving the Minutes, the Chairman called his restive colleagues to order.

'Now we have a long agenda before us this morning, gentlemen, concerning the course of operations in the Far Eastern theatres, but before that there is one item under Matters Arising, which goes back many years: Operation Determinate.

'What was that?' a new member of the committee whispered to his neighbour.

'It was something to do with that French chap, General de Gaulle!'

'The Prime Minister wishes to inform the Committee that he is recommending to the King that those involved in the planning and execution of this important and successful mission should be considered for high awards.'

There was a buzz of comment. Someone asked, 'What about that junior officer who carried the Protocol to Paris? French, wasn't he? Can't remember his name? Did he survive the mission?'

The Chairman looked through the file without success.

'Apparently not. But enquiries will be made, and if he survived he will be sought out. If not, a posthumous award will be considered.'

The Chairman, always attentive to detail, noted the file and passed it to his assistant, a Major Carter in the Intelligence Corps. After the meeting, Carter, equally diligent, set himself to make enquiries. He began by telephoning the Free French HQ in Carleton House Gardens and asking for a report on a junior officer.

'How could I trace whether he has survived, and if so, where he now is stationed, please?'

'You will have no problem, Sir, there is an official list, regularly kept up to date. What is the name of the officer concerned?'

'Captain Albert Leconte.'

'One moment please. Hold the line...*Yes, we have recently received a report about him. He is being held in a British prison at the present time.'

'In prison? What has he done?'

'He is charged with desertion.'

'Are you sure you've got the right chap? Captain Albert Leconte?'

'Absolutely, except he's been claiming he's a colonel!'

'Please give me all the details.'

When the Committee Chairman was handed the Leconte file, with Urgent red tabs stuck on it, he read Major Carter's minute, and scribbled in the margin: *For the personal attention of the PM on return from San Francisco.*

When he got to attend on his political master, he found Churchill tired after his transatlantic flight. Determinate was the last item on a long and complex agenda, so when they reached it, the Chairman said, 'Prime Minister, it's very late. Would you prefer to leave the one remaining item until our next meeting?'

Churchill always enjoyed Determinate, and reminder of it cheered him up. He poured out brandy for them both.

'Certainly not! Expound to me the current position.'

'The Committee was gratified by your appreciative message, but of course we are all aware that Determinate was personally conceived by you, and if any congratulations are due they are all yours.'

'You didn't put the item on our agenda to say that, did you?'

'No, Prime Minister. It's about Leconte.'

'Leconte? What is *La Conte*? Some French story you're going to tell me?'

'Very droll, Prime Minister. No. You will recall that Leconte was the selected courier who carried the Protocol to France. He escaped, remarkably, from the Gestapo, and then again from our custody at Mytchett Place, having, we believe, lost his memory of the operation.'

'Ah yes. I remember him. Agreeable young feller-me-lad!'

'Well, I've ascertained that he's now being held in prison yet again, surprisingly on a charge of desertion. But it's nothing to do with our people. And we don't know how he came to be arrested.'

'So what is the issue you are putting to me?'

'Rather a sensitive one. We can allow him to be convicted and sentenced, which will keep him out of harm's way...'

'Or?'

'Get him off, I suppose, in which case, he may be regarded as a liability again.'

Churchill gulped his brandy and roared with laughter.

'But, my dear chap, what an enormous moral problem you are posing! Let us consider the alternatives: on the one hand, we can make him into a hero, one who showed outstanding courage on a secret mission. The British people at this stage need a few heroes to help celebrate victory. We can get the charge against him – whatever it is – withdrawn on some legal pretext, so that he's released. Then we could award him a medal for gallantry – a decent one: a DSO, say! Citation withheld, of course. What do you think of all that?'

'That could be a dangerous course of action, Prime Minister.

191

If the papers get hold of him, he could make public matters best kept private. It would be safer to let the Court convict him and send him back to France in disgrace.'

'Ah, but if we do that, we will be grossly compounding our original deception, and poorly rewarding a brave young soldier who made a significant contribution to Victory in Europe. In 1941,' which was our darkest hour, the war was all but lost...'

Churchill always enjoyed his own rhetoric. '...the Nazis, successful on the battlefield, were well placed to invade our shores. We had been deserted by our Allies, left alone, struggling to continue the fight without proper resources. In 1941, our nation's finances were almost exhausted. The Americans had stripped us of our gold reserves and our overseas investments...'

'Quite, Prime Minister.'

'What's more, if we make him into a hero we will be securing another opportunity to outflank that fellow, de Gaulle!'

'Very good, Prime Minister, I'll see to it immediately.'

'Wait, we haven't decided yet. If, as you say, he tells his story to the papers, the world will know why that stupid fellow Hess was sent here in the first place – and what was his fate. And that's not all. We did what we had to do to survive, but what we did then might seem unworthy in the eyes of the world. None of us would come out of it well. Not well at all!'

It was getting late.

'Then what is your decision, Prime Minister?' the Chairman asked.

'About what?'

'About the disposal of the courier, Leconte.'

'Ah, yes...'

The PM gave his decision, and the Chairman wrote his instructions on the file. He'd had a long and tiring day, but at least one problem was solved.

7 May 1945

On the first morning of the adjourned hearing a young policeman took me up to the courtroom and put me in the dock. It was a relief to get out of the cell where I'd been living like a trapped subterranean creature, since having been arrested in my bedroom at the Savoy and dragged by two policemen from the loving arms of Lulu. I hadn't seen her since. Now I'd had three separate experiences of prison life, each one less comfortable than the last. First, I'd had a luxurious room at the Hôtel Crillon; then a bare attic in Mytchett Place, and now a dingy underground cell at the West London Police Court. I blinked in the lights of courtroom. My patronising young lawyer, George Strang, was already sitting there with his papers neatly arranged. It must have been Betty who had found him and got him to act for me. Now he nodded to me across the courtroom, but didn't smile. The previous day he'd addressed me at length about the cost of his services and the problems I was creating for him.

'I am in despair, Colonel, because you're not being frank with me.'

'I am sorry you should think that.'

'Unless you recount to me in detail the events that have caused this charge to be brought against you, I cannot mount a convincing defence.'

'What will be the consequences of that?'

'I shall be criticised by the judge, and that will be damaging to my professional career.'

'I am sorry to hear about your predicament, but what about mine?'

'You will certainly be convicted of desertion and sent to prison for at least three years!'

'I have told you how I was suddenly arrested at night in the Savoy hotel.'

'Yes, but that's all you have told me.'

'All right, Mr Strang, I will try again to tell you my story.

What had occurred must be an official error. When I came to England in 1940, I worked for General de Gaulle as an administrative officer. Then, in 1943, I retrained as a tank commander and landed on the beach in Normandy on D-Day. We fought our way through France; I was in Paris on the day it was liberated. Then I was, er, demobbed, as it's called, and went to work in a civilian office. Then a British bobby came to arrest me for desertion.'

'At night in a hotel?'

'Yes. I tried to explain it was an absurd mistake, but no one would listen.'

'And you've been in prison for some weeks?'

'Yes.'

'Didn't you ask to see a solicitor?'

'I thought it would all be straightened out.'

'Was it a friend of yours who called my office? A lady?'

'I suppose so.'

'What do you request me to do?'

'What is your advice?'

'Suppose you give me the address of your military unit and the name of an officer I can contact there. Then I can arrange for him to certify you have been released from military service.'

'My office was at 17, Carleton House Gardens. That is the HQ of the Fourth Bureau.'

'Very well, I will go there.'

Just what response he got, I never knew. Sitting alone in my prison cell, I had been reflecting on war and patriotism, and my views had changed. No longer would I be proud to be awarded a medal for gallantry. I'd come to recognise that war wasn't an honest game like chess, to be won by intellect, heroism and judgement. Heroism was a naïve sentiment, and acts of heroism had but trivial effect. War was played and won by deceit, treachery and betrayal. Otherwise there were no rules: the dominant element was chance. That was how I'd survived – chance and the goodwill of strangers. Edna and Freda had given me their love. Henri

194

Rouget, the hotel proprietor had given me a passport. Reindorf had effectively preserved me from the Crillon torture chamber. The fat policeman had told me how to get to Geneva ... and Lulu had taken me into her bed.

Over the last few months I'd passed through all the stages of anger and despair. Instead of confiding in my lawyer I was ready to fight a public battle for truth and freedom. During my three spells in prison I'd learned to suppress frustration and plan ahead. I'd decided that by allowing me to go into a courtroom and speak, they – whoever they were – had played into my hands. I'd made up my mind to tell the whole story: how in 1941 I'd been recruited personally by the British Prime Minister for Operation Determinate; how I'd been deliberately deceived about the nature of my mission and still didn't know exactly what it had been; how, after completing my mission, I'd been imprisoned and drugged so as to destroy my memory of these events; how, after I'd escaped and fought for my country, they'd tried to assassinate me. Now they'd imprisoned me again. My theory was that only after I'd told my story to the world would I be safe, because no one would then have any interest in suppressing it.

There was a crowd in the gallery of the Court: two French officers, a British Major with red tabs and several important looking civilians. The policeman nudged me to stand up when the judge entered. They'd told me he was called Sir Gerard Hogge KC; he was obviously a self-satisfied, pompous type.

A clerk intoned, 'The accused, Albert Leconte, is charged under Section 154 of the Army Act 1851 with being a deserter from the French land forces in Britain, which charge was first heard on 8th March 1945 and adjourned until today's date...'

Almost before he'd finished speaking, they went into one of those stupid rituals that the British so enjoy. One fat red-faced lawyer struggled to his feet saying he appeared for the prosecution, and my irritating little type, George, jumped up and told the Court in a strangled voice that he appeared for the defence. After that, I decided this was my big moment, so I pushed the policeman out of the way, stood up straight and opened my mouth to speak. I'd rehearsed exactly what I was going to say. I would give my account of events, starting with my 1941 meeting with Winston Churchill, no matter what the consequences. Everyone turned to stare at me.

'Sit down until you are told to stand!' the judge shouted.

Before I could utter a word, the fat red-faced fellow got up and said in one continuous, barely intelligible stream of words, 'There-has-been-a-development-Your-Worship-the-prosecution-now-wishes-to-offer-no-evidence-and-the-charge-against-the-accused-is-accordingly-withdrawn.'

Then he flopped down again. At first I didn't understand what he'd said. Neither, apparently, did anyone else. There was silence. The judge's face contorted with anger.

'Withdrawn?' he shouted.

'Just so, Your Worship'

'Withdrawn? No evidence?'

'That is correct, Your Worship.'

'No sir, it is not correct! It is most incorrect! I think, Mr Norton-Brown, you owe the Court some explanation.'

'Those are the instructions I have received, Your Worship, from those instructing me.'

'Nonsense! Absolute nonsense! You must secure from those instructing you some decent explanation.'

'If it please Your Worship.'

The room fell silent as the fat lawyer turned and whispered to another smaller lawyer sitting behind him. This one then turned and whispered to another one. I tried to stand up but the policemen pushed me down. Five minutes elapsed during which the judge fidgeted and could be heard muttering, 'Ridiculous!'

Finally the fat lawyer got up again looking embarrassed and said, 'Your Worship, I am instructed respectfully to say that, whilst there may be evidence of desertion from the Free French Forces, there is no evidence of desertion from the armed forces of The Republic of France. In these circumstances, I believe it is right to state that the prosecution cannot and should not proceed.'

Sir Gerard snorted with contempt. He glared at me and said: 'Case dismissed!'

As I still didn't understand, but continued to sit motionless in the dock, he shouted, 'Don't you understand? You are free to leave the Court.'

I opened my mouth, but no sound came out. The policeman tugged me by the arm as the Court rose to release Sir Gerard who strode off giving the fat lawyer a threatening glare. The policeman pushed me into the corridor outside, where my lawyer, George Strang, looking relieved and elated, rushed up and shook me by the hand.

'Congratulations, Colonel. In the face of our strong case, they capitulated.'

'I don't understand. Why wasn't I permitted to tell everyone my story?'

'There was no need for evidence because they admitted the case should never have been brought in the first place.'

I struggled with mixed emotions: relief at being free, anger that I'd been again prevented from telling my story, and fear they would again attempt to murder me. Betty appeared and we threw ourselves speechlessly into each others' arms.

She whispered in my ear, 'It was Germaine, the stupid bitch!'

'What was Germaine?'

'It was Germaine who tipped off the police that we'd be at the Savoy that night. She told them you were a deserter.'

'Why?'

'Because she hates you.'

'Why?'

'Because I love you.'

There was no time for any more questions. A crowd had now gathered around us: the two Free French officers, all the lawyers, including the fat one, who told me that my release had been an act of generosity on his part.

The senior French officer introduced himself as Commandant Duret.

'Leconte, I am here to apologise profoundly on behalf of the General and his staff for the error of your arrest. The General is most chagrined.' I was tempted to make a sarcastic reply but he went on, 'We recognise that you have been the subject of an unjust prosecution and those responsible, whoever they may be, will be sought out and disciplined.'

'On whose authority, precisely, are you here?'

'The General's Principal Private Secretary.'

'And who might that be?'

'Colonel Gaston Palewski.'

A British major launched into another version of the same text:

'Captain Leconte, I am here on behalf of His Majesty's government. The Secretary of State has asked me to convey to you his apologies for the involvement of the British police in this unfortunate affair. I am to tell you the government is particularly dismayed, having regard to your past distinguished service record which has now been examined. You may rest assured, however, that proper recognition will in due course be accorded.'

I found all this barely comprehensible and didn't know how to respond. However, my lawyer came to my rescue.

'On behalf of the accused, gentlemen, it is important I notify you now that compensation proceedings for false imprisonment may be instituted.'

'We shall make compensation as appropriate, Mr Strang.'

'And then there are my costs – I mean my client's costs.'

'You may rest assured that is a matter which will be dealt with. Your client is being recommended to the King for an award.'

'An award?'

'How much?' Betty asked.

'No, no, you misunderstand. An award of honour!'

'You mean Albert is a hero?'

'Certainly.'

'Not a deserter?'

'Of course not!'

I was struggling to decide what to believe. Was this yet another trick designed to give me a false sense of security or was my ordeal really over? Now one of the civilians stepped forward.

'Leconte, my name is John Colville. Would you please come with me immediately? We have to report to my political master who will have been waiting for some time to speak with you.'

I was confused by the sudden turn of events. Obediently, like a child, I followed him down a corridor, out of the main door and into a waiting limousine. Betty shouted something to me and I shouted back, telling her I'd meet her in the French pub and that she should wait for me there. The car quickly deposited us outside 10 Downing Street, where I was ushered into the presence of Winston Churchill, complete with cigar, sitting alone in an armchair, beaming at me.

'Captain Leconte,' he said, 'some years have elapsed since we met, but I am sure you will remember that last occasion and you will know why I have summoned you here. It is to express to you my personal appreciation for the way you successfully carried out the critically difficult and hazardous mission entrusted to you by my Committee four years ago, and to convey my admiration for your capacity to cope with danger and your courage....'

He went on like this for some time. Once, I might have felt proud to be honoured, and impressed by his eloquence: now I'd got so cynical about Churchill that I sneered inwardly at his hollow rhetoric and asked myself how, if at all, I should respond? Should I tell him that I knew it was on his orders they'd imprisoned me, drugged me to extinguish my memory, and perhaps even tried to assassinate me? That I thought him a liar, hypocrite and fraud? Or should I just smile innocently and thank him for his graciousness? Finally, he ran out of breath and stopped speaking.

I looked him straight in the eye and said bluntly, 'Mr Churchill, would you please tell me something important?'

'Yes, of course, my dear feller. Anything.'

'What *was* the message I took to France? Who was it for? What did it say?'

He puffed on his cigar for a long time.

'I have to tell you, Leconte, that I do feel a degree of guilt at having misled you – no – having deceived you about the purpose of your mission. If I tell you the true story, do you promise me you will respect the confidence and never repeat it? In 1941, absolutely everything – including our very survival – was at stake. Now, your mission has become part of history, but I readily confess to you it is a dark part. Do you give me your word?'

'I do.'

'Very well. I think you are one individual who deserves to know.'

He shouted to his typist in an adjacent office, 'Liz! It's tea time. Go for a short walk.'

He then told me a fantastic and complicated tale. On the 18 June 1940, he had declared that Britain would 'Never surrender!' But by the autumn of that year, Hitler was threatening to send a powerful force to invade England. He had named it Operation Sea Lion, and Churchill knew that German army commanders had been instructed to collect all available sea and river craft in their areas, to be used for landing. These craft and elite troops were being assembled in the French channel ports. Naval officers had been attached to the Army High Command as advisers. His spies had obtained details of a plan to land thirteen divisions in the first wave, to be followed by nine panzer and motorized divisions onto the south coast, probably between Ramsgate and Bexhill, Brighton and the Isle of Wight, and Weymouth and Lyme Regis. Airborne divisions would support the first wave. In three days a quarter of a million troops would have landed.

The British army had been defeated in France, and the Dunkirk retreat had left it short of vital arms, transport, ammunition and equipment. Furthermore, the army commanders had been demoralised by failure in France, and had advised Churchill that Britain would be unable to repel a landing force. The Battle of Britain, fought in the sky in 1940 had left the RAF hopelessly depleted, lacking vital spare parts. Again, Churchill had been advised it would be unable to withstand the Luftwaffe operating in support of beach landings. He had approached Roosevelt for help but the Americans had been determined to stay out of what they then regarded as a European conflict. A plan had been devised for the whole British Cabinet and government to be evacuated to Canada, to carry on the war from there, but Churchill felt that that would have been deserting his people.

To avoid certain defeat and occupation of his country, – subjugation by what he called 'the Nazi hordes', and the terrible suffering and humiliation which would have followed, he conceived the plan of secretly offering Hitler a Peace settlement. Not a capitulation, but a deal not far from one. The basis of it would be that if Hitler signed a secret Treaty promising not to invade Britain, but to invade the Soviet Union instead, he, Churchill, would make peace with Hitler and declare war on Russia so that Britain and Germany would become allies. Hitler had accepted this proposal and in May 1941 sent Rudolf Hess, his Deputy, with a draft treaty – a Protocol – for Churchill to sign, and return without delay. Hess had landed in Scotland and asked to be taken to the Duke of Hamilton, who, Hitler had believed, was head of a Peace Party in Britain. Actually, the Duke had been serving in the Royal Air Force, but he did meet Hess and conducted him to Churchill. Of course, Hitler had absolutely denied all knowledge of Hess's flight to Scotland, and had issued a statement to the effect that his Deputy had gone insane. This unlikely explanation of the event had been convenient for Churchill, and been readily accepted both in Germany and Britain.

After Hess had landed, and been captured, Churchill simply had him imprisoned at Mychett Place and, like Hitler, had explained away his visit by telling the Press that Hess had gone mad and was on a desperate mission to re-establish his failing career in the eyes of his master. Churchill had, as he put it, then selected me for the onerous task of returning the signed Protocol, Operation Determinate. He did rather shamefacedly admit that he'd chosen a French courier so that he could, if necessary, deny all knowledge of the document and claim it had been forged by de Gaulle and his staff.

None of this had been revealed to The War Cabinet, the Double Cross Committee, or anyone, except his Private Secretary. Churchill was well aware that the planned breaking of his contractual promise would be regarded as duplicitous conduct. (Whilst he was actually saying this, it occurred to me that there was a striking parallel in my own conduct: my equally dishonourable promise to Reindorf not to escape from the Hôtel Crillon, which I'd known I would break.)

This plan had been absolutely successful. Hitler had carried out his part of the bargain, had indeed invaded the Soviet Union on 22 May 1941, believing that in ten weeks – well before winter set in – his superior army would crush the inefficient Russians. Churchill, of course, had had no intention of joining forces with Hitler, so he had simply done nothing. He knew that when he declared that Britain and the Soviet Union had now become allies, Hitler would be furious at this enormous betrayal and – importantly – he would not be pleased with me, the innocent courier who had brought him the signed Protocol. That was why – Churchill claimed – they'd given me a false account of my mission, so that the true story could never be dragged from me by promises, threats or torture. What I didn't know, I couldn't tell.

I listened to all this for about an hour, with as much patience as I could muster, wondering all the time whether to believe it or not.

Then, summoning my courage, I said, 'Mr Churchill, I can understand why you feel a sense of guilt: you had me imprisoned and your doctors administered drugs to try to make me lose my memory of my mission. If I hadn't escaped from your prison, I'd still be there.'

He looked uncomfortable.

'And you wouldn't now be telling me how much you admire my courage.'

He recovered himself.

'Yes, but it was for your own good, my boy. So long as you were able to recollect your mission you would have been vulnerable to threats and promises from everyone – friends and enemies.'

'And now?'

'Now the war's over. You've played your part in our allied victory. It was a big part. An unique part. And you have given me your word that you will not disclose anything which I have confided to you – and I trust you to do that. You will be awarded the Distinguished Service Order, but no details of how you earned it will be revealed: 'Citation Withheld'. Now you can return, a hero, to your own country and your own city of Paris – the City of Light. Your general is, I believe, ready to welcome you back to his staff. Good bye, Leconte. God speed! And good luck!'

He stood up, and shook me warmly by the hand. I was about to leave the room, when I remembered something.

'What has happened to Rudolf Hess?'

'He is, of course, still a prisoner, and now that the war in Europe has been won he will soon be tried by a Military Court for his war crimes.'

That, I thought, was an unlikely conclusion to his tale, most of which I was reluctantly beginning to believe. His warmth and charm were absolutely irresistible. It was impossible not to be convinced by him. I also began to believe I had played an important rôle, no, an unique rôle, in winning the war. That, inevitably, made me feel much better.

He ushered me out with great friendliness, and his driver took me to the French pub in Soho, where Betty was sitting alone with an empty glass.

'Albert! I've been waiting so long for you. Where have you been? Who did you have to go and see?'

'It was nothing, Betty. Just some chap who said they're going to give me a medal.'

'Oh! They'd said that already.'

'Yes, let's have a drink, shall we?'

I sat down next to her, still absorbed by Churchill's account of my mission in 1941, which seemed to have relieved me of the gnawing sense of guilt I'd felt for an act of treachery, the detail of which I'd never known but which, once I'd recovered memory of it, had returned at intervals to worry me like an aching tooth. What I'd now been told was that I hadn't committed any wrong-doing; on the contrary I'd been commended for my magnificent heroism. But what is a hero, I asked myself? I remembered some stories from Ancient Greece that I'd read at school and the definition that went with them: 'Heroes are those celebrated by courage or feats of arms...' I didn't feel I'd been particularly courageous at any time during the past five years. When directly confronting the enemy in battle I had been struggling to understand what was going on around me, or else I'd been paralysed with fear. Or both! I couldn't recall any great feat of arms, except perhaps ending the siege and killing Erich Reindorf at the Hôtel Crillon. That didn't seem to be an act which qualified as heroic. All the war that I'd experienced had been too disorganised and undisciplined to lend itself to heroism according to that definition. Heroes could better be defined as those who are lucky enough to survive 'feats of arms'. I was going to be awarded a medal for being lucky! But what about all the other heroes of war who'd been awarded medals for bravery, self-sacrifice, rescuing wounded comrades under fire? Was I the only false hero. Somehow, I doubted it.

At least my 1941 mission hadn't been a game which I had myself been playing, nor had I made any cheating moves ... well, only one serious one – when I'd broken my promise to Reindorf. But Churchill had frankly admitted playing a dishonourable game in which I'd just been a pawn he'd moved around on his board. Had his conduct been justified, as he'd claimed, by the hopeless situation of his country at the time? He proved, if I'd needed any further proof, that war, unlike chess, was a dishonourable game, in which the rules could be broken at will.

I remembered that moment in 1941 in Ferney-Voltaire when I'd vowed to impose some discipline and order on my life. I needed to repeat that vow to myself at regular intervals. I also remembered I'd come to the conclusion that life was not susceptible to system and order. You just had to take it as it came.

Thinking of Ferney reminded me of the famous Voltaire lines I'd learned by heart at school. Daniel and I had debated them many times as we sat together with a glass of wine in the Café des Sports: *'Quoi que vous fassiez, écrasez l'infame, et aimez qui vous aime!'*

We'd argued about what was meant by *'l'infame'*. Was it limited to religious bigotry and superstition or did it mean all treacherous and corrupt behaviour? The history books said that Voltaire had spent his life battling against it. We'd looked up the words in *Larousse*, but it told us only that it meant conduct which was 'dishonourable', and that Voltaire had insisted that whatever you do in life you should set yourself against it.

Suddenly, I spoke the Great Thinker's words aloud.

'Quoi que vous fassiez, écrasez l'infame, et aimez qui vous aime!'

'What does that mean, Albert?'

'It means that you should do good in the world and love those who love you.'

'I love you, Albert.'

'And I love you, Betty.'

We walked hand in hand through the streets of London where news was spreading that the war in Europe had been finally won. People gave each other Churchill's famous V for Victory sign. We bought a newspaper, which reported that at 2.41 that morning, at Supreme Allied HQ in Rheims, General Jodl, representing the

German High Command, had signed the unconditional surrender of all German land, sea and air forces. That night we joined the celebrations. Throughout London, soldiers and civilians built bonfires and danced around them, singing, shouting, making love and giving thanks for victory. They called it 'VE Day'.

In one of his most eloquent and passionate speeches, Churchill paid special tribute to our Russian allies, saying they were: 'Our true comrades, whose magnificent prowess in the field of battle had been a magnificent contribution to our final great victory.'

It was adjudged to be time for celebration – celebration of a glorious triumph achieved by courageous soldiers, skilled generals and honourable statesmen. Why should I resist that golden illusion?

Appendix

VERBATIM EXTRACTS FROM THE DIARIES OF SS OBERFÜHRER REINDORF (1907–1944)

'... *a week ago on 13th December 1940, the Führer signed the Order for Operation Barbarossa, and today he issued Directive No 21 prescribing the conduct of the War in the East. His decision seems to have been based on one critical assumption: that in 1942 the United States will be ready to intervene actively on behalf of the Allies. The resources of that country are unmatchable and therefore we need to win the war in Europe in 1941. We have chosen to seek an alliance with Britain against the Soviet Union, rather than one with the Soviets against Britain. The Führer believed that both were possibilities but has concluded that the former is the better option. For once, the General Staff has immediately agreed with their Führer. They all have a deep hatred of Communism, and a belief in the natural superiority of the Aryan race over the Slav. And they believe that the Soviet Union is a weak and impoverished nation.*
But they may yet be proved wrong. Their decision has been made with complete disregard for the work of our intelligence services, who have reported, with detailed confirmatory evidence that Russia is not at all close to economic and social collapse. And that subjugating the country with the largest land-mass in the world will be a difficult and onerous task. The truth is that since our victories in the West, both our Führer and the General Staff have become over-confident...'
(18th December 1940)

'... I am now forced to the conclusion that the Operation Determinate Protocol has not governed, does not and will not govern the course of events. It is an irrelevance. I have already noted that the Führer had made his decision to launch Barbarossa six months ago, so that decision was not dependent on the Determinate contract, nor on the British performing their contractual obligations under it. Indeed it was a decision which seems to have been made before Determinate had even been conceived. So from the outset, Determinate has been a gigantic bluff and Churchill has fallen for it. It does give the British an excuse for seeking peace on reasonable terms, and having Britain as an ally against the Soviets can only be helpful to us. I believe that tomorrow we shall see a historic change in the course of events...'
(21st June 1941)

'I was totally wrong! Churchill has not fallen for the Führer's bluff. How could the Führer have been confident that the British would walk into so crude a trap and actually perform their side of the Determinate contract? It is now clear that Churchill is simply going to do nothing. The concept that Britain could have changed sides and that Britain and Germany could have suddenly become Allies which seemed plausible yesterday now seems absurd. The propaganda machines of both countries would have needed to revolve through 180 degrees. In Britain, public opinion could surely not have been so readily changed. However ... another thought has just struck me. The Führer's confidence must have been based on some earlier indication: a signal, perhaps, from Churchill that he was willing to enter into some such agreement. That is the only plausible explanation. So it wasn't a case of Churchill **not** falling for Hitler's bluff; but of Hitler falling for Churchill's bluff.
It is normal for incomplete information to be disseminated, and I believe there must be some undisclosed element which explains this event. After much consideration, I now conclude that the Führer had another underlying objective, which was to rid himself of Rudolf

208

Hess, Deputy Führer, who had become an embarrassment to him. Some of Hess's behaviour had been eccentric to say the least, and his loyalty was being questioned. I record here there was a rumour that the Führer and Hess had quarrelled and that the Führer had been heard shouting to him:

'Hess, you really are stubborn!'

So perhaps the Führer hadn't really fallen for Churchill's bluff. It was merely that he had nothing to lose by sending Hess as a messenger to Churchill, and, whatever Churchill's response, he had much to gain. As a one way bag-carrier Hess was perfect.

And Leconte has had a different role in Churchill's game. As a chess player he is a good beginner, but he does not have the analytical capacity to penetrate the layers of deception and recognise true motives in this convoluted and sophisticated game called 'The Diplomacy of War'. It is a game in which it is easy to get lost. He is the equivalent of an innocent onlooker and I am absolutely persuaded he cannot release harmful information, because he possesses none. He can present no danger to us because he was never told and did not understand the nature of the message he was carrying. In these circumstances, and because over the last few weeks we have become acquainted, perhaps even friends, I cannot allow him to be tortured to death by the Gestapo...

(24th June 1941)

209